BY THE SAME AUTHOR

The Half-Life

LIVABILITY

Stories

Jon Raymond

BLOOMSBURY

New York   Berlin   London

Published by Bloomsbury USA, New York

All papers used by Bloomsbury USA are natural, recyclable products made from wood grown in well-managed forests. The manufacturing processes conform to the environmental regulations of the country of origin.

LIBRARY OF CONGRESS CATALOGING-IN-PUBLICATION DATA

Raymond, John.
Livability: stories / Jon Raymond.—1st U.S. ed.
p. cm.
ISBN-13: 978-1-59691-655-5
ISBN-10: 1-59691-655-9
1. Family—Fiction.   2. Friends—Fiction.   3. Relationships—Fiction.
I. Title.

PS3618.A985 L58 2009
813'.6—dc22
2008030834

First U.S. Edition 2009

1 3 5 7 9 10 8 6 4 2

Typeset by Westchester Book Group
Printed in the United States of America by Quebecor World Fairfield

For Emily and Eliza

CONTENTS

OLD JOY

THE SOUND OF A BELL.

The vibrations moved outward from the wrought cup, dying sweetly at the edges of the room. I listened closely to the braided amplitudes, chiming and singing within themselves, waiting until the final ringing sound had narrowed and disappeared and the waters of my mind had fallen silent. When the vibrations ended, I raised the mallet again.

The sound of a bell. The dilating vibration.

And then the interruption—the shrill sound of the telephone, like a tropical bird in the corner.

I got up from my pillow and crossed the room, navigating the dismembered bicycle parts and piled shoes and ragged cat toys spread over the Persian carpet, then picked up the receiver and flopped onto the corduroy couch.

"Hey, Mark," Kurt said. "I'm calling you."

"Hey," I said. "So you're here."

I'd been expecting the call for about a week at that point. Kurt always called me when he got back into town. Usually there were a few sightings beforehand—someone would see him at a party or spot him hopping onto a bus—and within two weeks, the phone would be ringing. It took longer sometimes—I wasn't that high on his list anymore—but I always knew he'd make contact eventually. There was a time, back before Kurt was set wandering in the world, before he had finally burned too many bridges with his regular breakdowns and tantrums, that we had been very close, and there was still a certain duty from those days that bound us.

"When did you get back?" I asked him. This was always my first question.

"Two weeks ago," he said. "I've been staying with Pete."

"All right," I said.

We went back and forth for a while. Kurt said he had dreamed about me, which came out like an apology for something, and I caught him up on some of the goings-on around town. Mary had left Ben, Ben had found Naomi. The record store on Burnside had gone out of business and the last albums on the shelves were all by friends of ours.

Just as we were preparing to hang up, making plans to make plans at some unspecified point in the future, almost as an afterthought, Kurt came out with one final question. He asked me if I felt like going to some hot springs near the mountain with him that afternoon. He was leaving in a few hours.

"It's a great spot," he said. "Come on. We can camp. We'll be back by tomorrow night." The way his voice sounded, buoyant and boyish, seemed only distantly related to my own presence on the phone, and I wondered briefly how many other people he'd asked before me.

"Yeah," I said, surprising myself. Beyond the dark mouth of the front porch I could see the mailman slipping an envelope into the neighbor's slot. "Why not? I could use some time in the woods."

"You want to go?" he said. He sounded surprised, too.

"Yeah," I said. "Absolutely." I was already becoming attached to the idea. My friendship with Kurt was a point of some pride in my mind, after so many people had written him off over the years.

"Well, all right!" he said. "Let's go. I just got gas."

We hung up and I went back to the meditation pillow, pressing the fat mushroom between my knees. I tapped the bell and listened to its clean sound crumbling in the air, as my breath flowed in and out of my chest like the tides. I had trouble concentrating though. My mind had become full of loose, unfocused energy.

I arrived at Pete's place around noon. He was living on the ground floor of an eight-plex in Southeast, where humid exhaust from the laundry room hung in the air. After some sounds of obscure pounding around inside, the door rattled open, and I stepped back to let the screen door swing toward me.

"Hey!" I said.

"Hey!" Kurt said, smiling. We hugged and then backed up to take each other in.

Kurt was thinner than before, his cheeks slightly collapsed, and the knuckles of his hands were chapped and raw. He still looked all right though. His thick, black hair curled down over his ears, and he had big sideburns that fringed out like flames and fine stubble edging his square jaw. His nose was handsomely crooked, and his mouth, as usual, was faintly amused. He wore a wrinkled green T-shirt and a leather bracelet on his wrist, faded bluejeans that clung to his brawny legs. He could have been a movie star, I thought, if only his eyes weren't so close together.

"What've you been doing, man?" I asked, roughly rubbing his shoulder to show my clear happiness to see him.

"Farming. Down in Ashland," he said. Beneath long lashes, his eyes brooded with intensity, the same dark glint he had been cultivating all these years. "Living in a straw-bale house for a while. Before that I was delivering beer in New Orleans." Every year, Kurt migrated like a bird, to Denver or Mexico or Pittsburgh, depending. He had friends in every town, it seemed, who participated in his marvelous experiences, and who then went back to their regular lives when he moved on.

"It was all right?" I said, trying to parse his mood. Sometimes he came back from the road with grim stories to tell, feelings of desolation that still hung around him. Other times, he was skittish, eager to leave again as soon as possible. Today he seemed robust, and somehow scorched by wind.

"Amazing," he said, locking the door and swinging his backpack onto his shoulder. "Transformative. I'm at a new place now." A cryptic smile came onto his face, full of some deep meaning he refused to put into words. I had forgotten the mild struggle we fell into every time we found each other again.

On the way to the Corolla, Kurt told me about Ashland, and the woman he had met there who ran the organic farm, and the inevitable dissolution of their romance. "I was like one tooth, one curl, man," he said. What he meant, I realized, was that he had been sad, and crying like a baby. I told him about my dad, who had just left his wife, and the blood clots that had appeared and then dissolved in his brain.

"It was heavy," I said, and Kurt nodded knowingly.

By the time we hit the edge of the city, out past Tualatin where the buildings started to taper off and the freeway straightened, we were basically caught up. Filmy scenes of parking lots and sod farms passed by the windows. When we cleared Wilsonville—five minutes without talking and counting—I rummaged through my bag and rolled us a joint. I picked out the stems, mixed in some tobacco, and licked the yellow gum neatly. Kurt fiddled with the radio until he found the good oldies station.

I passed the joint to Kurt and he took a long hit. The smoke collected into a milky cloud in the slanting sunlight. The smell was sweet and rich, a little piney.

"You remember Yogi?" he said tightly. The smoke unfurled heavily and caressed the surface of the glass.

"Yeah," I said. He was a guy we used to live with, who had left town and never been seen again.

"I ran into him down in Big Sur last month," Kurt said, exhaling. "We had a really incredible night together. Really incredible." He took another brief hit and blew the smoke out his nose. "Out on the beach, dancing to these drums. We were all jumping through this huge bonfire. I've never seen anything like it, man. Everyone was so joyful that night. Beautiful women, dancing and singing. Really amazing bunch of people."

"No shit," I said.

"No shit!" Kurt said. "You should have been there. I think Yogi got laid." He giggled, and bounced in his seat, and passed me back the browning roach without looking.

At Salem, we cut east onto Highway 22 and stopped for lunch on the outskirts of town. We bought beer and Pringles and carrots and bread, some bottles of water and a cheap Styrofoam cooler with a bag of ice. Out in the parking lot Kurt made a noise like a chugging speedboat engine, bellowing and lightly pounding his chest. I twisted his arm in an Indian rope burn. We were starting to loosen up a little. Then we got back in the car and continued across the Willamette Valley, into the foothills of the Cascades.

The change from farmland to forest came quickly—the mangy fields and front lawns turned into dense woods, the colors going from beige and tawny gold to deep, impenetrable black-green. The air took on a colder, more mountainous vitality.

"This is a great spot," Kurt said as we began climbing. "I was here last summer. Totally private, no one around. And most of all, it's peaceful. You can really think."

"Sounds awesome," I said.

"You never get real quiet anymore, you know?" he said. "I visited some hot springs in Arizona where no one is allowed to talk. Total silence. It was fantastic. They want me to come back and work as a chef sometime. I've got a whole menu worked out for them."

I nodded, knowing the plan would probably never materialize, and if it did, it would likely end in some tragic mishap.

"I think I read about that place in a magazine," I said finally, then turned to stare out the window, letting the sound of the car engulf us.

We skirted Detroit Lake and began hugging the southern slope of Mount Hood, where the rain forest thickened and darkened further. We shot past trailheads and turnouts, runaway truck lanes on the opposite shoulder, as off to the side, volcanic ravines plunged and dipped, vast, frozen tidal waves of earth, spiked with innumerable identical fir trees.

Our plan was to find the stream we were looking for and set up camp before dark so we could wake up early and hike in to the hot springs first thing in the morning. Kurt claimed he knew exactly where we were going, but pretty soon it became clear that was not the case. We curved around a series of intersecting high-ways, through furrowed, wooded valleys, then doubled back, swung around again, and before long we were completely lost.

Eventually Kurt pulled over to the side of the road and took out the map, which clattered under his touch. He spread it on the dash-board and we tried reading it, but we were both still too stoned to concentrate. The colored lines and words fuzzed out, impossibly complex. The late-day sunlight made everything seem fragile and distressed.

"I know a place a few miles from here," Kurt said finally, crush-ing the map into the back seat. "We could camp out there and find the place in the morning. I know we're close."

"You know how to get there?" I asked him.

"Yeah, I know how to get there," he said, and banged the car into gear.

It got darker and darker, and soon the black trees were slipping by like ghosts. We turned up a logging road—white reflectors flashing as we raked by—and after a few scrapes and tilts and turns we ended up in a narrow cul-de-sac that was also an impromptu dumping ground. The headlights swirled with dust, which settled to reveal an old love seat, some kitchen chairs, and a smattering of soiled papers and carpet samples.

We got out of the car and peered into the gloom. The car was still idling and the dust was just returning to the ground. Beyond the garbage, we couldn't see much. The headlight beams shot out into stark emptiness. The air was cold.

"Well," I said, trying to keep positive, "we may as well stay here, I guess. Right? We can still get a good start in the morning."

"I'm cool with it if you are," Kurt said. "Looks fine to me."

We made a small fire and pitched the tent, pulled out some

beers and cigarettes. Kurt had a BB gun, a one-shot, air-pump pistol, which he got from the trunk, and we took turns aiming at beer bottles and metal cans. It was nice—the mellow rhythm of trading the gun back and forth, squaring up, and shooting, punctuating the drifting patterns of our talk.

We talked about nothing much for a while. We just tried to get something going between us.

"It's good to get out of the city," I said. "I forget all this is out here sometimes."

"No shit," Kurt said, and pegged an old square of carpet moldering a few feet away. "Not that there's any big difference between the forest and the city, really. You know what I mean? It's all one huge thing now. Trees in the city, garbage in the forest. What's the difference? You know?"

"I see what you mean," I said.

I aimed for a glinting tuna fish can, and dinged it.

We smoked another bowl and talked for a while about art and politics and some of the old people we used to know, and eventually, as the beers stacked up, we got into more theoretical territory. I told Kurt about some pots I'd been throwing. Kurt told me about some of the night classes he had been taking down in Ashland, where he had worked on the campus grounds crew.

"It was all right," he said. He was starting to slur, though he had not yet reached the wet incoherence of his final, clownish stages before passing out. "Some physics classes. But here's the thing, man. I knew more than they did. All this quark and superstring shit. I know all about that. It makes sense, don't get me wrong—I understand it. But that's not the final answer."

"You think you understand it?" I said.

"Basically," he said. "It's like this. Look. Sometimes things look like they don't have any order. Just a bunch of stuff jumbled together. But then, from a different level, you realize it does have an order. It's like climbing a mountain. See? You look around and just see a bunch of trees, bushes, rocks, pressing all around you, but then, you get up above the tree line and you see everything you just went through, and it all comes together. It has some kind of shape after all. Sometimes it takes a long time to get high enough to see it, but it's there. It's all about space and time, and how their rules change sometimes. It makes perfect sense to me."

He had another example, about two mirrors traveling through space and a single atom moving back and forth between them, but he lost the point and couldn't quite make sense of it in the end.

"So, anyway, I get it," he said. "I get it on a fundamental level. The thing is, I have my own theory." He held the BB gun in his lap, forgetting to pass it. Both of us were staring into the breathing coals of the fire.

"Here's my theory," Kurt said. "It's the universe is falling. That's what explains it all. The whole universe is the shape of a falling tear, dropping down through space. I'm telling you, man. I don't know how it happened, but that's how it works. It's this tear that's been falling forever now, man. It never stops."

I reached for the gun and pumped it a few times.

"So did you tell them that?" I said. I couldn't help digging at him for some reason. "Your theory about the tear-shaped universe?"

Kurt watched me lining up a shot at a milk carton propped on a broken desk chair. Orange light flickered on his face.

"Did I tell them? Shit. Who the hell am I? You think they care about my theory? It doesn't mean shit to them. I don't have any numbers for it."

We fell silent, and I locked the milk carton in the crosshairs, pulled the trigger, and grazed it.

Kurt poked at the fire and the light brightened, extending our hemisphere of visibility. A stuffed animal and some orange crates appeared from the darkness. Kurt's face looked clenched for some reason. His eyes were squinting, and his mouth appeared carved into a crude frown. A moment later, I realized he was crying.

At first I thought he was joking. The outburst was so sudden and unexpected. But then he leaned back in a racking moan, and I wasn't so sure anymore. His shoulders began heaving up and down, and big, snuffling sobs came out of his mouth.

Kurt looked up at me. "I miss you, Mark! I miss you so much. I want us to be real friends again. There's something between us now and I don't like it. I want it to go away."

Kurt stared at me as tears streamed down his cheeks. His face was like a grimacing stone idol. I watched him from across the fire and had a moment of blind panic, a feeling that the whole world was collapsing on top of me. I'd forgotten Kurt had that power over me sometimes. He could turn everything inside out in two breaths if he wanted to.

"Hey, man," I said. "What are you talking about? We're fine."

Kurt dropped his head between his knees and kept crying.

"Are you serious, man? Do you really think that?"

I got up and crossed over to Kurt's side of the fire and hugged his shoulders.

"Of course," I said. "Of course I do. We're fine. We're totally fine."

"I don't know . . ." Kurt said.

I left my hand on Kurt's shoulder—it would seem too significant to remove it—and stared at the throbbing embers.

I was about to say something when suddenly Kurt's fit was over. His shoulders stopped jumping and the mucousy noises faded away. He recovered immediately. He wiped his cheeks with his sleeve and sniffed loudly and cleared his throat.

"Oh God, man, I'm sorry," he said, rubbing his eyes on his shoulder. He fumbled for the gun and aimed it casually at a paper plate near his feet. He pulled the trigger and a BB pierced the white shell. "I'm just being crazy, I know. Don't pay any attention to me. All right? We're fine. I know. Everything is totally fine. I feel a lot better now."

We didn't sleep much that night. We just rolled ourselves into our sleeping bags, inside the tent, and stopped talking. I lay there with my eyes closed, feeling the damp forest air creeping around me, my hair going lank, the wetness coming out from the ground and the air and the trees. What was it about Kurt, I wondered? I heard some noises outside but I was too tired to care. At some point, maybe, a car drove up the road, but it stopped and turned around before it found us.

Soon the sky was brightening. I heard a birdcall. The rocks were biting into my spine, so I got up and crawled out into the morning. I took a deep breath—the smell of earth, distant rotting leaves, and ice.

I crouched near the tent as the colors began coming up on things. The landscape began to materialize from the darkness. All around the clearing, I could see now, past the litter-strewn shoulder, the earth fell away into a bending valley of broken snags and logging debris. A wide burn field covered with piles of splintered wood and dead, copper-colored needles ran down to a wall of meager second- or third-growth fir trees. The burnt stumps gleamed in the growing morning light, their blackened charcoal shining with a salty-looking white rime. The sun broke the horizon, and I stretched my spine toward the sky. I would try harder, I told myself. I would try harder to find some way to connect.

When Kurt got up, we packed our things quickly and edged back down the dirt road to the highway. We stopped at a café, where Kurt asked directions to the Metolius River, and it turned out we weren't that far away.

"Told you," he said, smiling and slapping a packet of sugar against his palm. He was acting playful that morning, I could tell, trying to put last night behind us.

"I never doubted you, man," I said, doing my part to keep things light, too. We both wanted to find our old chemistry again.

After breakfast we located the trailhead, an unassuming pathway marked by a wooden State Park sign. We parked and locked the doors, strapped on the backpacks, and marched off into the woods.

"All right, all right," Kurt said, rubbing his hands together.

"Right on schedule," I said, and poked him lightly in the ribs.

We hiked in a ways, upstream past dabs of orange spray paint on the boulders, past rebar jammed into the rocks where surveyors had been examining the stream for eventual restocking. We followed the bank as it rose and fell, slapping at the branches of hemlock and juniper that hung within arm's reach, and came out on a nice, flat, open stretch of water, with wide, pebble beaches on either side and an island tufted with sweet clover.

Above the trees, the peak of the mountain loomed in the air, streaked with late-summer dirt and haloed with morning sunlight. Frigid air billowed off the ice pack—you could feel it on the edges of your senses—which seemed to keep everything in the general area fresh and healthy and preserved.

"It's like nature's huge crisper," I said, and Kurt laughed.

We took a few hits from Kurt's pipe and kept walking. The light was feathery and soft, dappling in the rapids, the water nearly melodic as it rushed over the rocks. The dome of creation seemed centered right above us, fat clouds passing out of sight and then back again on the opposite horizon.

We let the wind brush against our faces.

"Look at that old guy," Kurt said, nodding toward the mountain. "That guy is so old."

"He's pretty old," I said. "Look at that big, white beard. How are you feeling?"

"Good. I feel good. How about you?"

"I feel good, too."

We ambled along, talking in short bursts. I told Kurt about the classes I'd been teaching, the community garden I managed—nothing that interesting, but all the small things I did to fill up my time in the city. Kurt listened with growing interest as my daily routine took shape in his mind. I told him about the homeless woman who sometimes sat with me while I weeded and the kids who used my backyard as a playground. Kurt nodded and smiled to keep me going.

"I'm so proud of you, Mark," Kurt said finally. He seemed genuinely moved by my little accomplishments. "You've really been doing something, man. Your house, your friends. You're giving something back to the community."

"Oh, I don't know," I said.

"No. Really. It's really something," Kurt said. "I'm really proud."

"Well." I nodded modestly as we stepped over the rocks. "I try. You know. Nothing you couldn't do if you felt like it."

"Hmm," Kurt said, kicking a piece of wood. A tone of strangled agreement sounded in his throat. "Uh huh."

Almost immediately I realized the small mistake I had made, and I tried to back out of it, but something kept sticking. "Not that you don't give to the community," I said. "It's just a different community . . ." My attempts to explain only drew the line more starkly though. Kurt nodded but I could tell his mood had soured again, and soon the undercurrents of the night before swirled back around us.

We kept walking, our shadows moving in shifting blobs over the ground. The sound of river rocks rattled under our feet. We turned along a bend in the stream and a curtain of poplar trees came into view, shivering in the distance, showing the white backsides of their leaves. I watched them for a while until an ancient, aching sorrow rose up in my chest. It was a familiar feeling. Something in the mute, unconscious trees resonated inside me, something so deep and fundamental it failed to remember its own source anymore. I watched the poplars flickering against the hard blue of the sky. What is sorrow? I thought. What is sorrow but old, worn-out joy?

I glanced at Kurt, his lips pursed, his eyes filled up with shadows. His strong brow was turned toward the ground. There was a cruel part of me still that triumphed in the truth that had been exposed.

Soon we parted from the stream and came to a ravine filled with lupine and heather, where we jogged down a twisting trail. Kurt moved easily over the ground, a healthy animal, taking the shocks into his knees and shoulders, and I followed him, tracing the nimble path he pioneered.

We crossed some unmarked boundary and entered the old-growth forest, where the air turned green and the earth mossy.

Everything was different there. The trees were gigantic and primeval. The ferns were prehistoric, their huge fronds like bending, wet eyelashes. We walked over the spongy, damp earth as the creek whispered and crows called from high above. These trees had been growing for hundreds, thousands, of years, I guessed, in the same place, side by side. I wondered what they must feel like, being rooted in place so long. I wondered if at some point they had come to resent each other.

Kurt pulled ahead of me and loped up the trail over the thick, snaking roots, brushing his hands over the hairy bark of the cedars. He stopped on the top of a hill, where I caught up to him. We had come to the end of the trail.

"Okay, Mark," Kurt said. "This is it. Hope you like it."

Down below, a handful of wooden structures had appeared, tucked into narrow ravines and groves of alder trees, each one sheltering a carved cedar hot tub. Straight ahead of us was a big, cylindrical tub, for large groups, and down to the left, a set of individual, canoe-shaped tubs separated into stalls. Farther down, there was a row of individual tubs on a platform without any walls between them, which was where we headed.

"This looks fantastic," I said, and gripped Kurt's shoulder with a happy squeeze.

The hot springs were fairly empty that day, just a couple of backpackers, a few teenagers, a pregnant woman and her bearded husband. I watched a man exit a stall, dripping water, and pace around the cedar deck. His belly was sagging and his legs were bent and atrophied, coming to gnarled, splayed toes on the end. When he turned around, his ass was a tiny crevice at the bottom of his back between two flattened, pinkish pancakes. He went over and petted a black Labrador tied to a tree, and then returned to his tub.

We staked out two tubs and put down our bags on the adjacent benches. The tubs were made of black, wet wood, with rubber stoppers on the bottom. They were a little slimy, but we didn't bother to scrub them out. We opened the sluices, wooden flippers that directed the steaming water into the canoe, and hauled over plastic buckets of cold water from a nearby well.

I felt strong, padding back and forth with the cold water. It felt good to use my arms and legs, tapping the last bits of strength left from the hike. I almost wished the preparation of the tub could have gone on longer, but quickly enough it was time to strip down and settle in. I pulled off my clothes, stashed my keys in my shoes, and eased myself into the water. I felt a shiver of warmth run through my body. I groaned, "Fantastic," as Kurt slipped into the tub beside mine and sighed.

We lay there for a long time, letting the hot water soak deep into our muscles. The birds were chattering in the trees, drunk on juniper berries. I watched my pale feet ripple on the opposite end of the tub, my pale arms flat against my hips. The walls of the tub rose on either side of me like a sarcophagus. I closed my eyes and sank down in the water until the sound of my own body was ringing in my ears.

I came up for air and wiped the wet hair from my eyes. Our little grotto was filling with afternoon shadows now. High above there was golden light on the tops of the trees, and beyond that a ragged circle of blue sky.

I heard Kurt rearranging himself in the tub beside me, a sloshing, slapping water noise. He propped himself up on his elbows and looked out into the trees.

"Do you want a beer?" he asked.

"No. Thanks," I said.

"Some more weed?"

"Nah." I closed my eyes and leaned back in the water. I heard the sound of a beer cracking open.

We let the previous hours wash away in the silence, until soon the dark rupture of the hike seemed like a strange, half-remembered act of imagination. Eventually, I heard Kurt laugh to himself under his breath, a gruff, amused chortle, which reassured me further. I hoped it signaled a return to our morning openness.

"What?" I asked. I kept my eyes closed, grinning in antici- pation.

"Did I ever tell you about that deer down in Big Sur?" he said.

"No," I said, eagerly. "What about it?"

"Well," Kurt said, and swigged from his beer. "This was pretty insane. The day after that beach party down there I borrowed Yogi's car. I wanted to go into town for some breakfast and stuff. Bring back some supplies. Everyone else was still sleeping in the drift- wood, so I took the keys and walked up to the parking lot and took off. It was a really beautiful morning, man. The poppies were blooming, the eucalyptus was really sweet. I was driving along this winding road, feeling good, when all of a sudden, out of nowhere, I hit this deer."

"Oh shit," I said.

"I know. It was awful. I stopped and drove back, and found her on the side of the road. This beautiful, brown deer. Her nose was wet and her ears were folded back. She was still breathing, but she had gravel and dirt all skidded up in her flank. She was knocked out. I didn't know what to do."

My eyes were still closed and the sunlight throbbed through the branches, playing on the orange screens of my eyelids. I heard the sound of water spilling onto the wooden deck, footsteps slapping on the ground. I heard Kurt walk to the other end of the deck, the scuff of a lighter. I smelled the rich perfume of the weed.

Then Kurt's footsteps slapped on the deck again. They seemed to be coming toward me. They got closer and closer, smacking on the wood, until soon I could feel Kurt standing right behind me. I could hear his heavy breathing and the leisurely cracking of his knuckles.

He kept talking while he stood there. "So I didn't want to just leave her there, you know?" he said. "I mean, if she was dead, maybe. But she was still alive and I figured maybe a vet could help her. So I dragged her over to the car and kind of pushed her into the back seat. I thought if I could get to the town fast enough, maybe someone could save her. I don't know what I was thinking."

I could feel him looming over me, making me paranoid.

I opened my eyes to see Kurt upside down in my vision, holding his hands wide apart. At first I thought he was going to box me on the ears, but instead he brought his palms together as hard as he could, making a single, pealing clap. Then he began to rub his hands together, back and forth, faster and faster, clasping and unclasping his fingers. The muscles of his arms flexed. His shoulders worked up and down.

The forest had darkened since I had closed my eyes. We were at the base of a shadowy, pear-shaped vessel now, topped with a pale blue lid.

"So I got back in the front seat and took off down the road," he said, panting a little. "I drove as fast as I could without sliding the deer off the back seat. I was checking the mirror every few seconds. I could see she was still breathing back there. And I could smell her, too. This terrible, sweaty, fear smell. It filled up the whole car."

Kurt lowered his palms toward my shoulders. I could feel the heat a good six inches away, a radiant, penetrating energy. His strong hands were almost burning.

Kurt gripped my shoulders. My back tensed up and I grabbed the underside of my legs. He didn't say anything. He just kneaded my shoulders for a second and then moved his hands behind my ears and held my head and twisted my neck carefully from side to side. I fought against him at first, trying to stand up, but he held me down in the water. I twisted but his hands were too strong. They held me in place. I could see my reflection snapping in and out of focus, and behind me, Kurt's face, blank with concentration, the white hole of the sun wobbling through spreading branches.

"I was getting pretty close to town," he whispered, "when suddenly the deer woke up back there. She was only stunned I guess. She woke up and just went crazy. She started kicking and thrashing all around. Making a choked sound in her throat. She clipped my head with her hoof and I almost swerved into a pickup truck."

"Shit," I said. I was succumbing to Kurt's plying hands by then. "And then what?"

"Then what? I pulled over as fast as I could and I just stood there. I stood there and watched the deer demolish Yogi's car. She went crazy. Ripped the upholstery into pieces, smashed the mirror. She kicked so hard that the back windows shattered. Right there in the parked car on the side of the road. Finally I crept over and opened the door, and she got out and split into the trees."

At this point Kurt pressed his fingers on my temples and it was like a portal opened at the base of my skull—a burst of energy flowing up the wick of my backbone into my brain. I felt like I was rising from an ocean of cobwebs, and a sickly light shone down, whitish-yellow. A warbling sound oscillated in my ears.

"Mmmmm," Kurt was chanting from his chest. "Mmmm." He made a long, sustained tone that vibrated though my body until my own chest resonated with his. When the chanting stopped, I lay back in the water. Kurt held me for a moment, rubbing my chest, and then let me go. I kept my eyes closed and floated in the luke-warm tub. My muscles felt light and emptied. My skin was a de-pleted husk.

Kurt went back to his own hot tub and opened the sluice for a new rush of hot water. We sat there without talking again, breath-ing evenly and listening to the crows calling each other in the sky.

His lighter flicked, and I could hear the butane feeding the flame. The harsh smell of tobacco floated over. "I see all kinds of shit out there, man. Most people never see anything at all. They don't want to."

When we got up to go, my body was pruned and waterlogged. We dried off in the sun and put our pants and shirts back on. I pulled on my limp socks. We yanked the plugs on the hot tubs and listened to the water cascade down to the rocks and dirt below.

On the way down the hill it rained, and we could hear the drumming shower on the canopy of ancient trees high above. The rushing creek beside us hissed and babbled to itself. It was almost evening when we got back to the car. Kurt started up the engine and we crept to the edge of the parking lot, where he flipped the blinker and turned out onto the main road.

The way back was all two-lane highways, winding through twisting draperies of national parkland. The setting sun spiked the wet asphalt, throwing up white sheets of glare, and the rising steam billowed in bright clouds. I put on the Stones. We had a long drive ahead of us.

The sun went down, and soon the land disappeared. We sailed past piles of sawdust lit by sodium lamps, and cement factories and junk shops, the rag edge of the road's shoulder flickering alongside us like firelight. The smell of wet trees blasted in the window— cold, strong, mountain trees. The yellow stripes shot toward us like laser beams.

I leaned against the window and watched the night floating by. A mailbox appeared and whizzed past in a blur. A gas station grew and receded against a backdrop of pitch-black. Kurt's face was half-lit from the dashboard, his eyes locked on the onrushing road. I pressed my cheek against the cool window. I couldn't tell if we were racing forward or plunging straight down into the void.

THE WIND

IT WAS AN OLD STORY, and Joseph had heard it many times before. In fact, ever since his grandfather's arrival a month earlier, he'd been hearing it almost every day, and it was always pretty much the same. The details might change a little, and some of the order, but the big picture remained intact. The beginning of the world, according to his grandfather, began with the wind.

"The wind was the first thing," the old man said. His voice was a throaty, desiccated rasp, and his eyes gleamed from the bottoms of deep craters in his head. He looked so brittle lying in bed that Joseph worried his soul would fall out of his skin before his eyes, dropping upward and rising into the air and splashing finally into the blue water of the sky. Joseph's grandfather's lips rounded and closed. His eyes seemed to read words on the ceiling.

"The wind was all there was," he whispered. "The wind would move inside the darkness, and touch itself, and try and hide. Before the world began, before . . . oh shit . . ."

He coughed, a resounding, catarrhal avalanche in his chest. His eyes bunched, and tears formed at the corners of his lids, and he pressed his yellowing hair into his pillow. Maybe this was it, Joseph thought. He didn't want to see his grandfather die. But he told himself that it would be okay, too. The cycle of being was a perfect circle, his mother said. Death was not a tragedy. Everything that entered the world naturally departed, only to come back again in some new form. He could see where the notion offered some kind of comfort.

His grandfather had lived a full life. He'd gone to war. He'd been married, more than once. And he'd spent the past decades prospecting in the Sierras. Now, at the end of his time, he stood as the last of his breed—stubborn, pure, and unbowed by the system. It was true, he'd missed out on some things along the way—his daughter's various graduations and weddings and such—but for all that she had long ago forgiven him. He deserved respect for the wisdom he had acquired, living out there in the mountains with his mule. It wasn't every day you met a free, wild man anymore, she said. It was just too bad he was so sadly lacking in health care.

"Oh, Jesus . . . Joseph," the old man eventually squeezed out, "I need some water."

Joseph filled a glass from the pitcher on the bed stand and re-sumed picking the cattails from his socks. The old man drank in loud gulps, his mouth a red circle inside the gray mass of his beard, his teeth gnarls of yellow stone. He reached a finger into the pill cup and pressed it to his wet lips. His chin shook.

The process took a long time. The old man had a lot of pills to take. Joseph blew on the window and carved a star in his condensed breath. He watched it disappear. He felt sorry for his mother. He felt sorry for his grandfather, too. He blew on the window again and the star reappeared, along with an old spiral, his initials, a face.

The hollow sound of glass on wood rang out, and Joseph's grand-father smacked his lips and wiped his long fingers on the quilt. The overcast light hung in the air, gluing everything in place—the suc-culents near the window, the limp batik drapes, the small city of pill boxes on the end table. Outside, the world was racing forward; inside, the time was crawling, entombed.

"Where was I?" the old man said.

Joseph shrugged.

"Oh yeah," the old man said. "The wind. The wind was restless, Joseph. It needed someplace to go. The wind was lonely before the world began. Do you understand what I'm saying here? The wind, it wanted a place to wander in."

"The wind was all alone," Joseph said, working a bur from the seam of his pants.

"Yes," the old man said. "The wind was lucky though. Water came. It was the wind's wanting that made the water come. It was the wind's wanting that made the world begin. That's how it all began, Joseph. The wind, then the water. When the water came, the wind had someplace to go. One wall and the world was made. Wind and water. One above and one below. And you know what happened then, Joseph? You know what happened when the water was there?"

"Nope," Joseph said. He clasped his fingers and dropped his hands between his knees, watching the veins plump with new blood.

"A cloud was born. You know that, Joseph. I've told you this a thousand times. The cloud was the first child of the world. You need to listen better. I don't want to have to say this again."

Outside, the air was electric. Joseph bounded from the porch and raced toward the trees, pounding on the path of dirt through the browning grass, finally free. "Back by eight!" his mother's voice trailed behind. "Yeah!" he said, and leaped over the chain drooping across the head of the access road.

He hurried through a field of yellow gorse, sucking in the sweet, bruised-peach smell, and continued to a low ridge overlooking the elbow of the nameless creek where the neighborhood boys collected most days. Black cottonwood and canoe birch arched overhead, and the white rock they called Alcatraz lurked on the opposite bank, half submerged. The smell of fresh water and rotting mud was clean and rank.

Ronnie and Tony were already there, as usual, working on their new raft. Ronnie, the pudgy, elder brother, was hammering on the frame, and Tony, the lithe, graceful blond one, was propping the raft upright. The raft was a simple construction—two sheets of plywood connected by two-by-four bracings, with hunks of Styrofoam wedged underneath for flotation. A round Plexiglas window set with caulking took up the middle of the platform so that the bottom of the creek could be visible during explorations. It was by far the most advanced watercraft they'd thus far attempted.

Ronnie and Tony were twelve and eleven years old, respectively, and the ringleaders of the neighborhood's population of boys, the main agents of the shared torpor and sudden enthusiasms that drove the group to its mischief. To Joseph they were fascinating creatures, clean of childlike naïveté and adult sentimentality alike. They were capricious, wrathful, funny, and knowing, and Joseph admired them more than anyone he had ever met. He emulated all the attitudes and desires he could attribute to them. Painters hats, plaid shirts, canvas shoes—he had adopted them all, and he was proud of the place he had established in their pack. He was a quick study of the code of conduct, a strict system of alternating sadism and empathy, whose poles, he had found, could reverse almost any time. "Are you in pain?" they would say, and then, when pain was admitted, they would say, "Good!" It was a form of affection, the taunts flipping into easy acceptance, the jokes suddenly turning evil, and Joseph found the whole unstable system exhilarating. He stood on the ridge, hoping for an invitation to come down. Part of his ready reception, he knew, stemmed from the deference he showed to the older boys whenever possible.

"What's up, Joe?" Tony said, not looking up.

"Not much," Joseph said.

The brothers continued their work, and Joseph took their indifference as the invitation he had been waiting for. He slalomed down and took a place on the bank, standing with his hands balled in his pockets. Tony continued jamming pieces of Styrofoam into the gaps beneath the platform, and Ronnie kept hammering. Joseph took the liberty of fishing the cigar case from the root system of a nearby cedar and plucked from it a pack of stale Winstons. He casually lit one and kept watching.

"How's the firefighter?" Ronnie said, still not looking up.

Joseph's father was a fireman, which made him an object of interest among the older boys. For Joseph, he was a source of fierce pride.

"He saw a bear," Joseph reported.

"I thought he saw one last year," Ronnie said.

"There's lots of bears out there," Joseph said. "He's in the middle of bear territory."

"You like felching, Joe?" Tony said.

Joseph appraised the question. He had never heard of felching before. But it didn't really matter. The proper response was double-edged, an ironic admission of ignorance attached to a slight change in terms.

"Love it," he said. "But only on weekends."

The boys laughed. They liked him. He was a good student of the rules.

"So are you ready or what?" Tony said. "You going to kick some ass tomorrow?"

"I guess so," Joseph said, tapping a long ash onto the ground.

The following day, Joseph was scheduled to fight Michael Hollingsworth. There had been no argument between them, no slight or misunderstanding, but they were going to fight nonetheless. The older boys had issued a decree, and as the two youngest kids in the area, Joseph and Michael had no real choice.

The past weeks had been devoted almost exclusively to preparation for the fight. A betting pool had been organized. A training regimen had been established, including exercises such as shadow boxing, push-ups, crunches, holding one's hand over a candle until it was too painful to continue, and eating raw eggs in the morning. The week before, Ronnie and Tony had loaned Joseph and Michael jump ropes and forced them to carry heavy logs from one end of the junkyard to the other, among other activities inspired by the training sequences in *Rocky* movies.

At first the training had been kind of fun. Joseph had enjoyed the attention and the feeling of camaraderie. It had never occurred to him that the fight would actually occur. He had assumed some unforeseen circumstance would intervene. A flood would come, or an earthquake, or a wave of summer bronchitis. If nothing else, the neighborhood kids would simply lose interest and forget, as they often forgot their more elaborate schemes. They had never stolen a car, for instance, or built a pipe bomb. But as the day drew closer and the excitement increased, it was becoming hard to deny it was really happening. Tomorrow, he would fight Michael. There was no stopping it.

"Mike's been training hard," Ronnie said. "He's a little fucker. He's going to be tough."

"You do your push-ups?" Tony said.

"Yeah," Joseph said, though he hadn't. He hadn't done any crunches or deep knee bends either.

"You gonna take any shit?" Ronnie said.

"Fuck no," Joseph said.

Tony seized the cigarette from Joseph's hand and enjoyed a mighty toke, letting the smoke curl inside his mouth. His blushing cheeks and feathered hair were like an angel's. "Don't nig-lip it," he said, and handed back the burning cigarette. On his next drag Joseph was careful to curl his lips over his teeth before touching his mouth to the filter.

He understood that it was his duty to fight Michael, and that he had been selected for a reason. Michael was not very well liked among the boys. It was Joseph's task to humiliate him in a novel fashion, to serve as a tool of Michael's further disgrace.

"That little turd," Tony said. "You're gonna kick his ass, Joe."

The affection in his voice was almost too much to bear. Joseph was relieved when his mother's voice came drifting through the trees, rising and falling with its sad, evening lilt, calling him back home for dinner.

It was taco night and the table was filled with bowls of beans, hamburger, grated cheese, diced onion and tomato, and a basket of corn tortillas. Joseph greedily assembled his meal, trying to put the fight out of his mind. It was no use though. It kept coming back in the form of questions. Where and when would the fight happen? Who would be watching? How long would it last? What if he bled? A lot? The questions were unanswerable and led only to more questions.

A part of Joseph longed to tell his mother everything about the fight, but he knew that would be wrong. What happened at the creek was not discussed with grown-ups. On the contrary, what happened there was specifically opposed to their world. Without secrecy the world of the boys would not function at all. No one had to tell him that. And besides, she had her own problems to deal with.

After dinner it was time for his grandfather's weekly bath. Joseph's mother filled a metal bucket with steaming water and handed Joseph a stiff sea sponge and together they entered the room. The old man was still talking about the cloud as if Joseph had never left.

"The sun arrived and all the colors came out," he said, as Joseph's mother lifted him from the bed and placed him on a wicker chair. "After the sun, the earth arrived. The dirt rolled out and quartz and agate and salt came up. Salt was a modest element. It brought out the best in other things. Salt alone is no good though."

Joseph pulled the sheets off the mattress and rolled them into a bundle, catching glimpses of his grandfather's chest, tufted with white hairs, and his pelvic bones protruding like carved shelves of stone. The old man pinched Joseph's cheek, and Joseph politely accepted the pain, hoping his mother recognized the great effort he was making.

Joseph's mother dipped the sponge into the bucket and ran it over her father's bony arms, swabbing his shoulders and rib cage. Joseph stretched the fitted sheet over the mattress and smoothed the regular sheet on top of it, tucking in the edges. He caught a glimpse of the old man's withered nether regions, the copses of tangled hair and shapeless flesh.

"The rainbow is a devilish thing," the old man said. "You can spend your life trying to catch a rainbow. Don't get mixed up with the rainbow, Joseph. It only leads you to nothing in the end. The moon is devilish, too. Don't expect anything from the moon."

"Okay," Joseph said.

Joseph's mother toweled off her father, patting him along the shoulders and along the chest, and together she and Joseph lifted him and tucked him back into bed. They pulled the quilt up around his shoulders and fluffed the pillow behind his thin neck. As soon as the blankets had been pulled under his chin, he fell asleep and began snoring. His mouth dropped open and his arms lay straight along his sides. The furrows on his forehead relaxed and his ears seemed to droop back on his head. Quietly, Joseph and his mother slipped from the room.

Joseph's mother went to the living room and flipped on the TV, hoping for news of the forest fires.

"Night," Joseph said.

"Night," his mother said, and before the commercials were over she was asleep, too.

In the morning, Joseph woke early. He tried falling back to sleep but he couldn't, so he got up and watched TV—a robot cartoon, then a quiz show, and then a superhero cartoon. He tried to forget what was in store, but it was impossible; every show only underscored the grim fate that awaited him. Coyote crushed by an anvil. Spiderman thrown through a wall. Joseph imagined the coming body blows, the bloodshed, the stinging pain. The possibility of breaking something was not insignificant.

Midway through the first quarter of a college football game, his mother appeared, groggy from sleep. She made a pot of coffee and returned to her bedroom and came out wearing her sheepskin coat and faded blue jeans, which meant it was time to go somewhere. She punched the power button and the screen's image contracted into a white pinprick, then died in a final spasm of popping static.

"Come on," she said. "We've got errands."

"I don't want to go," Joseph said.

"Too bad."

"I've got plans."

"We're not arguing about this. Let's go."

Joseph gave up easily enough. In reality, he was happy to go. He now had a plausible excuse to tell Ronnie and Tony if he missed the fight. He had tried his best but his mother had forced him to leave for the day. What could he do?

Pulling onto the paved street Joseph saw Michael Hollingsworth's mother taking the garbage to the curb. The two mothers waved, oblivious to the secret destiny their sons shared.

The first stop was Webb Ranch, a fruit market where campesinos collected each morning to look for work. Joseph's mother toured the bins, filling plastic bags with broccoli and green beans and selecting a bucket of raspberries while Joseph wandered the perimeter of the parking lot, watching his shadow change shape. Next was Safeway, where they piled the cart with cans of black beans, mango juice, frozen pizzas, and Tater Tots, and after that, Rozzati's, a roadside restaurant where they ate Swiss cheese and grilled onions on sourdough rolls at a wooden picnic bench gouged with rough initials and crude hearts.

Out in the world, the fight seemed like the dream of another life. Away from the house his mother was more cheerful, too. She told him a story about living in Hawaii for two years and getting to know a dolphin in a sheltered, turquoise bay. Her stories were no better than Joseph's grandfather's, but at least she didn't repeat herself all the time. They talked about his dad, and imagined him out in the mountains, spotting bears, saving deer, digging ditches faster than any other man alive.

"When does he get back?" Joseph said.

"When the job's done," his mother said, and Joseph waited to hear more, but his mother had already begun collecting their trash.

"Do we have to go home now?" he said, pausing at the garbage can.

"We do," she said. "Grandpa needs us."

"There's nothing else to do?" he said.

"I thought you had plans," she said.

He had plans, it was true. He followed her with resignation to the car.

They got back in the mid-afternoon and the street was empty. The fight had no preordained hour, but Joseph knew the other kids might be waiting for him even as he helped his mother carry in the groceries. He still hoped more than anything for some reprieve. If there was any way to beg out and maintain his honor, he would have, but there was not. He understood that any mercy had to come from without or not at all.

Maybe the test was entirely in the lead-up to the fight. It was all about the demonstration of loyalty to the idea. At the last moment the command would be rescinded and the tragedy averted. Very possibly, the mind of the neighborhood had spared him. He hoped.

For the next hour Joseph stayed close to home, making himself available but keeping a low profile. If they wanted him, they could come find him, he figured. There was no dishonor in not actively seeking them out.

He crouched near an oak tree, fascinated by the fine dust in the grooves of the living wood. The tree's posture was mournful, the way it spread and swayed in the smallest breeze. The sunlight on aspen leaves and the smell of blackberries in the late summer heat filled him with nostalgia for the brief past he knew. He wondered if the desolate feeling in his chest would lessen over the years. Perhaps it was just the feeling of childhood itself.

The day aged into late afternoon. He practiced his fighting techniques, holding his fists high, keeping light on his feet. But then he got tired and sat down, letting clods of dirt crumble through his fingers. His father's truck's tire tracks were beginning to grow grass, he noted, and the old oil spots were beginning to disappear from view.

It was almost four o'clock when the contact finally came.

"Joseph," a voice said.

He looked up. At first he saw no one. But then, at the edge of the yard, like apparitions, two figures appeared. They were the girls from Stowe Lane, Sarah and Rebecca, six and seven years old, with rosy makeup on their cheeks and gobs of mascara clinging to their lashes. Their long, floral dresses were dirty from the forest floor. Sarah, the older one with black hair and a big gap in her teeth, watched him intently. Her lips were coated with orange lipstick. She stepped from behind the forsythia bush into the open sunlight.

"Ronnie says you're supposed to go to the creek and get ready now."

Joseph's stomach curdled. The news, entirely expected, still came as a shock. He got to his feet and brushed off his pants. He had no choice. The group had spoken. Dutifully, he followed the girls into the woods.

Joseph heard the boys well before he saw them, their voices banging in the trees, the hard snapping of branches in the underbrush. He heard a heavy rock plunge into the water with a goofy, plopping kerplunk.

He was surprised to find how many boys had come out. Ronnie and Tony were there, of course. But also Patrick and Steven and David, rich kids from the development over the hill, and a pair of fat kids he remembered from the last school year whose names he didn't know. Off in the brush he spotted another handful, and far downstream he could discern two more, slapping the water with alder branches. How had the word gotten out? What elaborate network of communication existed unbeknownst to him? It was hard to comprehend.

Michael Hollingsworth himself prowled the shallows. From a distance, he looked less than intimidating. He was a full year older than Joseph, but he was gaunt, sallow, and spindly-armed. His skin was chalky white. He might even have weighed a few pounds less than Joseph. Joseph watched him clamber over the rocks in the pumpkin-colored down vest he wore every day. In his right hand he held a butterfly net, and every few steps he jabbed the net into the water, raised it, and jabbed it again, like an Indian, unaware or uncaring that anyone was observing.

Patrick, with his freckles and buck teeth, was the first to approach. "Dude, you reek," he said. "You smell like perfume."

"No I don't," Joseph said, and turned to find the girls, but they were already gone, mere messengers.

"Hey, Joe," Tony said, flicking a cigarette butt into the creek. "Where you been?"

Joseph shrugged as the boys moved around him in a tightening circle.

"You ready?"

His throat made an audible click and gulp. "You better be," Tony said. "This is hard-core. Are you hard-core?"

"Yeah," Joseph said, but he lacked the strength to add the additional curse words that would have gone over well.

Down the creek, an unknown boy held a stick with six crawdads dangling from white strings. He raised it above his head and began whirling it around, whooping, until one by one the bodies of the crawdads came loose and sailed off into the water, leaving behind a staff of twelve dead claws.

"Fight! Fight! Fight!" he chanted. The other boys joined in. "Fight! Fight! Fight!" And en masse they adjourned the creek, headed for the ring.

The boxing ring was a blue square spray-painted onto the gravelly, oil-soaked parking lot behind Ronnie and Tony's house. A fleet of broken cars hid the spot from view, and the bougainvillea on the walls made a fragrant pink backdrop. The group of boys trooped into the lot with Michael and Joseph at the center. On the out-skirts there was much pushing and cussing and tossing of Patrick's orange hat back and forth above his outstretched hands.

"Two bucks on Joe! Two bucks on Joe!"

"He's gonna waste Michael."

"They're both pussies."

As it turned out, there was only a single pair of boxing gloves, which meant the boys would have to fight with one glove apiece. Joseph received the left glove, and Michael the right, Michael's ten-month seniority in age giving him first pick.

Lacing the glove, Joseph scanned the group for allies, only to find that he had none. As if by some magic, the normal alliances had all broken down. Ronnie was in Michael's corner, whispering in his ear. Tony was taking bets from two unknown interlopers. The other kids were all just hooting for the fight itself, the spectacle, with no preference as to who landed what punches on whom.

Joseph had misjudged his place. In the space of mere hours, the whole arrangement of the neighborhood had capsized. He was not the instrument of Michael's embarrassment at all, but rather a pawn in a much bigger game. He was a fool.

An upturned plastic bucket marked his corner, and he was guided to sit down. Tony became his manager again, but only out of perverse duty, not friendship, and his gleeful talk about strategy in Joseph's ear was purely to feed his bloodlust. He put his arm around Joseph's shoulder and patted him on the chest.

"You can take him, man," he said. "You can totally whip his ass. Keep your head down and your hands up, like I told you. All right? You can take this kid. Make him bleed. Go for the nose."

"I don't know . . ." Joseph said.

"That's right, man. You're a fucking champ," Patrick chimed in. He was stalking from corner to corner, stoking the fear and anger on either side. "Michael says you're a faggot," he said. "You going to take that?"

Joseph glanced across the ring at Michael. His dingy yellow hair floated around his skeletal face. His hollow cheeks were flushed. He nodded violently at something Ronnie was saying, his whole frame shuddering as one of the boys massaged his shoulders. He smirked, unaware that the attention he received was poisoned. He welcomed it, and for that Joseph despised him.

Michael looked up and met Joseph's gaze, his half-lidded eyes cloudy with hate. He banged his bare fist against his glove, then banged his glove against his chest. Joseph was numb. This was not what he had signed up for.

Steven, a nearsighted, asthmatic redhead, strode into the center of the ring holding two hunks of wood. Normally nervous and tightly wound, he was radiant with excitement today. He turned around in a slow circle and raised the blocks of wood above his head.

"All right," he said. "All right." The crowd quieted a few degrees.

"All right. It's time for the main event! The battle of the century! Only one of these fighters will leave the ring victorious. This is a battle of strength and courage. Each round is two minutes. We'll go until we have a winner. No biting. No scratching. When I hit these blocks together, you men come out fighting. All right?"

The crowd roared and Michael made a bestial sound as Ronnie kneaded his back. Tony, seeing the massage strategy, clasped Joseph's back and began pinching and prodding as well. Steven banged the two pieces of wood and scurried off, and the boxing match was underway.

Before Joseph could even think, Michael was racing from his corner with his arms flailing. Somehow Joseph managed to evade him, awkwardly shuffling off to the side, and from there the boys began circling each other. Michael pranced, making tight, exploratory jabs, and Joseph ducked to avoid the punches. Michael turned his head and spit hard onto the ground. The spectators screamed.

They circled the ring three times before Michael finally pulled within arm's length and began swinging wildly. Joseph couldn't quite believe it. The fists jumped all around him, to the left and right, falling wide, and he held his glove with both hands before his face, trying to protect his nose and mouth and eyes. For a moment he thought he might come out untouched, but then the first blow connected. He felt the heavy, dull weight of Michael's arm on the bone of his skull.

The crowd roared and Joseph stumbled back, swinging blindly in self-defense. He had trouble aiming his gloved hand but his bare right fist clubbed Michael on the side of the face. Joseph felt a surge of hope, but a second later Michael was back, windmilling and shoving, elbowing and kicking.

Joseph was on the verge of falling when the wood blocks

clacked and Michael was pulled away. Joseph staggered to his corner and sat down on his bucket, breathing hard. His mind was empty and alert. His arms were exhausted. He felt his lip swelling and tasted blood in his mouth. He passed his tongue over his front teeth and felt it slide like oil. He saw the whole situation with clarity. The boys were forcing the universe to turn on itself, to vanquish itself, and that was demonic somehow.

"Keep your hands up," Tony said. "You're letting him land every punch, all right? Don't take that shit. You're awesome. You're a killer."

"I'm bleeding," Joseph said.

"It's nothing," Tony said.

The wood clacked again and Joseph was pushed to his feet. He wanted only to flee, but Michael was already crossing the ring with renewed intensity. His glove and bare fist were in motion, his damp hair sticking to his sweat-glazed forehead. Joseph tried to ward off the next round of blows, but his arms seemed to crumple under the force. Michael's punches landed repeatedly on Joseph's head and neck until Joseph curled over to protect his stomach and take the worst on his back. Through the din of his body he could hear the rest of the boys chanting his name, urging him to fight back.

"Joseph! Come on!"

"Michael! Waste on him! Waste that puss!"

His mistake was trying to stand up. Given the smallest crevice of an opening, Michael managed to land an uppercut and knocked him backward. For a long moment, Joseph's entire body was catapulted into the air. His feet leaped out from under him and his weight redistributed from bottom to top. He hit the dirt, and pain shot through his spine. His arms slapped the earth and he could hear the scuttle of pebbles under his outstretched legs.

For a second the whole world became still. The crowd waited. Michael staggered, slightly shocked by the dexterity of his own punch. He loomed over Joseph, hips thrust forward, glove hanging at his side. Sweat beaded his face. His victory was all but complete.

Joseph tried not to cry but the twitching muscles were beyond his control. He swallowed, holding back, but he was too far gone. He felt his shoulders shudder and his face erupted in hot tears.

"Jo-seph! Jo-seph! Jo-seph!"

Ronnie pulled Joseph to his feet and tried to get him to keep fighting, but his body refused to cooperate. He was sobbing too hard. Eventually Ronnie gave up and left Joseph huddled in his corner and crossed the ring to declare Michael the winner.

Michael was not a gracious winner. He pumped his fists and hollered as the gambled money exchanged hands. Then, mercifully, the boys swept off to 7-Eleven for celebratory candy and Big Gulps. Joseph, defeated, ignored, sat in the dirt. A few of the boys ambled by and patted him on the back on their way out.

Tony was the last to approach. He sidled over and crouched down. Joseph wiped his nose with the back of his arm and wiped his arm on his shirt. Through the shame and exhaustion his spirit surged with gratitude at Tony's attention.

"You all right?" Tony said.

"Yeah," Joseph said.

"You did good today," Tony said.

"I did not," Joseph said.

"You did. You fought hard. You got in some good hits."

"Barely."

"No way, man. You nailed him. I saw it. You couldn't see his face. He was out of it."

"Nah."

"I'm telling you. I saw it."

Joseph sighed wetly and hid his smile in his shoulder.

"Hey, just don't tell anyone what happened today, all right?" Tony said.

"I wouldn't," Joseph said firmly.

"What are you going to tell your mom?" Tony prodded.

"I don't know."

"Well, think of something," he said. "Don't tell her anything. We don't need that."

"Of course not," Joseph said. "I wouldn't."

"Cool. I'll see you later, man." Tony ruffled Joseph's hair. "You kicked some ass out there, man. He's older than you. You were great." And then he jogged away toward 7-Eleven.

Joseph didn't say anything to his mother. He didn't have to. He came home covered with dirt and blood and his lip almost big enough to cover his nose. She wasn't that stupid.

She called Ronnie and Tony's mother immediately, and when he came out of the bathroom, she was still on the phone, bawling her out.

"You shouldn't have called," he said.

"What do you mean?" she said, but he didn't answer. There was no point.

For the rest of the night Joseph brooded. He took a hot bath and ate a pork chop and a baked potato. Then he watched an old western on TV. He considered calling Tony and telling him what had happened, how his mother had acted against his will, but he had never talked to Tony on the phone before and he knew it would seem strange. He could only hope that the group understood he had done his best. He had kept the day's secrets as closely as possible. During commercials he imagined sitting on Michael's chest, pounding his face into a mush of blood and crushed bone.

Every half hour Joseph's mother checked on him and he refused to acknowledge her. Finally, to escape her attention, he slipped from the living room to his grandfather's bedside.

The old man was sleeping. His beard moved softly on his chest. His eyebrows were bushy gray caterpillars. Joseph sat at the window, relieved to get out of his mother's sight for a while. He watched the woods, powdered in moonlight, a bluish, barely moving world of branches and leaves.

When the old man awakened, he seemed frightened at first, but then his red eyes sparked with recognition. He saw Joseph and seemed to remember something, and the fear seemed to recede. Joseph's fat lip didn't register at all.

"Animals," the old man said huskily. "The animals. We'd come to the animals, hadn't we? We are all animals here, Joseph. We are all animals on this earth together."

"That sounds about right," Joseph said.

"They came and built their nests and molehills everywhere," the old man said. "They lived in their caves and in their coral reefs. The animals made the earth their home, which was good for the earth, because the earth was hungry. The earth ate them all in the end."

Joseph watched the moonlight in the yard. The distant city emitted the palest glow. Faint shadows were moving at the edge of the yard and at first Joseph thought nothing of them. He knew the darkness had a way of playing tricks sometimes, having been spooked many times in the woods by piles of leaves and half-hidden stumps, thinking they were dead bodies or sleeping hobos. Even when the shadows moved again, he assumed it was just the trees. But then dark shapes emerged from the brush and took on human forms—Ronnie, Tony, Michael—carrying paper bags.

The old man coughed, tapping deep pockets in his lungs, a hissing, rattling susurration appended to each hack.

Joseph gazed out the window as the boys drew close to the house and pulled rolls of toilet paper from their bags. Silently they began to hurl the rolls into the air.

Long white strands unspooled in the darkness, crossing paths, falling to earth like shooting stars. The ribbons sputtered as they rose, catching in the branches of the plum tree in the garden, coating the bushes and plants along the side wall. Joseph heard the soft flumph of the rolls striking the shingles and tumbling down the opposite incline. When the boys depleted their loads, they opened backpacks to reveal more and cranked their fresh rolls high into the gloom. Then, as quickly as they had materialized, they were gone, leaving Joseph at the sill.

"Just a little longer now," the old man said, rubbing his chest. "And you know what happens then? You know what happens when the world is done?"

Joseph stared at the maple tree's mummified trunk and made no reply. His breath clouded the window.

"The wind," the old man said. "The world ends, and we become wind. I thought I'd told you that before, Joseph. You have to listen."

THE COAST

MY WIFE, JUDY, loved the coast. When we first met, back in
our twenties, we went out there all the time. She was a paralegal
then, and I worked at a bookstore, and we'd take off in the late afternoon so we could make it to Oswald Park by sunset, and end the
day roasting hot dogs and playing guitar under the pulsing stars. In
the winter we prowled from Astoria all the way down to Coos Bay
looking for cheap hotel rooms, and took midnight walks alongside
the frigid surf in search of glass buoys and whatever else the current might wash in. We spotted our share of deer, eagles, whales,
and burnt-out ceramists on those trips. One night in Depoe Bay
we befriended a teenager and his pet rat, and saw a barn owl swoop
down in the moonlight and pluck the animal right off the kid's
shoulder.

Over the years things changed a fair bit. The Californians came in,
building their angular beach houses and yoga centers. The galleries
got more expensive. But it stayed largely the same, too. The battered
shore pines gripping the road shoulders never left and the old nauti-
cal bars kept serving their watery beer. No matter what happened, or
how many people came, a certain hovering mystery always remained,
coaxing us back.

In 1986 we got married at Cape Lookout, accompanied by a jazz band, a crowd of picnickers looking on from the side. Judy wore a white cotton dress and a white bandanna in her red hair and the freckles over her pug nose shone brightly in the hot July sun. Afterward we moved the party to the Eagle's Lodge in Netarts for homemade tamales and blackberry pie, unbothered by the fact that the nuptial sand castle had been destroyed by the incoming tide.

Over time I came to imagine Judy and the coast as somehow the same. It was like her spirit seeped into the manzanita and yellow swamp lantern, the clapboard chowder bars and the chapped whale murals. Driving along Highway 99 a dozen memories were always waiting: the birdhouse we bought from the rattled Vietnam veteran, the flapjacks in the logger bar with the Paul Bunyan sculpture, the fly-plagued hike up Saddle Mountain. In the city, she could become tense and judgmental. But out among the sandstone and basalt headlands, the funny, spontaneous person I'd always known could be counted on to reemerge.

We couldn't afford a beach house—I ended up teaching fourth grade, she worked for the state—but in 1993 our rich friend Bill bought a cottage in Newport attached to a defunct hotel and kindly let us use it whenever we felt the need. The cabin had a drafty, double-mouthed stone fireplace, a galley kitchen, and a living room bulging with bay windows facing the lighthouse on the far side of Nye Beach. Maybe it was the positive ions in the sea air, or the white noise of the crashing waves, but I had no memory of Judy as anything but happy there. We went out to the cabin at least every few months and talked almost every time about someday retiring nearby.

It was only two days before our regular trip that Judy was riding her bike along Interstate Avenue and a dump truck turned without signaling, veering across her path. The driver never saw her and she was crushed under the rear tire along with the bike and her groceries. I got the call at work and rushed to the hospital as fast as I could, but by then it was already too late. She had no idea I was there. She held on for a few hours, her ribs broken and her brain badly swelling, and that night, with only the two of us in the room, she passed away. After twenty-five years together, close to half our lives, she was gone, right on the cusp of our fall vacation.

Three months later I drove out to the coast, hoping for what, I wasn't sure. If nothing else, I told myself, I just needed some space. Ever since the funeral it had become almost impossible to leave the house without running into wet-eyed well-wishers, and staying at home had become an unpleasant option, too, what with all Judy's things staring at me from the corners. I appreciated the support I'd been getting from friends and family—it kept me alive— but in a way even the charity was a burden, a constant series of obligations to fulfill. What I needed was real privacy, and the cabin was the first and only thing that came to mind.

In the back of my head I also had the idea that the coast might hold some kind of message for me. I didn't know what it would be, or how it would be expressed, but I imagined some kind of reckoning to be done out there. It only seemed fair. Judy had been taken away so quickly, without anything like a proper good-bye. I felt I deserved at least one more chance to communicate with her, and the coast seemed like the only place where it might actually come to pass.

I left on a Friday afternoon. The minute I pulled away from the house it started raining and it kept up, on and off, the whole way out. Rain doused the windshield, followed by bolts of sun, followed by rain again, intermixed with patches of fog, sleet, and buffeting wind. The weather might have seemed ominous if I hadn't driven the route so many times before and known there were at least eight microclimates between the city and the ocean. For a drive to the coast in the wintertime, this was just par for the course.

I crossed the Willamette valley, passing the fallow fruit farms and groves of oak trees, and climbed into the moist coastal mountains. The thin stands of Douglas fir barely shielding the blasted clear-cuts whipped by on either side, making me wonder, as always, whom the loggers thought they were fooling with their trick. Not me.

I arrived in Newport just before dark, under a clearing sky, and turned off the highway into the old section of town. It was a cute town—there were cobbled streets and wrought-iron lampposts—but thankfully not too cute. The grip of tourism hadn't quite latched on this far south, which was part of the reason we'd always liked it so much.

As I turned off the main street, I caught sight of a young girl's face in the window of a shingled beach bungalow. She was a moony girl, with sandy blonde hair pulled into tight pigtails and ruby lips against her pale skin, and the way she stared made me think she was waiting for something, possibly even for me. Maybe she had something to tell me, I thought. She was offering herself as some kind of sign. Passing along, though, seeing the flicker of the TV in the room, I realized she was just incredibly bored.

The hotel was a dilapidated box with broken windows and ragged shake siding, partly hiding the cabin at the end of an over-grown alleyway. The key was in the fake rock, as usual, and inside the door the smell of aged wood and ocean brine was reassuring. I dropped my bag on the floor, turned up the heat, put the whiskey on the shelf, and then promptly turned around and walked back out. Our routine had always been to hit the beach directly upon arrival. I figured I should stick to our patterns if I expected Judy's spirit to pay a visit.

It was only four o'clock, but already the winter sun was heading down. The wind was blustery and the sky was all over the place—dark in one quadrant and pale blue in another, with splashes of magenta, orange, and streaks of hot pink in the lower regions. The billowing cumulus clouds gliding over the ocean were like slow-moving buildings of water and air.

I skirted the edge of the tide, avoiding heaps of bullwhip kelp and seagull carcasses and blobs of broken jellyfish, and tried to imagine Judy walking alongside me. I thought of her rounded shoulders, her full lips, the lilac smell of her hair. I picked at memories of New Year's in Brooklyn, our month in Morocco, our last phone conversation about whether or not we needed fresh half-and-half.

I waited for something to happen, but nothing did. Her voice didn't whisper from the rocks or the sea. The sky didn't open. I felt no tingles down my spine. I couldn't say I was surprised, really. Judy was a practical person, and ghostly visitations didn't seem like her style. Our love had never been the flamboyant kind.

I came to a giant rock and watched the waves smash against its wall, pulverizing into mist. The orange sun touched the horizon. Overhead, the stars were beginning to speckle the dark shell of sky and a flock of gulls keeled near the trees.

It was fully dark when I got back to town. I ate dinner at a vegan place with live folk music, the fruit of the hippie diaspora that had reached Newport decades before, and almost despite myself, I started to relax. The people were friendly there, my tempeh tacos were excellent, and the beer improved my mood considerably. By the second pint I was actually feeling pretty good. The grief had started to unclench its teeth a little.

Eating alone wasn't always so bad, I had to admit. Nor, for that matter, was waking up in an empty bed or going to the movies in the afternoon or sitting in a coffee shop watching the traffic go by. On some level, if I was really honest with myself, I was beginning to relish my newfound solitude. I enjoyed making the small decisions about which way to turn on the beach or what restaurant to try. I liked the slight puzzle a single man my age seemed to pose. I couldn't exactly admit these feelings to anyone—I was supposed to be in despair after all—but out on the coast, away from my daily routine, I could at least begin to admit to myself a glimmer of optimism was kindling.

After dinner I wasn't ready to head for the cabin yet, so I wandered around Newport, fending off the nagging guilt about my own lack of unhappiness. Maybe I should have taken my little vacation elsewhere, I thought. Someplace new, someplace unhaunted by memories. Passing the bookstore-café and the brick-oven bakery where we used to eat, I was reminded again what a selfish person I was simply for being alive.

Once I got back to the cabin, I realized, I'd be inside for the night, so I took my time meandering around. I peeked into a smoky bar and window-shopped at the knitting store, which was closed for the evening. I coaxed a cat from a hedge for a little petting.

The streets of Newport were desolate in the off-season, so it came as a mild jolt when I turned the corner and saw my old friend Alissa Donegan in the window of the Seagull, the neighborhood's overpriced Italian place. At first I doubted it was even her. I'd only seen her once or twice since the funeral. But on second look there was no question. She was sitting alone, eating a bowl of soup, and reading a paperback she seemed to be having a hard time keeping open. The window framed her grandly, the low candlelight etching a fine outline along her bare neck. For a moment, motionless, pinning the book's spine in place, she could have been a stuffed display in a carefully composed diorama.

I'd begun looking forward to my whiskey and television at the cabin by that point, but before thinking I rapped on the glass. Alissa looked up, startled, and we gave each other questioning expressions, then smiles. And the decision was made. I went inside to pay my respects.

Alissa was standing beside her table, waiting for me. She had long, black hair, narrow, graceful eyes, and cinnamon skin, testament to her mixed background of Filipino and Irish. Her mouth was bracketed by deep dimples and her body was petite but shapely. She might have thickened a little over the years, and some of the youthful sheen had worn off, but she remained, to me, a beautiful woman. At her table we hugged warmly.

"So bizarre," I said.

"I've been thinking about you!" she said, which I knew to be an old trick of hers. She had always just been thinking about everyone. You could run into her at the library or at the DMV, and always you had just been on her mind. Another trick was the constant touching. Touching your shoulder, touching your elbow, an incessant subconversation of gentle brushes and cradlings. "What are you doing here?" she said, tugging my sleeve. Alissa could have been an actress, I thought. She was such an expert at tapping people's affection.

I told her I came out to the coast pretty often, and asked her what she was doing there.

"Working," she said. "I can't concentrate in my house anymore.

I need some peace and quiet. I really can't believe you're here, James. This is so amazing. Really, I was just thinking about you, and you showed up. I summoned you."

I laughed. In the city Alissa was generally so distracted by social obligations she could barely stay in one place long enough to complete a conversation. In this case though, in an empty restaurant in an empty town on the empty coast, she was focused and present and I believed her charms. I wanted to believe.

We didn't talk long, just enough to catch up on the recent news: Karin's new restaurant, Dan's new dog. When her dinner arrived, she asked me to stay, but I decided I'd been there long enough. I figured I still owed it to my dead wife to despair a little this evening.

"But maybe I'll see you around?" I said.

"Definitely," she said. "I'm here until Monday."

"I'm here until Monday, too," I said, and hurriedly, as her plate steamed, we exchanged cell phone numbers and hugged one more time.

"I really can't believe you're here," she said again.

"Your food's getting cold," I said. "I'll talk to you later."

"You better."

That night, sitting in the cottage, drinking my whiskey and watching the moon, I found myself thinking not about Judy, but about Alissa Donegan. Seeing her had stirred something up in me.

I'd known Alissa a long time, almost as long as I'd known Judy. We'd all met through Jill, the former roommate of my former girlfriend Amy, and for a few bright years we had spent a lot of time together. We'd shared the same clique, gone to the same parties, passed the same gossip. Before Judy and I had finally committed, I'd sometimes even wondered if there might be something more between Alissa and me. I could still remember a few times when the line had almost been crossed: a late-night back porch after a birthday party; an afternoon riverbank, alone on the rocks. We'd always had other things going though, other commitments. And, I told myself, I had never wanted to play the game that getting her would have entailed.

Then the pairings had been set and the tribe had dispersed. Amy and Jud. Addie and Sean. Myself and Judy. Alissa and I had remained friendly, but over time we had drifted apart. The fact that we'd known each other over two decades now was hard to comprehend.

I sat in the bay window, reluctant to admit just how often I'd nursed thoughts of Alissa over the years. I used to imagine us together someday in an alternate life, in a house full of hanging ferns and succulents and at least one beautiful Persian rug. I could remember nights when I'd thought of her with such longing that her name was like a bell gonging in my brain. I figured everyone had this kind of person in their heads. A phantom of missed possibility. An almost lover. We all lived with them, knowing they were just figments of our imagination, but never entirely getting rid of them either.

The lights of the ships burned on the horizon, steady and evenly spaced. I imagined the lonely men on their wet, treacherous decks, looking back at the lights along the coast. I got up and poured myself another glass of whiskey. When I returned, I pushed Alissa from my mind. I told myself I was here to mourn, after all. Not to pine.

I woke up in the morning to the sound of booming waves and the unflinching horizon line of the water meeting the sky. I stood at the window awhile and watched the clouds shift, contemplating the warp of the earth's roundness extending just beyond my frame of perception.

I knew Judy would have been outdoors already, and she probably would have dragged me with her. So with her in mind I pulled on my jacket and headed into the cold air. I tried to retrace my walk of the day before but I didn't get far. Well before the giant rock I turned around and found a breakfast place with decent pastries and fresh-roasted coffee.

When I got back, there was a call from Alissa waiting for me. Her work was not very pressing, she said, and I should call her if I wanted to make some plan. I dialed immediately and we agreed to meet in an hour or so and take a drive to a bookstore I knew down in Florence, about fifty miles south. Hanging up, I felt a twinge of fresh guilt. Was I betraying Judy in some way? Was I being diverted from my ritual of remembrance? I decided if I was, I didn't care that much. I'd come to the coast for something magical and this was what the coast had provided.

Around noon Alissa showed up. She was wearing a bright orange anorak, a canary yellow mohair scarf, faded blue jeans, pink socks, and powder-blue clogs. The spectrum was almost blinding, but somehow it all held together. She'd always had a way with color.

"Morning," she said. "It's still morning, right? Or no?"

"Close enough," I said. "Come on in. I need to get my crap together."

On the way through the door, she tripped over the threshold. She had a bumbling, comic way of comporting herself. The two parts, the artfulness and the klutziness, clashed in a way that was hard not to find winning.

"I packed us sandwiches," she said, holding a brown bag. "But look." She opened the bag to show me two sandwiches that were mangled almost beyond recognition. "I don't know what happened. The peanut butter was really hard."

"They don't look that bad," I said.

"They look terrible."

"We don't have to eat them."

"But I made them for us. We can't waste them."

"Okay. I'm sure they'll taste good."

"I can't believe I can't even make a sandwich. Who does that?"

"They're not so bad," I said. "They just, you know, have character."

"Pathetic."

We kept the conversation light as we headed out of town. But soon enough, wheeling around the wild vistas of the coastline— the volcanic protuberances, the haystacks and sheer basalt cliffs— we were more at ease. On a deep level we had always remained close; it was only on a day-to-day level we hardly knew each other. I didn't even know what her job was anymore.

"I'm working at a home and garden magazine," she told me, "doing layout for Albert. He's the top editor now. About time."

On the topic of romance, Alissa said she was dating around, but not very seriously, which wasn't surprising. Early on, Alissa had committed herself to what she thought of as an artistic lifestyle, and on principle she had never settled down. Not that she had pursued her artwork with much ambition either. She'd just cultivated a certain serendipity in her daily routines. She made friends in grocery stores; she took sudden trips. Her sense of adventure had come at the cost of both her creative impulses and some of the normal intimacies of life, as far as I could tell, although maybe she was more diligent than I realized—I wasn't sure. I went ahead and asked her if she had taken any pictures lately.

"I'm more into gardening now," she said. "I haven't picked up the camera in over a year."

"I still have one of your pictures," I admitted. "I got it framed, actually. Not too long ago."

"You did?" She seemed incredulous.

"Yeah. It's in my dining room."

"Oh God."

"What? Why 'Oh God?'"

"I'm sure it sucks."

"It doesn't suck," I said. "It's good. I think so anyway."

"Which one is it?" she said.

"It's one of the cops." For a period, she had been taking pictures of police at leisure, some of which I genuinely liked very much. "It's a cop eating an ice-cream cone."

"Oh yeah," she said. "That one wasn't so bad."

"It's better than not bad," I said. "It's good."

"You're my one fan."

We paused, passing an inlet rimmed with finlike rock formations. The waves repeatedly glazed a tabletop of stone, the lacey whiteness draining over the black edge and back into the sea, only to reappear moments later with the next swell. For a moment we were both transfixed by the world of strange, gleaming surfaces and seeping froth.

"How about you, though?" she said. "How are you? It's been a big year."

"It has," I agreed.

"Tell me about it."

"That would take awhile."

"What are we doing? We're just driving around. I want to hear."

So I told her about my year. The initial trauma of Judy's death, the slow acclimation to the loss, the outpouring of generosity from all our friends. I talked about the pangs of dread, the drying-up of generosity and the dwindling invitations. I tried to sound matter-of-fact, knowing that I would hold together better that way, and also that philosophical acceptance was the more attractive posture in general.

"It's just so unfair," she said, shaking her head. "I still can't believe it."

"What can you do?" I said. "It's out of your hands."

"They say it's all good," she said, "but it's not all good. It's not all good at all. She was so young. She was so great."

"No," I agreed. "It's not all good."

We passed a seagull hovering over a rocky cliff, perfectly still, pinned in the confluence of cold wind draughts.

"Not all bad either, though," she said, touching my leg. "That's something to remember."

Climbing a hill, we zoomed past a once-colorful billboard for something called the Sea Lion Cave, a tourist trap for coastal RV traffic. A few minutes later we passed another sign, and soon enough, the building itself appeared, perched on a bluff, looking just crappy enough that it might be worth investigating. I had driven by the place with Judy more times than I could count, but we had never really thought to stop. The roof was pebbled with gravel and the signs in the window looked like they had been there at least fifty years.

"Families Welcome!" one said. "World Famous!" touted another. The parking lot was almost empty.

"Have you ever been there?" Alissa said.

"Nope," I said. "I've driven by but I never went in. You?"

"No. Maybe we should check it out."

The decision had to be made immediately or else the twisting, shoulderless road would shoot us too far and there would be no turning around until Florence. What kind of day was this going to be, I wondered: an adventurous one or an efficient one? Fuck it, I thought. I cranked the wheel, sending us sailing into the field of asphalt.

We locked the car and trudged through the blustery wind to the glass doors. Inside, the building was mainly a gift shop full of the usual Western trash: thunder eggs, key chains, posters of whales, bear mugs, moose T-shirts. For nine dollars, an elevator would deliver us three hundred feet downward for a glimpse of what was advertised as the largest sea cavern in the world, populated by wintering sea lions.

"Are there lions down there right now?" I asked the girl at the counter. She was a prude-looking teenager, wearing a frilly blouse and safari hat.

"The monitor says currently a few hundred," the girl said.

We asked a young couple emerging from the elevator if the descent was worth the price of admission, and they said no, not really. But we decided to go down anyway. We paid our money and entered the elevator. The smell of salt and hairy mammals was thick and only got stronger as we plunged downward. The speakers played a Burt Bacharach orchestral-type number.

Finally, the elevator came to rest. The strings swelled and the door opened onto a rocky passageway. The walls were almost perfectly modeled, like a prop from *Star Trek*. The cave smelled powerfully like a zoo, a mixture of sweat and fat and hot breath and piss.

We followed the signs to a few displays explaining the world of sea lions, and then, unceremoniously, to a fissure in the rock covered by a cyclone fence. Through the natural window, the hollow of the advertised sea cavern was visible.

The arching cavern roof rose about a hundred feet over a watery cove where at least two hundred sea lions lounged on the rocks. They were sleeping, barking, slithering, and playing, and in the very center a single bull stood posed on a pedestal of wet rock. The light falling from the mouth of the cave diffused over the animals, and on the far wall a hole led out to the ocean, a single square of bright silver. It was a pretty incredible scene. Like a living history painting depicting some Oriental harem. The composition was weirdly perfect.

I stood next to Alissa and for a minute neither of us spoke. We were both fascinated by these monstrous, half-formed creatures. These turdlike mountains of flesh, groping with their flippers. They were like unfinished humans, struggling in their fat, heaving bodies. The hellish victims of some terrible curse.

"Those people were idiots," I said. "How is this not amazing?"

"People are insane," Alissa agreed.

She huddled nearby, and for a second I contemplated putting my arm around her, but that seemed like too much. I knew I could have though; she would have been happy if I had. She would have leaned into me and pressed her weight under my arm. For a brief instant our arms touched, then pulled away.

Standing there with Alissa, I had the distinct sense that nothing in my life would have been different no matter what I'd done. I'd been fated to end up here, in the same place, with Alissa, regardless. My long years with Judy had only been one long diversion, a preparation for this eventual encounter with my true match in a briny cave full of sea mammals. Maybe I'd even wasted years in the wrong place.

The bulls barked their rough, violent syllables, unable to say.

Florence was less charming than I remembered. The majestic coastline petered into sandy plains, and most of the town was just a long commercial strip, with all the same stores we had in the city. We found the bookstore, though, which was all right, and I bought an old atlas. Alissa stumbled across a nice collection of Carleton Watkins photos, but the price was too steep. There were no bargains anymore. With the Internet, everyone knew exactly what everything was worth.

After the bookstore we walked to the dunes, scrabbling in the beach grass. Cresting the slope we came to a view of more dunes. Far away, some kids were tooling around on buggies and recumbent beach bicycles.

"You want to do that?" I said.

"Fuck no," she said. "Let's go home. I'm hungry."

After dinner we returned to Alissa's hotel room, and to my surprise, we made love for the first time in our decades of friendship. I would have felt strange using the cottage in that way, and without my having to say anything she understood.

· I had often imagined Alissa's body over the years. I'd watched her change gradually from radiant youth to beautiful adulthood. Removing her clothes, I still remembered that young body, the graceful neck, the fine legs, but I wasn't sorry to be arriving so late. Her small breasts were lovely. Her hips were supple. My own body was hairier and heftier than it used to be. We did all right though.

I had never cheated on Judy, and I was pretty certain she had never cheated on me. We'd always been firm in our commitment to the convenience of monogamy, if nothing else. Whether fucking Alissa while still in mourning really qualified as infidelity I wasn't sure, and at least for the moment I decided to suspend my judgment.

Afterward, we lay in the window seat of the hotel room, watching the tide. A gang of gulls lurked on the sand, keeping themselves company. Wispy clouds skidded across the sky, fringed in moonlight.

"So strange," I said, my hands wandering over her skin, cupping her breasts, tracing the bone of her hip. I kissed her behind the ear, smelling minerals and flowers.

"What?" she said.

"I've thought about you a lot over the years," I said. "You'd be surprised how much."

"I don't think so," she said. She craned her neck and I held her face as we kissed.

The wind kicked up that night, rattling the windows in their mullions. I woke up in the early-morning hours, worrying a pane might shatter, and then, fitfully, fell back to sleep.

In the morning I went back to the cottage. Alissa had a few layouts to turn in by the end of the day, and thanks to me, she had fallen behind. We kissed at the hotel room door and I left her to her laptop.

I spent the next few hours in the cabin reading, but I had trouble concentrating. I read the same paragraph seven times before putting the book aside to stare at the water, at the flotsam each wave deposited, the flotsam each wave reclaimed. The darkening and lightening of the pounded sand. The crabs rising from the

beach, scurrying, disappearing. Gradually the coastline was eroding, but I couldn't perceive it.

I held back from calling Alissa as long as I could, not wanting to
push anything. But then, around noon, I called anyway.

"How's the work going?"

"It's going."

"You need any help?"

"No!"

"Are you busy later?"

"No."

"I'm just down the street if you need me."

"Yeah. I know where you are."

We made a plan for dinner at the Seagull, where I had first seen
her, and after that I was finally able to calm down. I finished a chapter in my book, ate lunch at the vegan place, and took yet another
walk on the beach.

This time I headed away from the lighthouse, marching toward
the bluff that sheltered the inlet from the southern wind gusts. As
I walked beside the roaring surf, I remembered my mission. I was
here to ritualize Judy's passing, to remember her, wasn't I?

She would not have been pleased with how things were going.
She was a person who demanded fealty, doting attention. She
nursed petty hurts. She had a tendency to pout. Unless death had
transformed her into a different person, she would most probably
disapprove of my behavior.

"Sorry," I said into the wind.

"You could have waited," I could hear her say. "Or at least do
this somewhere else."

"I have the chance now," I said. "There might not be another
time."

"It's disrespectful."

"It doesn't have anything to do with you." Though it did.

The breeze stiffened and I turned back, following a young family wandering from driftwood to rock, dwarfed by the surf and sky.

Near the cabin, I came to a pile of driftwood. As commemoration of some kind, or perhaps as apology, I stacked some rocks on one of the larger slabs of wood. The clouds parted, and a band of sunlight fell onto the water. The faraway whitecaps became more vivid than the ones closer in.

I was waiting in the restaurant a few minutes before seven. Alissa's hotel was directly across the street, so I could read the paper and watch the door from the corner of my vision. The waiting was much as I remembered from long ago, before Judy. I was nervous. I wondered if we would spend the night together. I wondered when the next kiss would be coming. I tried not to think about where our whole thing was going, but I couldn't help toy with the idea that it might be more than a weekend tryst.

Fifteen minutes after seven Alissa still hadn't shown up. Judy was never late—it was against her constitution. We both considered lateness a form of elitism, a sign one valued one's own time more than others'. In this case, though, I knew it was just how Alissa was. She had been late her entire life. She always would be.

Sure enough, five minutes later, she emerged from the hotel and crossed the street, waving. She was wearing a new batch of clothes, equally festive as those the day before, and I was pleased to see she had taken the time to make up her face for me, with a little lipstick and a trace of rouge.

"Howdy," she said, touching my shoulder. Her flowery scent wafted in her wake.

"Howdy," I said, folding the sports section.

"Sorry I'm late," she said. "God. What's there to drink?"

"Tough day?" I said.

"Deadlines," she said. "It's like I can never get everything done. There's always more."

"What's the assignment again?"

"It's so boring. I can't even tell you."

"Come on," I said. "I'm curious."

She gauged my interest with a look and decided it was genuine, or at least genuine enough. "It's a thing about furniture stores," she said. "It's a holiday guide. For the holidays."

"Actually, that does sound pretty boring," I said.

She laughed. "I told you. What about you? What did you do today?"

"Not much. Read."

"I saw you on the beach."

"Yeah, I took a walk," I said.

"I could see you from my window. It looked like you were building something."

"Ah. You were spying on me."

"I was spying, it's true."

"I was making a pile of rocks."

"Uh huh?"

"For Judy," I explained. "It's been three months. Almost to the day."

"Oh. That's good. That's a good thing to do."

I took a sip of wine. I knew I should stop talking before I said too much. I might end up going too far, revealing intimate details. The events of the night before might not have counted as infidelity, but talking about our old secrets would. We had waited too long, Alissa and I. We had grown parts we would never share. Plus, I was feeling protective of Judy for some reason.

"Anyway," I said.

"Anyway," she said.

"So you finished your work though?"

"We'll see. Depends what Albert says."

"Is he pretty tough?"

"He's all right. I'm just never sure what he wants. You know? I can't seem to get it right."

"I see."

"I need a new job is what I need."

"Oh."

"I try and be a little creative, you know, and he's always like, no way."

"What would you want to do?"

"I don't know. That's the problem."

"I guess that makes it harder, doesn't it?"

That was probably the wrong thing to say. Thankfully the waiter came and pressed Alissa to scan the wine menu. After a minute of flustered indecision, she went with the Syrah.

We had a hard time finding a new topic to discuss. I knew she didn't follow politics so I didn't bother with that. Or sports. The Raiders' draft picks held no fascination for her. She told me a story about Albert I'd heard before, which bought us a little time.

For a minute we devolved to talking about the weather, and then, as a default, we entered an ancient conversation, the genius of Weegee. We had rehearsed it for many years. We both loved Weegee and we could always bond over his images—the blackness of his blacks, the casual precision of his compositions. I was able to carry on my side of the conversation while tracing a whole other line of thought in the back of my head. I thought about the parent-teacher conferences I had to reschedule. The shoes I had to return to the mall. The small ways that Judy would have been bored by this topic.

The Weegee conversation followed its normal path. It was reassuring but also disappointing in a way. Afterward, Alissa excused herself to go to the bathroom, squeezing my shoulder on the way as a kind of morale booster, but I could tell she was disappointed, too. I felt dull. I couldn't seem to think.

Out on the street, a car crawled by the window, scaring a gull that had been picking at wet crusts of bread. For the whole day I'd been assuming we would eat dinner and then go back to the cabin together, but now, suddenly, I wasn't so sure. I wasn't sure we would stay the night in the same bed at all.

I watched the candle's flame float on the top of its wick, battered by the smallest air currents. I was finding it hard to breathe for some reason. My arms felt heavy, and a cold, dry energy poured through my nerves.

The candle flame wobbled and reshaped itself. I wasn't sure what was happening at first, but then I realized: it was Judy, at last. I couldn't see her or smell her or hear her or touch her, but I could sense her nonetheless. Her absence touched everything in my world, pressing itself to all that wasn't her. The absence settled against me and, for a moment, I felt the weight of everything that existed pitching toward her sucking gravity.

I missed her so powerfully I thought I might collapse. It was like an imploding star in my chest. I wanted only to hear her voice on the phone, her incredulous guffaw. I wanted to wait at the door while she searched for her keys. I wanted to feel her hand on my back while I dried the dishes. The thought of her final moments, the fear she must have felt in the road, was almost too much to bear. I could imagine the hard asphalt against her cheek. The sight of her own blood. The vibration of the passing cars, and the streaking lights. All of it, sucked into the past, never to return.

The waiter came and filled my water glass. The ice tinkled against the rounded walls. I could hear Alissa laughing with the hostess near the bar. They laughed again, two jolly women, and the candle's flame shivered. I sipped my water, trying to calm myself down. Already, the moment was passing. Already, I could tell, we were moving on.

BENNY

I WAS VISITING MY MOM in Clackamas when she told me Benny's dad wanted to see me. She mentioned it in passing, in the middle of making us turkey sandwiches for lunch, as if there was nothing more to it than neighborhood pleasantries.

"Benny's dad?" I said warily. I hadn't seen him in years, but I remembered him well. He was a real asshole, as I recalled, full of big ideas about honor and propriety that he'd dutifully inflicted on his sons. When Benny and I were kids, I'd witnessed my share of pyrotechnics in that house, and I'd come to think of his dad as one of the main causes of all Benny's problems over the years.

My mom knew how I felt. According to her, though, Benny's dad had mellowed since I'd last seen him. She said he spent most of his time tutoring at the library now.

"He just wants to talk to you about Benny," she said. "That's all."

"What do I know about Benny?" I said. "I haven't seen him in ages."

"He's worried," she said.

"Probably for good reason."

"Do what you want," she said, handing me my plate, a few spears of carrot on the side. "I'm just telling you. He's sitting over there and he'd love to see you."

She didn't have to say anything more. She was a peacemaker and she'd always had a soft spot for Benny, like she did for all underdogs. I told her I'd check in with Benny's dad when I had a chance.

After lunch I installed a new thermostat, and then, conveniently, my mom took a nap. With nothing else to do, I wandered out the back door and before I knew it, I was crossing the yard to the rear gate.

The way to Benny's house was still hardwired in my brain. As a kid I'd walked the route at least four times a day. We'd stayed at each other's houses most nights in the summer. We'd played football in the street. Benny even lived with us for a while back in junior high school when things first broke down badly in his household. I could have walked the path between our places in my sleep.

I passed through the fence, skirted the neighbor's manicured yard, headed across the retirement village parking lot, and turned right on Sunset Drive. His house was down the block four driveways, just where I'd left it. It was a drab ranch-style number with fogged storm windows, rusted wind chimes hanging from the eaves, and damp cardboard boxes piled in the side yard. The fir trees in the back choked out any sunlight, and mold had crept into the seams in the vinyl siding. Everything seemed wet, decaying, though it was hard to put a finger on where the real problem lay. The house wasn't really that much different from any of the neighbors'. But the fact the mess I remembered could remain so permanent was a kind of miracle.

I rang the bell, hoping for no answer, but Benny's dad appeared right away. The curtain rustled, and then the door cracked open, and a warm, stale smell rolled out from indoors.

"Daryl," he said, smiling. "How are you?"

"Hi Mr. Reger," I said. We shook hands.

My mom was right, I could tell from a glance. Benny's dad was a lot softer than he had been. Part of it was physical: his face was fleshier, and the line of his jaw had become indistinct. But mostly the change was in the eyes. The old glint of menace was gone, worn away by the years of unrelieved disappointment. All the noble ideals he'd entered fatherhood with had been proven wrong, and he'd at last come to the point where he no longer trusted his own instincts. I felt a little sorry for him, but in a way I imagined he was better off now. He'd become kinder and maybe even wiser in his long-term failure.

Men should spawn their children late in life, I thought. They did better as fathers that way. Only after they'd been beaten up by the world for a good, long time were they ready. So much pointless violence and unwarranted discipline could be avoided if they just waited.

Benny's dad invited me inside and I crossed the threshold into the funky gloom. I'd forgotten the distinct odor of Benny's house, that combination of freezer burn, air freshener, and ground-in cigarette smoke. The collection of sleeping Mexican campesino sculptures was still in place, well dusted, and the family pictures on the wall were unchanged. I was in one or two of them myself, skinny and shirtless and laughing in the sun.

Benny's dad sat down in his ancient recliner, the beige fabric discolored by his body's oils, and waved me to a wooden chair across the room. In the half-light he looked exhausted. His skin was pale and papery and the remaining hair on his head had been reduced to patchy, reddish wisps.

"How's Mrs. Reger?" I said. I figured we might warm up on the easier topics. Benny's mom had always been sweet. Everyone liked her.

"She's doing just fine," he said. "She sees your mother at the grocery store. She always asks after you."

I managed a friendly chuckle. "My mom loves passing along the news. I hear all about you guys, too."

"I should say congratulations on your wedding," Mr. Reger said. "We were so happy for you."

"So far so good," I said. I'd been married for almost three years. It occurred to me I probably should have invited them to the ceremony, and I felt a momentary stab of guilt.

"She's Chinese?" he said. "Is that right?"

"Vietnamese," I said.

"Well, it sounds wonderful," he said, and we avoided any embarrassing comments by moving along quickly.

Benny's brothers were doing well, he said. They worked in the trades and they still liked to surf. My dad was thinking about retirement, I said; my mom volunteered at the animal shelter. His wife had gone through a health scare a few years back, but she was fine. We moved on down the list, eliminating one name after another, narrowing our focus until only the one name remained, by which time Mr. Reger's question almost had the innocuous feeling of cocktail party chatter.

"Have you seen Benny lately?" he said.

"Not for a long time, sir," I said. It might have been the first time I had said "sir" in my whole life.

Mr. Reger sighed and shook his head. He gazed out the filmy window. "That's too bad," he said. "I was hoping you might have seen him. You were always so close."

"I used to run into him more often," I offered. "I don't get out much these days. I guess you haven't heard from him in a while?"

"Not for a very long time, no."

We sat in silence for a few moments, honoring the gravity of Benny's wayward path. The wake of destruction was long and twisting. The money that had been wasted in trying to help him was alone monumental to think about. I could only imagine what his last stay at the rehab in Newberg had cost them.

"He should really come home," Mr. Reger said. "We just want to know he's okay. He should check in."

"If I see him, I'll be sure to pass on the message," I said.

"I thought you might know where to look," he said, pushing gently. "We don't even know where to start. Maybe it wouldn't be too much trouble to do a little looking around . . . I don't know what I'm asking."

Mr. Reger sat slumped in his ancient chair. A defeated general, the only good kind. He turned his eyes away and stared at the blank television set. It was a lot to put on me, but I said I'd do my best.

It should have been his brothers looking for him, but his brothers were probably sick of trying. They'd already found him in every shitty situation you could think of. Jail. Sleeping under bridges. Bleeding in the street. They didn't have the time for it anymore. Benny had long ago used up their patience.

That didn't leave too many people for the job, I guessed. Benny rarely had a girlfriend anyone knew about. He didn't have a job, and thus no coworkers. It was possible he didn't even live in town anymore. We didn't know. He might have gone to Seattle or San Francisco or Montana and gotten stuck there. If he was in town, he had drifted so deep into his own galaxy that finding him wasn't such a simple proposition.

The last time I'd seen him was almost two years before. We'd both lived in the same neighborhood at the time, and every once in a while we made the effort to hang out. He came over one day holding his striped rubber ABA ball, looking generally rattled and unkempt. His hair was a mess, he was sweating yellow ooze, and his eyes were bugged, but I didn't say anything. It wasn't my business. We walked over to the covered court at the junior high school and shot around and bullshitted.

Benny had never been a great basketball player, but that day he was truly terrible. His hands seemed almost detached from his arms, slapping together full seconds after the ball had passed him by. His shots only vaguely arced toward the rim. He had his excuses, but he wasn't really bothered by the lousy efforts, and neither was I. We were there more to relax and catch up than to play ball.

Still, we ended up in a game of two-on-two, against a pudgy teenager and a midget with a rat tail. The midget was literally three feet tall—the top of his head came up to Benny's belt buckle—and yet he scored on Benny at will. He dribbled around Benny's knees and blew past him and sank layup after layup. Benny fell down at least twice trying to keep up with him. Before we knew it, we were beaten. The kids high-fived each other and looked at us with something like pity.

Afterward, Benny complained that the lines on the court were askew. He went home and came back with a tape measure and made sure they were parallel, and then he measured the rim's distance from the ground. He got it in his head that he would ask the Trail Blazers for a grant to fix up the neighborhood court. I doubted he had slept in a week.

Later, I joked with our friends that Benny's tweaking had finally started to impede on my own lifestyle. The humiliation on the court was the final straw; he needed help. I was only kidding, but the fact was, I hadn't seen him since then, and I had no idea where to start looking.

My search began in our old neighborhood a few weeks after my talk with his dad. I finally couldn't put it off any longer. I hated to be the ambassador from a world Benny was trying to escape, but on the other hand I did want to see him. And it was a good excuse for getting out of the house, too. It was easy to get stuck in there once the rain started.

The old neighborhood had changed a fair bit over the years. New houses and condos were popping up in all the vacant lots, sprouting like mushrooms. They were mostly skinny, in-fill buildings—a decent-sized garage with a little living space padding the roof and rear wall. But some of the new places were a little fancier, too, with raw cedar siding, broad, overhanging eaves, and glass doors that opened onto trim, second-floor patios. They were pretty handsome, actually, with young, handsome owners to match.

The neighborhood still had some of its flavor though, I was glad to see. I was almost run over by a bum on a bicycle dragging a baby carriage, and behind that a rusted lawnmower.

Benny's old apartment building was a crummy box off Killingsworth called the Cynthia Arms, and the guy living in Benny's old unit was about my age. He said he had never heard of Benny before. He talked to me through the cracked door, his white eye underlined by the taut golden chain. He told me there had been a few residents in the apartment since Benny's day. The last people were a Mexican family of eight.

"Sorry to bug you," I said, but the door was already closed.

From there I tracked down the manager. He lived on the ground level in a unit that resembled a dirt cave. The windows were covered with dark blankets and the TV was like a primitive fire casting blue illuminations on the wall. I almost expected to see bones scattered on the floor.

"I wonder if you remember Benny Reger?" I said. "He lived up in 206 a few years ago?"

The manager, a plain, forehead-heavy dude with greasy eyes, remembered Benny well.

"He left a real fucking mess," he said. "I had to call in movers. It was like an electronics store. But everything busted. What was the point?"

"You haven't seen him lately though?" I said.

"He's long gone. He had a roommate at the end. He might know something."

"What was the roommate's name?" I said. I had never heard of a roommate before.

"Blue," the manager said. "I guess that's not helpful. Blue was a black guy. For what that's worth."

"Any idea where Benny went?" I said. "Did he leave a forwarding address or anything?" It was a long shot, but I had promised an honest effort. And anyway, I was kind of enjoying the detective work.

The manager rubbed his chin and pinched the flesh of his neck. He leaned from his dark doorway into the daylight and squinted skyward. I had the feeling he might be on the verge of plucking some helpful tidbit from the air, like a gnat, but then he retreated, stepping back inside the mouth of his living room.

"No idea," he said. "He never said a word. He was just gone one day. That was it."

My knowledge of searching for people came almost exclusively from old *Law and Order* episodes, and so I knew that after checking

Benny's former address, I should probably track down his last workplace for clues.

I knew Benny had worked construction in the past, and I'm a carpenter myself, so it wasn't hard to ask around at the Local for any leads. Benny wasn't a union guy, but it was a small town. There were only so many contractors out there, and Benny got around. Bill Sandstrom had a dim memory of hiring him once. At least the name sounded familiar. And after I described Benny—his black, tightly curling hair, his stick arms, that crazy laugh—he was pretty certain we were talking about the same guy.

"That was at least a couple years ago," he said. "He'd just quit the Plaid Pantry."

"Three, more likely," I said. Benny had been out of work for a while the last time I'd seen him. If it had been two years, it had been three since he'd worked with Bill.

"Shit." He whistled under his breath. "Time flies. I guess you're right."

"So I guess you don't know where he is now?"

"I doubt he knows where he is."

"So he wasn't doing so good?" I said. It was practically a rhetorical question. Was Benny doing good? Was Benny *Benny*?

"Put it this way," Bill said. "He wore shades the whole job. I don't think I ever saw his eyes. I finally had to fire him."

"How come? Anything in particular?"

"We'd had some trouble, but I thought we'd got through it. He was showing up on time, putting in good days. Then one day he goes off and wastes five hours cleaning the moss off a fence in the backyard. This fence was crap. We were going to rip the thing out. But we come back and he's scouring the thing. I mean, it's practically destroyed by blackberries and he's out there scrubbing every plank.

He's cleaning garbage, man. He was a tweaker. I wanted to give him a chance. I've been there, you know? But he had some time left with it. I hope he's pulled out, man, I really do."

I'd already done a pretty good job of looking for Benny, I thought, having visited his last known address and employer. But according to the TV logic I was following, I had a little more work left to do. I had to visit at least one bar.

I chose Mork's, a punk bar we used to frequent, and where his ex-girlfriend Janet might still work. I doubted they were in touch, but it was possible she might have some recent news. And then there was always the outside chance the man himself would walk in the door.

Mork's was on Albina, in a formerly sketchy neighborhood, but parking the car I saw those days were now over. I was confronted by new condos on two corners and a half-dug foundation on the third, which wasn't surprising, and not even that depressing either. Build it up, I thought. No big loss. Maybe the neighbors would get a grocery store someday. Still, I remembered when it had seemed impossible the middle of town could ever creep this far out. A few years ago, Mork's had been the very edge.

The smell of beer and cigarettes inside was almost comforting. The walls were familiarly plastered in posters and stickers and the ceiling was spray-painted with sloppy whorls. The kids, for their part, were the same as always. They wore the same flannels and jeans, the same haircuts, the same mechanic's jackets. It could have been 1973, 1985, or 2004 in there.

None of them gave me a second look. They had no idea I was one of them. Which was to say, I wasn't one of them anymore.

I sat at the bar and waited around, nursing my beers. The jukebox was pretty good, still stocked with a lot of my old bands. In a way it was even kind of relaxing sitting there. It was conducive to thinking at least. I got to remembering some of the better times we'd had. Benny was a funny guy. The things he did often made no sense, but there was a kind of genius there. I thought about the time he ate the photograph of our friend Eric. He pulled the school picture from his pocket, and placed it inside the bun of his hamburger, and gobbled the whole thing down. What did it mean? I doubt even he knew, but it was hilarious. Or the time he discovered the mummified cat corpse under his porch. Most people would have left it alone. Benny, however, chopped it in half, attached a pair of baby doll legs to the body, and sewed the beast a little striped shirt and beret. He displayed the cat on his mantel for years. Everyone had Benny stories.

He should have been an artist, I thought. He just had no means of expression, no discipline. The best parts of him had trouble getting out. Plus, he liked being high too much. And the idea of the future had never held much weight for him.

Around eleven, Janet came on duty. I'd always liked her. She was big, with Betty Page hair and laughing cheeks. She hadn't seen Benny in months, she said, but she was glad to reminisce with me. She reminded me of the time we'd all gone to the river together and Benny had climbed the tree on top of the cliff to make his jump even more treacherous than necessary. I'd forgotten that day, but sure enough, with a little prodding, the memory was waiting in the back of my brain. I could see Benny, frozen in midair, a scattering of leaves floating behind him and the water shining below.

We found other memories, too. The basement parties, the fireworks shows. The time Benny passed out eating a Whaler and woke up with a cheek full of wet fish and bread. We had an easy time talking about him. There was something about knowing Benny that tended to bond people for life.

Benny, of course, didn't show up. Janet mentioned a few other places to check, but my time was limited. I knew I wouldn't make the rounds that night, or possibly ever.

Well past midnight I walked back out into the cold air, passing under a streetlamp's yellow cone of light. Across the street a crane rose from the gaping pit. I could see they had a new kind of self-propelled boom lift on the site, but I wasn't that interested.

There had been a time when every new building that went up seemed to change the city a little. When every new restaurant and every new club made some minute difference to the city's character. But we'd moved beyond that point now. The changes were arriving too fast to register anymore.

Pulling away, I had to admit the new town rising around me just didn't seem real most of the time. I might as well get used to it, I thought. I was one of those people stuck in the old town for good.

I gave up searching for Benny for a few months. I'd done my due diligence, I figured, and I had my own problems to worry about. My job took a lot of time. We were busy, which was better than the alternative, and then there was my own house to work on. Minh and I had managed to put a down payment on a place in St. Johns, which had cleared us out, and there was still a lot of work to be done. Being my own client and lone employee, I had to crack the whip on myself. I built some new cherry shelves in the dining room. I painted the upstairs bedroom forest green. I fixed the leaking pipes in the downstairs bathroom. There was always something.

On weekends Minh and I cruised estate sales and used-furniture shops, rarely buying anything but enjoying the vague purpose of the drives. Gradually, I was assembling a cool tiki bar in the basement, and whenever I came across interesting paintings or bamboo furniture, I tried, with her permission, to indulge. I wasn't sure when I'd gotten into the tiki thing, it'd just kind of happened, but over time I believed I was becoming a connoisseur.

One Sunday afternoon, after a long day of shopping on Eighty-second Avenue, my mom called. Benny's dad was sick, she said, and he wanted to know if I'd had any luck finding Benny. I told her no, I hadn't, and she told me he'd been spotted at a bus stop in deep Southeast. She had the intersection written down on a coupon.

So the next weekend I trekked out to the bus stop on Ninety-eighth and Foster, hoping to pick up the trail. I was like a cop on stake-out duty, what with my supply of danishes and coffee. I settled in with my headphones and watched the day's dramas unfold on the street.

I saw some weird shit during my hours at that bus stop—a man with tattooed tears commanding his woman never to look at him again; a woman serving her kids hamburgers straight off the plastic bench. I saw lots of Benny's people. Fucked-up people, with no place to go, and no compass to get there anyway. The sidewalk filled and emptied, filled and emptied, collecting wrappers and soda cans, and then on Monday the trash was swept away.

I went back two weekends in a row without any luck, so I tried a weekday. I arrived before work and spent an hour, and then I came back after work and stared down the same patch of concrete. I saw the commuters head out in the morning and come home in the evening. But Benny, my friend, never showed.

One Sunday night I witnessed a fight between two Salvadoran dudes. It was an ugly brawl. I had no idea how it started, but suddenly one of them had a knife and then there was blood on the sidewalk. The cops showed up seconds later, lights strobing, and cuffed a handful of onlookers. The ambulance came a few minutes after that. God knew if those guys made it out all right. It was a sad sight, the whole stupid thing. I couldn't help but think how those kids were both so far from home.

I called a few friends, hoping for further leads, but no one had any ideas. I told them to tell Benny I was looking for him, and they all said they would but they doubted he'd turn up. It was good catching up with most of them, and I would have called more if I'd had their numbers. People had moved on, or dropped out, and their digits were tough to track down. Also, it turned out I didn't even know most of their real names. Who was Jack Vile? Or Amy Starpower? I'd know them if I saw them, but there were no such listings for those people in the phone book.

We lived in a small town though. Eventually you ran into most everybody out there, like it or not.

A month after my stake-out I was downtown doing some errands, walking on Sixth Street, which I barely recognized anymore. The new lofts, the widened streets, the storefronts full of green architects and graphic designers were all new to me.

I might not have recognized Benny either, if I hadn't had him on my mind so much lately. I was looking for a print shop I'd once liked, and there he was, standing outside a gay bar on Davis. He looked like shit. He was skinnier than ever, his face pitted and caved-in. His shoes were two sizes too big and he wore a garnet hoodie under a letterman jacket with a rearing horse on the back. He was digging for a cigarette butt in the sand of an outdoor ashtray.

When he saw me, though, his face brightened, and in his eyes I could see the little kid I had known practically since I had known myself.

"Daryl?" he said. "Whoa, man. What the hell?"

"Benny," I said. We hugged. I didn't care about his dirty clothes or the fetid smell that came off him. I was just glad he was finally there in front of me.

"What are you doing here?" he said, as if this corner were a private world he inhabited. Or as if his life were so distant from mine that the very fact of shared space and time was impossible.

"Just walking around," I said. "I've been thinking about you, man."

"Yeah?" he said, and for a moment a flicker of suspicion crossed his face. He'd never been able to hide anything, and his eyes seemed almost misshapen from the years of uncontrolled emoting. I could tell he was prepared to bolt, to deny, to lash out. But then the moment passed. Even he could figure out I had no ulterior motives in mind.

"You want to get some coffee?" I said. Across the street beckoned a characterless coffee shop with plate-glass windows and fluorescent lights. Benny agreed.

We went inside and ordered drinks and muffins and took seats at the yellow plastic table in the window. Like anyone who had lived in town more than a few years, we talked mostly about all the changes happening.

Benny had many insights into our shared civic life. He wasn't stupid, after all. He might have been undisciplined, self-deluding, manipulative, and unreliable, but he had never been stupid. He read the newspaper. He gleaned things from TV. He had well-developed theories about almost everything, if you got him at the right time.

He said the housing market was going to crash. "Mark my words, man," he said. "Next year. It's over."

"You think so?" I said. The upward progress of real estate values was an article of faith to most people at the time, something unstoppable, inevitable. But Benny and I had always been pessimists together. We took any opportunity to doubt, and the more fatal the doubt, the better. I was glad that much had stayed the same.

"Do you know how much the median house price has gone up this year?" he said. "Fucking one hundred fifty percent. Same last year. It's a classic bubble economy. They say that's not the case because it's real estate, but it is. There's precedent. It's called the Great fucking Depression."

"It would only make sense," I said. "Since I just bought something a few months ago."

"Ha!" he said. "The landed gentry."

We talked about music, politics, friends, the weather. Benny had learned a lot about nutrition he wanted to pass on. He knew all about herbal supplements and non-Western medicines, which was ironic, considering his lifestyle, but his interest was genuine. He refused to finish his muffin because of the processed sugar and corn syrup.

I told him a little about my new house, my wife. He said he had heard the news, and offered heartfelt congratulations. And then it was back to him.

He couldn't stop talking that day. He talked so much, in fact, I wondered if he was high, but he claimed more than once he was clean. He'd been clean for three months, supposedly. The talking was just him being himself. It was as if he was frightened of what someone else might say in the breaths between sentences.

"I'm talking to a friend about opening a music store," he told me. "This guy, he used to run Apple Music. He knows the business upside down, man. He knows all the vendors. And he knows, I mean knows, this town could use another good music store. Kids are moving here all the time. They need to buy their fucking guitars somewhere. This place is overflowing with trust-funders—pockets full of mommy and daddy's cash. We're talking about taking a space over on Grand Avenue. Good traffic over there."

"That's great, Benny," I said. "That's a great idea."

It had begun raining outside, and the sun had gone down. The plate glass was spattering with droplets. Compared with some of the past plans I'd heard, the music store sounded almost plausible. From someone else, it might even have sounded inspired. But coming from Benny, I knew it would go nowhere.

"So I saw your dad a few months ago," I said, partly just to change the subject.

"Cool for you," Benny said.

"He said he'd like to see you."

"What for?" he said. The mere mention of his relations made Benny uncomfortable. The train of thought led too quickly to regret, resentment, recrimination. Better never to climb on board.

"I don't think he has a reason," I said.

"He always has a reason," he said. "Believe me. He has a thousand reasons."

I didn't want to argue. Besides, Benny had already launched into a rambling story about his family's failure to help him during his last flame-out. He said something about a deed, a loan, an uncollected inheritance he was owed. He might have been confessing something, but the facts didn't really add up. The story changed even in the telling, and anyway, I barely listened. I'd carried the message I was asked to carry. I'd done my job. Now I just watched his teeth flashing in front of the blackness of his mouth, the life of the hard lines near his eyes. I wasn't about to add to the weight of Benny's trouble that day.

Out on the street, just before saying good-bye, Benny hit me up for money, slipping in the plea as if he hadn't been waiting the whole time for his chance. He told me he was getting paid in a day and he just needed some cash to tide him over, but it was obvious there was no paycheck on the way. I had been expecting this on some level, but still, it came as a disappointment.

"I'm sorry, man," I said. "I'm broke," which was true, to a degree, though I had a lot more than Benny did.

"Come on," he said. "Just a few bucks."

"Dude, I'm running on fumes right now," I said.

"It's just a loan, man."

I shook my head. "Sorry, man. Maybe next time."

Benny's face clouded. He tossed his hair and jammed his hands in his pockets. For a second I thought about giving him something just to avoid the coming hassle, but it turned out I had drawn my own line. I didn't want to be used. I didn't want to become just another anonymous mark on the sidewalk. I was hurt that Benny would mar what had otherwise been such a thoroughly decent interaction.

"Whatever, man," Benny spat.

"I wish I could help out—" I said.

"Don't give me that rap."

"Dude. We're having a good time."

"You always looked out for yourself, didn't you, Daryl?" Benny said. "We both know that."

And then, without another word, he turned and walked away. He was done with me. I could have hurried and caught up with him and pressed a few bucks into his hand, but I didn't budge. I just stood there, watching him overtake a limping black guy and hurry down the sidewalk, getting lost in the light of the oncoming traffic.

High above, the moon was full. The sky was colorless but beautiful. Thin clouds moved along the glassy slate.

As Benny slipped around the corner, I had the strong feeling that something had just missed me. Something had blown from the earth and swirled around and now, at last, it was rising upward into the white hole of the moon. I didn't know what it was. Some crackly, invisible force, parting as it blew by me. I could only hope it passed Benny, too.

For the next few weeks I replayed our conversation in my mind, tested the rancor in his voice. I wondered if we could have ended on a different note if I'd done something else, but I doubted it. He was unreasonable.

I'd looked out for myself? Fuck you, Benny, I thought. When had you ever helped anyone? I considered it testament to my respect for him that I had refused to treat him like a child that night.

Still, Benny rattled in my head while I caulked the windows or raked the yard. Yeah, I said. I'd looked out for myself; it was true. Was that such a goddamn crime? You looked out for yourself, too, Benny. You just never did a very fucking good job of it.

It was a long winter that year. The gray days stacked up, month after month, and over time I stopped thinking about Benny so much. I retiled the kitchen; I patched the leak in the roof; I went down to Minh's sister's wedding in L.A. I figured we'd catch up again at some point and get back on good terms. We'd start over again, like we always did.

In the spring the dogwoods in the backyard half bloomed. The sunny sides made their share of pink blossoms, but the shady sides remained patchy and skeletal. The oregano and the mint choked out the lilac and the lavender. The fennel shot up in a shaggy, purplish wall.

I was out laying railroad ties when the phone rang one day. I could tell from the look in Minh's black eyes when she handed me the receiver that something was wrong. It was my mom calling. She was crying, and she said it was about Benny.

"They found him," she said.

"What? Who found Benny?" I said.

"He was in Washington Park, just off the trail," she said. "Lying under a blooming rhododendron bush." She said he'd OD'd, whether by himself or with someone else they couldn't be sure.

My mom went on to tell me what more she knew. Benny was only four days out of jail, she said. According to a story on the radio, the week after release was the most dangerous time for an addict. The body wasn't prepared for the new freedom it found, and accidents happened.

"This is how we take care of our people," she said. "It's shameful. Utterly wrong."

I hung up and handed the phone to Minh. She told me to call his parents, so I did. I left a message on the machine, and then I wasn't sure what to do. If I were religious, I'd have gone to church or read the Bible. But I wasn't.

I finished laying the railroad ties. Then, lacking any better ideas, I went down to the basement.

The tiki lounge was almost complete now. After the holidays I'd installed a fake thatched roof over a small bar upholstered in leather, with colored track lights that caught on the tumblers and shot glasses. I had velvet ocean paintings lit by matching brass fixtures and rice-paper fans artfully placed on the wall. I even had a jar of vintage paper umbrellas for the specialty cocktails I would someday mix. At some party in the future. I wasn't sure what for.

I poured myself a Scotch and took a seat at the bar, strangely thrilled that my oldest friend was now dead. My own story was somehow burnished by the sordid drama. But the better part of me was utterly humbled by the news. I'd always thought I'd know Benny until the very end. I was glad his folks hadn't seen him in those last few months. It probably would have broken their hearts.

For some reason, my thoughts kept coming back to one memory in particular. It must have been when we were about thirteen, hanging out in the forest near Reese Road. I could still see the scene clearly. Benny was sitting over on the white, fallen snag, shaded by broad maple leaves, wearing his combat boots and the heavy, black raincoat of that period. I was sitting on a stump, loosening the shingles of a dried pinecone. The air between us was milky with cigarette smoke.

As usual, we had nothing to do. We had no way of getting anywhere, and we could rarely think of anything worth trying close to home. Mostly, we just killed our time smoking in the woods and talking, though I don't remember about what.

At some point that day we decided to throw some rocks. We had no reason, but we didn't really need one. Throwing rocks we discovered, was its own reward.

We started with small ones, winging little nut-sized stones and waiting for the distant knock if we were lucky and hit something. From there we progressed to bigger things. We went a little crazy that day. We lifted rocks and banged them against the trees, chipping into the yellow meat. We rolled small boulders down the incline of ferns until they cracked angrily against something at the base of the ravine. We pounded the woods until our arms ached and our breath was ragged. We taught the woods a lesson they would never forget.

I could still see Benny sweating in that ridiculous oiled trench coat. The eyeholes on the belt, the huge flaps of the collar. He wore that coat for years. Even in the heat of that dappled, late-summer day, he seemed to be preparing himself for the worst.

Upstairs, the door opened and Minh called down to see if I needed anything, and I told her no, I was alright. She closed the door and a few minutes later I heard a pot filling with water and the chopping of something on the countertop. Soon I could smell frying garlic.

I refilled my glass and stared at the bottles in back of the bar. I was a pretty lucky guy, I realized. My life was holding steady so far. I had a good woman, a solid roof over my head. Minh might not understand where I was coming from all the time, but then I didn't understand her all the time either. I figured we weren't too different from anyone else in that regard.

I heard her walking around in the kitchen and I knew she'd be happy enough if I came up and told her what was on my mind. I stayed put though. I had plenty of stories about Benny I could share, but I didn't really see the point. Why bother? Minh had never lived in our neighborhood after all. She'd never seen the shed behind Benny's house or slept on the thin carpet in his parents' den. The memories I had wouldn't mean anything to her, no matter how long I talked or how many old snapshots I pulled out. Those days were gone. They'd been gone a long time already. It was too late for Minh to understand what Benny had meant to me. It was too late for her to understand that we might as well have been brothers.

THE SUCKLING PIG

ON HIS FIRST pass by the labor corner, Tom Chen was just browsing. It was Thursday afternoon and the half-block between Burnside and Ankeny was crowded, as usual, with Latino men in diverse poses of waiting. There were men half asleep, slouched against the bowed cyclone fence, and men in pairs, drinking from wrinkled brown paper bags. There were men leaning on the retaining wall of the Plaid Pantry parking lot, scanning the traffic for potential jobs, or cops. A few feet away, a man in a grubby Raiders warm-up jacket stood alone, eating a hamburger.

Tom turned and circled the block, and once again the group of men swung into view. On this pass some of them noticed Tom's car, a white, aging Porsche, and gamely climbed to their feet, waving their hands. "Hey! Hey!" they called, coming to the edge of the sidewalk. "What you need? Over here." Tom pulled over and a small crowd mobbed the car.

"I need two," Tom said, holding up two fingers. He spoke in a low, modulated, mildly ironic voice, amused by the flare-up of activity his arrival had caused. How often did a balding, middle-aged Asian guy in a Porsche hit the labor corner? Usually it was Russian contractors and gay guys and local farm bosses in pickups who did the hiring. Asians dealt with their own yard work. Or they had their kids do it. Or they paved the yard so there was only the occasional hosing to do, and you didn't need Mexicans for that.

"Whatever you need, boss," said a moonfaced man in the passenger window. "I'm your guy."

"Painting? Yard work?" said another man with reddish eyes and an unshavable cleft in his chin. "You need work? I'm ready."

Among the selection—the wiry and the potbellied, the tattooed and the tired—Tom's eye landed on one man in particular, a big guy with shaggy, black hair, mocha skin, and a beefy, squared-off head, like a gallon jug set on broad shoulders. He was not fat but wide all the way through, with a barrel chest and thick arms and a face that was fleshy but handsome, dominated by heavy, liver-colored lips and long eyelashes. He seemed slightly older than the rest of the guys, and he held a glimmer of self-possession in his eyes that suggested he was somehow above his current circumstances. He might be selling himself on the corner, but he was prideful, even regal, in his clean white T-shirt and blue jeans.

"How much?" Tom said, meeting his eye. "You. How much?"

"Ten an hour, boss," the man said. He shifted his weight to indicate his readiness, but not so far as to assume he was yet hired.

From behind him another, slightly younger man appeared, squatter and darker, with severe Mayan features. His face was all harsh angles and flat planes. Black bangs cut straight across his broad forehead, and his mouth was a wide gash, parting to reveal tiny, well-spaced teeth. He wore a soiled yellow T-shirt with a logo too faded to read and high-top sneakers at least six years old. He crossed his arms and stared at Tom's car with glowering intensity, and then he squatted, a signal of his own readiness to be hired.

Tom scanned the group again. Already, a few of the men were turning away, retaking their positions along the fence. He came back to the big man and his smaller, darker friend. It seemed his decision was being made for him.

"How much, you?" Tom said to the small one.

"Ten dolares," the man said.

Tom gestured at the passenger door, waving them both inside. "Come on. Hop in, both of you. Los dos. We go."

With some delicacy they climbed into the Porsche. The small one, who was named Javier, took the tiny back seat, and the big one, named Diego, the front, bringing with them a masculine smell of earth and gasoline and cheap deodorant that almost overpowered the interior's scent of sweet leather and old sunlight. For a moment Tom felt a pulse of trepidation—two strange men were squeezing into his car and he was taking them home—but the feeling passed quickly. The men were utterly polite, even demure, and when Tom instructed them to buckle up, they obeyed immediately.

He pulled into the traffic of Grand Avenue and motored toward the Ross Island Bridge. On the way he asked Diego, the apparent spokesman, where he was from. Diego was from Puebla, he said, south of Mexico City, and Javier, his friend, was from the state of Michoacán. They lived together in North Portland, and they liked the Northwest, except it was too rainy. Diego had a strong accent, but he spoke slowly and clearly and seemed comfortable making conversation with the boss, holding his rounded, weathered hands in his lap without fidgeting.

"So you guys have been here awhile?" Tom asked. He was always curious to hear the outlines of his hires' stories. His own career managing an insurance company gave him a special interest in the hazards that buffeted the majority of the world's population.

"This time?" Diego said. "Two months for me. Five months for him."

"And you always work together?"

"Nah," Diego said. "Only sometimes. Sometimes I don't see him for days. What about you? You've been here a long time?"

"I've been here all my life, Diego," Tom said, accelerating. The supple action of the gear shaft under his palm was pleasing. "My dad came over after World War II. From China. He owned a grocery store not too far from where I just picked you up. He did pretty well for himself. And I'll tell you something"—Tom paused, signaling to Diego that he should judge the merit of his coming words for himself—"He never could have done it anywhere else, Diego. Only here. Only in America. You work hard and you can get somewhere. That's the truth."

The clean wind battered the windows. "Good for him," Diego said, without guile. He rested his big hand on the lip of the glass. "So you're a native. You're very lucky."

Tom headed south on I-5, toward the leafy, affluent suburbs of Lake Oswego, exiting at Mountain Park, a maze of nested cul-de-sacs named after Renaissance artists and scholars—Da Vinci Court, Magellan Lane, Medici Circle—a pretension on the part of some long-ago developer that, like many dumb, obvious gestures, had actually worked out. The street names had attracted those they were meant to attract, and over time the development had aged into genuine prestige. The Mexicans, watching the bloated, first-generation pocket mansions roll by, with their hard-edged lawns and SUVs parked in front, were silent.

Tom's house was on Bernini Circle, a three-story '70s modern extending from the hill on cement stilts. The architecture was

vaguely Western, with a steeply pitched roof, angular front windows, and exposed cedar siding all around. A narrow driveway cut
down to a carport beside the basement, bounded on one side by a
laurel hedge and on the other by a rocky incline that became the
front yard, tufted with azaleas and hardy rhododendrons. A year before, the garden had been vibrant, a series of raised beds filled with
neat, bushy arrangements of wildflowers and native grasses. Since
Tom's divorce, however, the garden's fortunes had declined. The
laurel hedge had gone without shearing and the beds had grown a
diverse population of weeds. In the fall, a ten-foot cedar near the
bathroom window had suddenly died, losing its needles and turning brittle and white. The tree doctor had come to look at it and
could find no explanation for the event other than bad vibes.

Since then the dead tree had mocked Tom, a constant reminder
of all the life that had once blossomed in the household, and which
now, with the children grown and the wife gone, was resolutely in
the past. With spring coming on, he wanted the house back in order. He wanted the tree removed. He wanted all the light that it
continued to block from his bathroom for his own.

He zipped over the lip of the driveway, guiding the Porsche to a
stop in the carport, and for the next fifteen minutes walked Diego
and Javier through the afternoon's tasks—the weeding, the bark
dusting, the pruning, the excavation of the dead cedar. He showed
them the pile of mulch that had been delivered the week before
and the new wheelbarrow he had bought especially for the occasion, and then he found them trowels and hedge clippers. Then,
without ceremony, he went inside, leaving them to solve whatever
problems arose on their own.

From the kitchen, he peered out the venetian blinds to observe
the Mexicans assembling their tools against the wall. He saw

Diego eyeing the yard, plotting the best mode of attack, and Javier more or less following his lead. Satisfied, he poured himself a glass of white wine, tuned the kitchen TV to the day's bike race in Norway, and got to work himself. He had guests coming, and much work on dinner left to do.

Tom opened the refrigerator and crouched before the deep shelves, filled with bowls of leftovers sealed like drums with Saran wrap. On the bottom shelf a large metal tray humped with aluminum foil took up the entire space, and with some effort Tom slid the bulky mass from its cove and transported it to the countertop.

He peeled back the foil and had a look inside. Underneath the foil, huddled in a pool of marinade, lay the body of a small, white suckling pig. Its legs were tucked tidily under its torso, its empty eyes bunched tightly shut. It looked almost fetal, curled on its haunches, and strangely peaceful. Tom drizzled some marinade over the length of its spine, and the fluid trickled and spread through the goose bumps. Then he returned the foil like a shroud and pushed the tray toward the oven.

On Thursday nights Tom hosted a regular dinner party—his friends Lana and Conrad came over around eight, along with whomever else they had in tow, selected from the handful of neighbors who had not already slipped into the premature senescence of suburban family life. The evenings were generally bachelor chic— meatballs in a Crock-Pot, macaroni and cheese, chili, copious amounts of good Scotch—but tonight, in honor of the one-year anniversary of his divorce, Tom had decided to concoct an elaborate, surprise feast. The day before, he had spent the afternoon preparing the shark's fin soup that was currently resting in a porcelain tureen in the refrigerator. A bag of fresh scallops would become a stir-fry with ginger and green beans. He had wontons and shredded papaya salad yet to make.

The centerpiece would be the suckling pig, a dish Tom had never attempted, the main ingredient of which had been difficult enough just to find. There were no whole pigs at Albertsons, or Fred Meyer, or Safeway, and so he had been forced to order one through a specialty butcher in Old Town. It was locally raised on organic slop, they told him, and it had been killed only the day before. Dirt from the farm's pen had still been clinging to the pig's knuckles when Tom took possession, in an exchange that had seemed more like a kidnapping than a purchase.

Tom had brought the pig home and cleaned its hide and emptied its cavity of packed organs just as the recipe had instructed. For the past twenty hours the body had been soaking in a mixture of garlic, shallots, sugar, red bean curd, and bean paste. It would cook for at least four hours and come out of the oven radiant, shining crimson, a succulent demon.

It was almost four o'clock now—he had gotten a late start—which meant it was time to get going. He wiped down the kitchen counters and collected his cooking implements from the cupboards: the glass mixing bowls, the tin measuring cups, his favorite, all-purpose chopping knife. And again he unveiled the pig, this time turning it over to reveal a belly split down the middle, and set to stuffing the cavity with sausage from the refrigerator. He enjoyed the mindless, preparatory work, and the wine wasn't bad either. Occasionally, he glanced through the blinds to check on the Mexicans.

He was surprised to find how much progress they had already made. The weeding was practically done, and the bark dust was almost spread. Diego was crouched near a jasmine bush, pulling out dead leaves, and Javier was high on a ladder clipping the flattop of the laurel. It was a small yard. In its disuse it had come to seem much larger. Tom remembered how his sons had managed to finish the weeding in a matter of minutes by the time they were teenagers. And their work habits paled compared with those of this peasant stock.

"You want a beer?" Tom stood on the concrete path running through the front yard, holding two cold Budweisers. The men had only been working for an hour or so, but it was past five o'clock and the sun was hot. Tom believed that hard menial labor should be rewarded quickly and often.

"Sure, boss," Diego said, rising from the beds. He tossed his weeds toward the growing pile and wiped his hands on his jeans. Silently, Javier climbed from the ladder and followed him.

Tom stood around as the men cracked the cans and took their first sips. "Looks pretty good," Tom said. He leaned over and plucked an errant weed from the walkway and tossed it on the pile. "The tree's the big thing though. That's going to be a real bitch. I want it out all the way at the roots. Nothing left. I'd give it some time."

"You got some picks, boss?" Diego said. "Shovels? That would be good."

"There's a shed under the deck in the back," Tom said, pointing. "It's open. Whatever you can find in there is yours to use. And if you need something else, we can go get it. There's a hardware store down the hill."

Drinks in hand, the men drifted over and surveyed the dead tree, pushing on the trunk, inspecting the ground to comprehend the root system. Diego said something in Spanish and Javier snorted.

Tom saw no reason that his role as the boss should bar him from inclusion in the day's jokes.

"What's so funny?" he said.

"Nothing, boss," Diego said, his smile fading. Javier retracted his smile, too, and scowled at the dead tree.

"Come on. What is it?" Tom said, gruffly but with obvious warmth. Diego comprehended the tone and relaxed a little, letting him in.

"His girl," Diego explained, jabbing his thumb at Javier, "she won't let him play football this weekend. Soccer. She thinks he might get hurt. It's true. He might. He might get hurt right now, too. Look at that tree. It might fall down on him. Break his little fingers." He winked in the direction of Tom and Javier both.

Tom chuckled. "Don't let her get the upper hand, Javier," he said. "Believe me. Once she does, it's all over. You both play soccer?"

Diego affirmed that they did.

"My kid played soccer," Tom said. "The younger one. He was good, too. All-state. I always told him he should play tennis though." Tom fixed the side of Diego's big face in his gaze, watching the hired man stare at the ground. "Tennis," he said, "you can always get a game going. You don't need twenty guys out there running around. You just call up a buddy and you find a court."

"That's true," Diego said, eyeing the tree.

"He was good at tennis," Tom said. "But soccer is what he plays. He's in a league or something. They play in the park. What can you do?"

From the kitchen Tom watched the Mexicans disappear around the back and return with two picks and two shovels, approaching the tree and beginning to dig near the trunk.

The pig was sewn up, the skin had been rubbed with oil, salt, then oil again, and a small piece of wood had been placed in its mouth. The whole thing had been fitted onto a roasting pan which Tom slid into the oven, and then he set the timer.

He turned to the ginger for the stir-fry, peeling the gnarled fingers and dicing them into stringy cubes. He beat some eggs for the wontons. He poured himself another glass of wine. The Swede had begun attacking the leader on the final leg of the bike race when the phone rang. The caller ID told him it was Lana.

"Lana," he said, cradling the phone so he could continue whisking the eggs and watching TV at the same time.

"I can't make it tonight, honey," she said. "I'm real sorry."

"Nothing to be sorry about," Tom said. "You're making it."

"I can't tonight," she said. "I've got certain . . . obligations." Tom understood this meant she had to stay home with her husband, whom she despised, due to some hysterical episode on his part.

Tom switched the phone to his other shoulder. Lana was an old friend, and once, years before and very briefly, a lover. She was now a successful banker in town, and her husband worked at the daily newspaper, having stalled out long ago in the suburban office where the driftwood collected. It was Lana who brought in the bulk of their family's income and also captained the ship of her household—she maintained the books, did most all of the parenting, built their retirement fund—and as such, she was an object of great admiration in Tom's eyes, a kind of hybrid creature, woman and man, all-American in her abilities and attitudes. Like him, she was impatient with any obligation outside family realms; and like him, she had an appetite for louche, operatic behavior. People who worked as hard as they did, they figured, were

allowed certain latitudes; they were allowed to cut loose sometimes. It was an unspoken credo between them, a mentality of
prosperity and reward. What was the point of making this money,
of working so hard, if there was no pleasure to be taken in the
victory? No privileges?

"I'm cooking tonight," Tom said. His tone was placid but he
knew she knew he was putting the screws on her. "You're going
to regret it if you miss out. This is not a meal to miss. I'm going all
the way tonight."

"Fuck. If it was up to me . . ." she said.

"Of course it's up to you."

"It's not, really."

"You're punishing yourself, and there's no reason. Listen to
yourself. Listen to the true desire in your voice."

"I know, I know, but I can't do it. Shit. I might be able to do it.
We'll see. Don't count me out, okay? But don't count me in either. God. I know that's so weak."

"There you go. You're coming. I'll see you around eight."

"Don't count on it."

"How am I supposed to eat all this pig?" But she had already
hung up.

Tom hung up and a minute later Conrad called, also to beg out,
which came as little surprise. Most likely Lana had given him the
heads-up. Conrad was an old friend at this point, and good
company—willful and crude, uncensored in his absurd opinions—
but the rapport between him and Tom was still somewhat soft
around the edges. Lana was their common denominator, their
shared affection, and without her they were easily lost to each other,
prone to uncomfortable silences and misunderstandings. They both
loved Lana; each other, they happily tolerated. Conrad was out, he

said, due to a prior engagement, which downgraded the likelihood of Lana's appearance as well. Tom hung up, both relieved and annoyed by Conrad's departure, but mostly just confounded by the sudden turn of events. The pig was already cooking, releasing its oils. The alchemical process had begun. Such was the cost of a good surprise, he told himself, cradling his wine glass, the risk of a genuinely grand gesture. The chance always existed that the surprise might not go off.

Tom poured himself more wine and tasted the distant trace of pear. He could find no good object for his anger. Lana and Conrad couldn't be expected to read his mind, after all. But the pig would be done soon enough no matter what. He looked out the window at the Mexicans shaking the dead tree.

The tree had a deep moat around it, and the men were rocking the trunk back and forth, loosening the roots in the earth. The tendrils popped and sprung, like snapping bones muffled in flesh, but the thick ones remained fastened securely in place. When the hole was wide enough, Diego took a swing at one root with the pick, revealing the white insides under the caked skin, and chipped away until it was thoroughly severed.

Tom hovered on the front steps with his wine glass, watching the action. The big roots were dispensed with one by one. He enjoyed watching the labor, the spectacle of young, energized bodies exerting themselves. Each body held a different power, a different style of release. This was the lesson of tennis and bike racing as well. Diego was strong and fluid, and Javier quick and harried. They rotated the use of the pick, making a game of the awkward chopping angles. Finally, the tree listed and drooped, the underground cables shuddering. With the major roots split, the trunk came out easily, ripping from the dirt, leaving a gaping socket where the tentacles of wood had been.

The yard suddenly appeared huge. The sun poured onto the ground and hit a section of wall that had not been touched in years. A seemingly indelible shadow was erased and Tom raised his glass. "Well done," he said. The men raised their fresh beers in return. Before losing momentum they knocked what dirt they could from the tree and dragged it to the side of the house. Tom would get the neighbor kid to help him chop it to pieces. "You guys did it," Tom said. "That was a big deal, the tree coming out. I've been needing to do that for a long time. It came easier than I thought it would."

"Not so bad," Diego concurred, inspecting the new hole in the yard. He kicked some clods of loose dirt into the basin.

"You've got some more time today?" Tom asked. "Or you guys have somewhere you have to be?"

"We have some time," Diego said, squinting at the sky, happy to squeeze a few more dollars from the day. The long Oregon twilight always allowed at least one more task to be done.

"It's your lucky day then," Tom said. "I'd like you to stay for dinner tonight."

The Mexicans shared a quick look. They were accustomed to all manner of unexpected events on their jobs. Sexual passes, family dramas—they saw it all. This was but a small disruption in the turmoil of their lives. Diego laughed off the invitation though, assuming Tom was joking.

"I'm asking if you two would like to eat with me," Tom explained. "What do you say? The food here is very good. You won't regret it."

"I don't know, boss." Diego wiped his hands on his pants and placed them on his hips, reluctant to commit. "We've got some things to do. We maybe should get back to town soon . . ." His refusal was halfhearted though, Tom could see, more an act of etiquette than real regret. He was merely giving Tom a clear opportunity to retract the invitation should he have second thoughts.

"Don't worry," Tom said. "You'll still be on the clock. All right? We'll count this as work. Believe me, you'll have a good time. You haven't eaten like this before."

"You're sure, boss?" Diego said. But Tom was already at the front door, giving a final, impatient flip of his hand.

"Get in here," he said. "You're going to like it."

The boys followed, conducting a rapid conversation in Spanish as Javier got up to speed. At the door Tom told them to take off their shoes and then he led them down the narrow, shadowy hallway toward the kitchen, passing old pictures of the kids, the dogs, the mountain cottage that had been sold before the divorce. He stopped at the bathroom door and let them each wash their hands, Javier first.

"Very nice house," Diego said politely, waiting for Javier. "You've had it for a long time?"

"I've been here twenty-five years, Diego," Tom said.

"Very good," Diego said. And they stood awkwardly until Javier reappeared behind him, patting his damp hands on his shirt.

Tom and Javier stood in silence as Diego pissed loudly and washed his hands. When he was finished, Tom led the men the rest of the way down the hallway and guided them to barstools at the counter separating the open kitchen area from the TV room. They perched lightly on the stools, examining the architecture, awaiting further instruction. Tom went into the kitchen and headed directly for the faceted glacier of alcohol bottles under the cupboards.

"What's your pleasure?" he said. "Another beer? A margarita?

I've got some very good tequila I've been saving. We've got anything you want."

"A beer?" Javier managed. He was busily admiring the interior of Tom's house, eyes darting from appliance to furniture to art to appliance, taking in the layers of wealth.

"Straight tequila," Diego said, shrugging. He smiled broadly. "Why not?"

"Now we're talking," Tom said, tying on his apron. "That's more like it. I like you, Diego. You know what you want and you're not afraid to take it. That's the idea. Javier, I'm pouring you some tequila, too. If you don't like it, too bad."

Tom poured out the drinks. "I'm making a few courses tonight, boys. I think I can guarantee that you're going to like at least one or two of them. This is a real Chinese feast you'll be eating. My father taught me how to make most of these dishes. You guys like Chinese food, right? Doesn't matter. You'll like this. We're having shark's fin soup. This is a real delicacy in China. We'll have a scallop stir-fry, too. That's what I'm working on right now. You see these scallops?" He shook the bag of white buttons. "They're going to melt in your mouth by the time I'm done with them. The main course is a suckling pig. You can smell it, can't you? Maybe you have something like suckling pig in Mexico. In China, it's a traditional wedding dish. It symbolizes virginity, for what that's worth."

"Smells good," Diego said. "Really good. It cooks a long time? The pork?"

"It's got a ways to go," Tom said, chopping a bunch of scallions with flashing speed, swiping the fragments into a bowl and chopping another batch.

"It's a funny thing about Americans," he said, continuing to slice. "You should know this since you live here now. They think cooking is women's work. Which is ridiculous. I don't know where they get that idea. The fact is, women don't really belong in the kitchen at all. They never have."

Diego laughed and Javier attempted a belated, half-comprehending grin. They were already nearly finished with their first glass of tequila, and Tom, noticing, shoved the bottle within arm's reach.

"I'll tell my mother you said that," Diego said. "She'd wring your neck."

"No offense to your mother," Tom said, peeling the white inner rind from a pepper. "I'm sure she's a very good cook. I'm sure she's very competent at what she does. But what I'm talking about here is real cuisine, the art. That's a man's job. You think I'm joking but I'm not. Scullery work, that's one thing. Anyone can make a taco. Spaghetti. But real cuisine, it's too complex for women to comprehend. They don't have the attention span, the rigor. That's why most great chefs are men. Isn't that right?"

"That's right, boss," Diego said. "Whatever you say."

Tom diced the chili peppers and wiped the blade with his finger. "Well, there you go. The boss is always right. But in this case I really am right."

"I worked with a cook in Santa Rosa," Diego said, tipping the tequila bottle into his glass. "He wouldn't let women even clean the plates."

"He was an artist," Tom said, returning to his chopping board. "That's my guess."

When Tom was finished chopping the ingredients and mounding them into piles along the cutting board, he led Diego and Javier outside onto the deck to take in the sunset, midway through its slow, gradient change into night. The sliding glass door opened onto a pine expanse overlooking a distant cow pasture and a deciduous forest dotted with glass office buildings, a new housing development, and an old farmhouse half devoured by blackberry vines. To the southwest, an enormous white spire rose in the woods, surrounded by lacy scaffolding. The sky was hot pink and plum. Tom handed out cigars and brushed the fir needles from the railing.

"It's a little early for cigars, I know," he said. "But we've got some time to kill before I heat up the wok. That pig has a good ways to go. It'll come together pretty fast in the end. You like cigars?" He struck a match and lit the men's cigars. "I'm only recently a fan myself."

Diego got his cigar going and savored a few puffs. "I could learn," he said. Javier inhaled and coughed loudly.

"Don't inhale," Tom instructed. "Just let it sit in your mouth. Roll it around. Can you explain to him, Diego?" Diego explained the cigar-smoking protocols to Javier, whose next drag was expertly done. Over the pasture a flock of sparrows pulsed and scattered in the trees.

"It's a very beautiful view," Diego said. "You can see everything up here."

"That's a Mormon temple they're building down there," Tom said. "Those white spires. You have Mormons in Mexico?"

"We have Mormons," Diego said. "Oh yeah. They come down, they set up a church, they go out with their little papers. Lots of souls down there. Lots of work."

Tom laughed. "I hate the Mormons. I don't see the appeal. No drinking. No boning. Their church looks like fucking Disneyland. 'It's a Small World.' I don't get it. When did you come to America, Diego? Your English is pretty good."

"I come here all the time. This time? I been here two months now."

"And you've come to Oregon before?"

"This is my first time in Oregon. He's been here though." Diego gestured at Javier, who looked startled, and Diego did a quick translation of the conversation.

"I have two times," Javier said. "Two years ago, one year ago." Satisfied, he went back to his cigar, rolling the smoke in his mouth, getting comfortable.

"And then you go back?" Tom said.

"Back, forth. We come and go," Diego said.

"I don't get you guys," Tom said. He rested his feet on the empty lounge chair and rattled the ice in his glass. "You have to commit. You have to stay put. This back-and-forth thing. It's bullshit. How do you think you'll get anywhere with that? You get here, you stay, you make your fortune. What is it with you?"

"Coming and going. It's not so bad. I love Mexico."

"I hate fucking China. It's a fucking nightmare over there. Ignorant, arrogant people. Dirty cities. Corrupt government. I spent a year over there on business. In Hong Kong. You couldn't pay me to go back. My dad, he wouldn't go back either. This is our home now."

"Where I'm from in Mexico," Diego said, "it's very beautiful. Mountains, farms. I come up here, work hard, go back. It's good. I've got friends everywhere now."

"You have kids?"

"I have a daughter. She's very young. Three years old. You?"

"No daughters for me. Just boys. Two boys. They live in New York and Minneapolis now. They're big shots. The younger one's in the restaurant business. He dates models. The older one works on Wall Street. He's a real high roller. They left me behind, Diego. They couldn't wait to get out of here when it was time to go."

"Big cities. Big success. I'd like to see New York someday," Diego said.

"They buried me," Tom said. "That's how it should be though. They should make their own way." He drained his glass and stood up. "You talk to your family when you're up here, Diego?" he asked. "You keep in touch?"

"Of course," Diego said. "All the time."

"That's good," Tom said. "That's how it should be. Keep in touch."

Tom went inside and poured another round and checked on the progress of the reddening pig. He could hear Diego and Javier talking outside, a low babble of rapid-fire Spanish. He opened the oven to find the skin turning a golden pink and brushed more oil on the spots that seemed to need it. He used a needle to prick the skin and let out the excess oil. The smell of the pig was almost stunning in its savory power. He delivered the boys their drinks and returned to the kitchen. He pulled down the wok and placed it on the burner.

He was slicing some garlic into paper-thin slivers when he was surprised by the sound of the doorbell, a chiming clangor from cylindrical bells installed near the bathroom. The clock on the stove said eight fifteen, which seemed late for the parade of canvassers and proselytizers that normally hit up his neighborhood, guilting the rich for Greenpeace or the Sierra Club, but perhaps they were on some special campaign this month. The doorbell rang again, too soon, and Tom revised his prediction. No canvasser would be that impatient. Most likely it was the neighbor kid with some school fund-raiser or magazine deal. He would make quick work of him.

To Tom's surprise, though, it was Conrad, looking slightly jaundiced under the growing power of the yellowish porch lamp. His thick, crude lips were set in a regal smirk, and his flaxen hair was swept across his forehead. He could almost be an SS officer, Tom thought, the corruption of his Teutonic features was so pronounced. His eyes were blue and cruel, his nose fine, his skin well-preserved, but webbed in the cheeks with delicate lines of debauchery. He was wearing a madras short-sleeved shirt and khaki pants with loafers, his uniform, and holding a slim brown paper bag at his hip.

"Surprise," Conrad said, a croak of sarcasm in his voice. There was always something sideways in his way of talking. "I'm ready for dinner after all. I faked you out."

"You made it," Tom said, widening the door. "Very nice, sir. Very nice."

"Lana's behind me," Conrad said, stepping inside and kicking off his shoes as he'd been trained. "Lana! Come on, you wench! Let's go. Our host is waiting."

A car door slammed and moments later Lana's blonde hair peeped into view. She emerged from the gloaming and stomped down the walkway between the rows of garden lights. She was short-waisted and squat but adamantly seductive in her way. As she came closer, shoulders squared, her face resolved from the shadows. Her eyes were small and almondine, and her face was almost pretty, well-formed on top but becoming crimped at the bottom, pocked with the remnant of childhood acne. On this night, she wore a tight black dress with a scoop neck and fishnet stockings with patent-leather pumps. Her sex appeal was palpable, and a product of pure willpower. She was in a party mood, Tom could tell immediately, likely owing to a blowup at home.

"I had to get out of there," she said, kissing Tom on the mouth as she stepped through the door. "What a fucking jackass. I'm not missing my one good night of the week for him. I hope we're not too late, honey. I brought wine."

"Never too late, my dear," he said, shutting the door gently behind her. "The invitation always stands. It's good you made it. We're getting close on dinner."

"Goddamn, this smells good," Conrad said from down the hallway. "Tom, man, why did that woman leave you? Who cares what a bastard you are. She's fucking crazy."

The three of them converged in the kitchen, and Conrad and Lana deposited their bags on the counter and found their own glasses while Tom finished tending to the garlic. The night was shaping into something after all, he thought, much better than he'd even imagined. Sometimes, he told himself, a surprise surprised itself. He looked forward to the coming revelations, promising himself to allow the introductions to unfold naturally. No need to hurry anything along.

"You want some tequila?" he said. "We're drinking tequila tonight."

"I'll help myself," Conrad said. He pulled a narrow bottle of Scotch from the sheath of brown paper. "I got this baby in Scotland last year. Thought I'd break it out for the occasion."

"Suit yourself," Tom said. "The rest of us are drinking tequila." He couldn't help himself.

"The rest of us?" Lana asked.

"We have some other guests tonight," Tom said.

"Tequila and Chinese," Conrad said, ignoring the cues. "Does that work? Seems weird to me. I'm sticking with Scotch."

"Murray?" Lana said, accepting a tall glass of tequila and ice. "I thought he was out of town this week."

"Not Murray," Tom said.

"Who then?"

"I don't think you know them," Tom allowed. "I think I can guarantee that."

Drinks poured, the trio adjourned from the kitchen to the deck, passing in single file through the dining room on the way.

"Chinese and tequila," Conrad continued, prodding for conflict. "It seems weird to me."

"The Chinese invented tequila," Tom said, sliding the glass door on its rubber track. "Everyone knows that."

"Chinese didn't invent tequila," Conrad said.

"We invented everything," Tom said. "It was just so long ago we forgot about it. If you don't know that by now, I can't help you."

Out on the deck Diego had moved from his lounge chair to the wooden railing and was staring out at the half-finished housing development in the trees. Javier was ensconced in a wicker chair, savoring his cigar, obscured by a hanging cloud of smoke. Both of them hastily came to attention as the new company arrived, standing up and putting their glasses aside for introductions.

"I see you replaced us," Lana said, unflappable. She brushed the needles from a deck chair and took a seat. "Such a great view, Tom. Really spectacular."

"Conrad, Lana," Tom said, "this is Javier and Diego. They worked on the front yard today. You may have noticed the dead tree is gone. At last. They did an excellent job, too. Not like all the lazy, snot-nosed teenagers around here."

"Nice to meet you," Lana said, inspecting the two Mexicans as she shook their hands, gauging in her mind the vectors of inappropriateness already traveled, and those yet left to go. The warmth in her voice was genuine though. She was democratic in all her dispositions.

Conrad shook the Mexicans' hands enthusiastically. His warmth was sarcastic. To him, they were an excellent novelty and not much more.

"Boys," he said. "Welcome to Tom's house. I hope the neighborhood is treating you well. You're getting everything you need."

Diego and Javier murmured uncertainly, unsure what was expected of them next. They remained standing, prepared to exit, aware that the circumstance of their invitation had likely just changed.

Briefly, Tom entertained the thought of whisking them home. Clearly, they felt out of place and it wouldn't take long to drive them back to town and deposit them on the corner where he'd found them. On the other hand, though, the food was nearly ready, and they had been having a good time. Furthermore, there was a principle at stake. He had already extended an invitation, and the invitation could not simply be rescinded now that it was inconvenient, now that the real guests had arrived. The Mexicans were his guests, even if paid to be so, and the idea of turning them out seemed wrong. They remained on their feet, ready to take his lead, which only made their continuing presence seem more integral.

"Sit down," he ordered. "We've got a pig to eat. You boys need a new drink. Give me those glasses."

Diego and Javier remained standing, giving Tom yet one more chance to change his mind. "I'm okay on the drink, boss," Diego said. "Thanks though."

"Sit down," Tom said firmly "You're my guests. Javier? You want a drink? You look ready."

He pried Javier's glass from his fingers, and Conrad stepped into the conversational void. "So you guys pulled that tree out? Nice job. About time. Tom was dragging down all our property values around here. Must've been a real bitch to extract. Was it a bitch to extract?" The boys stared at him. The cynical tone and the word "extract" were meant explicitly to trip them up.

"Conrad's never worked in his life," Tom said, reentering the house. "He has no idea what it means to use your own hands. He was born rich. What he's got is called passive wealth. He just sits back and watches his stocks sweat for him."

"I work my ass off, Tom!" Conrad said, unoffended. He turned back to the Mexicans. "He's got some kind of Chink work ethic. I use my brain. No shame in that."

Tom continued to the kitchen without comment, but he could hear the conversation through the screen door. Lana asked where the boys were from and a soothing murmur soon spread among the group when it turned out she had visited Puebla herself. "It's a great city," she said. "Beautiful zócalo, as I recall. My car got broken into down there. They stole all my CDs."

"It's a tough city," Diego said ruefully. "A lot of poor people there. They don't know any better."

"It didn't seem that tough," Lana said. "It was beautiful. I just got unlucky that trip. That's all."

From the kitchen, Tom listened to the rise and fall of conversation, the monotone of exposition and the ensuing spikes of laughter, all of which pleased him greatly. A good party always contained some minor catastrophe, he believed—a small grease fire, a broken coffee table. In this case, the catastrophe was the guests themselves.

Tom checked the pig, which was progressing nicely, its skin

blushing, grease sizzling below. He closed the door to find Lana in the room, holding four empty glasses.

"You left them with Conrad?" Tom said.

"He's talking about his housecleaner. He says she steals from him and he wants to know how to deal with it. Incredible. I couldn't really handle it. But Diego doesn't seem to mind. And Javier has no idea what's going on. His glass is empty though. So's mine."

"That was quick," Tom observed.

Lana positioned herself at the counter, inspecting the array of bottles. "Don't monitor me," she said. "I get enough of that at home." She poured four tall drinks and dropped a handful of ice in each.

"Extra for Diego," she said. "You're almost out of tequila, Tom."

"There's more in the pantry."

"I'd bust it out if I were you," she said. "I doubt this is going to be anyone's last." She headed back outside, sipping her drink, clutching the other three in one hand.

Tom set the table with the good, gilded china, moving agilely around the smoked-glass tabletop, folding the napkins, placing the burnished silverware, arranging the cut-crystal wine glasses, not fussily but with an eye for the symmetries of presentation. Outside, he could hear Diego talking, and judging from the responses, Lana and Conrad were rapt.

"I was living in Los Angeles," Diego was saying. "I was working on a beautiful, beautiful house. Spanish style, white stucco walls, with the black iron fences. The red tile roof. Bougainvillea. Very beautiful, very handsome house."

Tom dimmed the light on the chandelier, its marbled globes softening, and scooted the chairs to their settings. He began bringing out the side dishes and placing them on the teak credenza he had kept against his ex-wife's virulent claims of ownership. The wontons in their moist basket, the haystack of grated papaya. In a flurry of final preparation, he chopped a handful of peanuts, decanted the wine, and put a Coltrane CD on the stereo, moving from task to task smoothly, all the while catching swatches of conversation from outside.

"The man who owned the house," Diego went on, "he was rich. A really famous man. You know him, I think."

"Who was it?" Lana said. "Tell us."

"What was his name?" Diego said. "Peter Fonda?"

"Peter Fonda? The actor?"

"Yes. That's it. He's a nice man. Very generous. We were like this, spending some time together. At the end of the day he fed us, too. I put on his leather pants. The famous ones. From *Easy Rider*."

"You wore Peter Fonda's leather pants from *Easy Rider*?" Conrad repeated. "Is that what you're telling us?"

"They were tight. I almost ripped them."

"Diego, you're insane!" Lana said. "He's insane."

"Here's to Peter Fonda," Conrad said. "That fucking hippie. Tom, where did you get this guy? And when is dinner? We're starving out here."

Just then the buzzer sounded and Tom swung out onto the deck. The four faces of his guests looked at him expectantly in unison. Oven mitt in hand, he addressed them as one, "Dinner, my friends, is ready. It is time to get your asses inside."

The table was gorgeous, the stir-fry a swirl of glassy noodles hiding jewels of scallops and green vegetables, the dipping sauces a spectrum of earthy fluids, elemental juices trapped in wrought clay. Mounds of cottony white rice in cobalt-colored ceramic bowls dotted the length of the table. At the center of the composition was the suckling pig, resplendent on a gold platter covered in sprigs of parsley. The skin was a perfect surface of glazed crimson, the jowls plump, the ears folded. In the pig's mouth Tom had replaced the wood with a tiny apple.

The guests clapped spontaneously at the sight.

"That pig looks fucking pissed," Conrad said.

"Tom, this is incredible," gushed Lana. She sat facing the windows, and pulled Diego beside her, as Conrad took the opposite side, leaving Tom and Javier at the heads. The pig's snout ended up pointing at Diego, which made him the guest of honor, and that seemed appropriate.

"I've seen better though," Conrad said, opening his napkin onto his lap, and the group laughed more wildly than necessary. Only Javier seemed at all confused or out of place, but even he was obviously pleased by the table's camaraderie.

"You know they used to call humans 'the long pig'?" Conrad said. "We're not that different from the pigs. As fetuses we're almost indistinguishable. The long pig. I can see it. I bet we'd make good bacon. Right, Javier?"

"To the new yard," Lana offered, raising her glass.

"Hear, hear, the new yard," Conrad said. "And to divorce. The great liberator of men."

"To divorce," Tom said. "To second acts."

"To the cook," said Diego.

They all touched glasses and drank, and Tom set to carving with a special knife and prong. The plates were passed toward him and he sent them back heaped with meat, and for a moment a brief lull in conversation descended. The sound of silver on porcelain filled the room and the group was reflected in the black windows of the dining room.

"You hear Murray is selling his side lot?" Conrad said, passing a steaming plate to Javier. "He just put it on the market yesterday."

"For how much?" Tom said. He was sorry to be lapsing into the inanities of neighborhood real estate so soon, the subject of last conversational resort, but he was curious for the figure.

"Five hundred grand."

Tom whistled. "Good for him. Good for all of us. Keep it going. Let the bubble never burst."

"There's no bubble," Conrad said. "Not here anyway. We're in a hammock is what we're in here. Until we get up to Seattle and San Francisco levels, we're still undervalued. We're still the crummy neighborhood of the West Coast."

"I ran into Elaine yesterday," Lana said, already bored by the topic. "She was at the wine store. She looks relaxed."

"Great," Tom said, hacking out a rib and going back for another. Elaine was his ex-wife. He had managed to avoid her over the past few months, although there were probably more near misses than he realized. They still shared a fair number of friends and similar habits, and the town was small. "She should look relaxed," he said. The pig's body was quickly getting whittled down, cratered with large divots. "What's she got to do?"

"Elaine is a beautiful woman," Lana informed Diego. "Real Swedish farm girl. Big knockers. Nice legs. She was a stewardess. They met on a plane. Can you believe it? They were such a beautiful couple. It's sad when a couple like that breaks up. They were really something to look at. She said Billy's having a kid, Tom. Congratulations."

Tom had finished the carving and placed the knife and prong on the platter, taking his seat. "I don't think she was supposed to tell anyone that," he said, "but thanks." He opened his napkin onto his lap and smoothed out the wrinkles.

"Oh God," Lana said. "I'm sorry. I didn't know it was a secret. Don't tell her I said anything. All right?"

"Boy or girl?" Conrad said, unfazed by protocol. "Have they scanned the bugger?"

"They don't know anything yet," Tom said. "It's too early." To Diego and Javier he explained, "This is my son in New York. He's married to his high school girlfriend. They own a place in Brooklyn. Now that's a real estate market."

"Congratulations," Diego said, raising his glass again. "Very good news, boss. Your first grandchild?"

"To my knowledge," he said.

"Fantastic news."

The table toasted again, with more solemnity this time, and then set to eating with gusto. All agreed the pork was delicious, perfectly soft and smooth, clean and well seasoned. The baby fat was almost too gelatinous, but one adapted to the texture. "Beginner's luck," Tom said. "Don't know how it happened. Thank the pig."

"I don't see the problem scanning the kid," Conrad said, returning to the last uncomfortable moment. "Why wait until it squeezes out? You know? It's a surprise whenever you know."

"I wouldn't want to know," Lana said. "Diego, will you pass the soy sauce?"

"I guess it makes sense," Conrad said. "They'd probably abort it if it was a girl. Right? That's the Chinese custom, right, Tom? Toss the girls in a pond?"

"That's why we'll rule this continent one day," Tom said, his

chopsticks hovering with a scallop near his mouth. "We're building an army, Conrad. Only the strongest will survive."

"Tell him what your mom used to say," Lana urged. "It cracks
me up." Tom shook his head, refusing to indulge, but Lana pushed
him. "Come on," she said. "Don't be that way."

The table's attention settled on him, and he took his time chewing his food, letting them wait.

"When I was a kid," Tom finally obliged, "my mother used to
come into my room at night and talk to me before I fell asleep. I'd
be there in bed, nodding off. And she'd come in and lean over and
whisper in my ear. She'd always say the same thing." Here Tom's
voice changed into a shrieky, marble-mouthed register, muted in a
whisper. "She'd say, 'Tommy, Tommy. Listen to me. One day—
China rule the world.'" He bugged his eyes and drew out the word
"world" to give the full Chinese-mother effect, and Lana and Conrad cackled with laughter. Diego chuckled politely and Javier
grinned as if some of the meaning had penetrated from the side.

"Jesus Christ," Conrad said. "No wonder you're such an asshole.
What do you say, Javier? You think that's funny? You like the pig?
You haven't said much tonight. Good food, right? I bet you understand everything we're talking about. You're just sitting there judging us."

Javier, caught off-guard by Conrad's sudden address, gave a
warped smile. Then, to everyone's surprise, he raised his finger in
the air, signaling he had something to add. He cleared his throat
and lifted his glass, bleary eyes darting sloppily around the room.

"Someday," Javier said, holding his glass above his head, struggling to lean into the shared space of conversation, "someday,
Mexico rule the world!" His gapped teeth flashed a wide smile

and the laughter boomed throughout the room. Conrad laughed so hard he almost choked.

When the wontons were gone, and the pig had been reduced to a pile of bones in a puddle of grease, the group, leaving everything on the table, migrated into the living room, with its high, peaked ceiling, cream carpet, and stone fireplace. Lana and Diego took the couch, sinking into its soft cushions, and Javier drifted to the fireplace, attempting to blend into the surroundings. Conrad wandered the outskirts of the room, looking for something to seize his attention, picking up various coffee table books and jade figurines. Tom crouched at the stereo, searching for a good soundtrack to accompany the next phase of the evening.

"Javier," Conrad pestered, holding up a carved wooden dragon, "what do you think of this? You like it?" Javier smiled wanly and shrugged. "You don't care," Conrad said, releasing him. "You've got other things on your mind. I know."

From the bookshelf Conrad pulled down a volume on primitive erotic arts and flipped through the pages. "You know, I think of you as a Mexican, Tom," he said, "You're my Mexican friend. You should see this guy in a cowboy hat, Javier. He could be your brother."

Tom didn't respond. From his small CD collection he chose *Bitch's Brew*, dimly aware that its humid powers, its steeping black magic, might be appropriate for the night's mysterious chemistries. He was already delighted by the license the guests were taking and hoped to see them push even further. Let's see where it goes, he thought. Feed the flames. He loaded the CD into the magazine and the first sultry notes slid from the speakers, coiling in the air like smoke.

He stood to find Lana and Diego already dancing, Lana clinging to Diego's beefy frame, and Diego holding his hands loosely around Lana's waist, slightly embarrassed by the spectacle they were making. There was something undeniably sordid in the scene. The two blundered around the room, knocking into the edges of the coffee table and the sides of the couch, as the three other guests watched.

Conrad leered and raised his glass.

Tom raised his glass in return. The trumpet was like a slithering, multihued snake. Lana tucked herself against Diego's broad chest. Tom approved. What better way to heal yourself than the cauterizing fire of bad decisions? What better way to reclaim whatever eludes you in day-to-day life?

The pair stumbled along until Diego seemed to think it had gone on long enough and released Lana, gently but firmly. Lana looked confused, as if she had just awakened from a dream, and Conrad clapped four bleak claps, breaking what remained of the spell. Diego grinned sheepishly and took the opportunity to evacuate the room. On the way he lumbered into the wall with his shoulder and knocked a framed picture of Mount Hood askew.

Lana, finding her drink, glared hatefully at Conrad, blaming him for some unformed slight, and exited as well.

"You and me next?" Conrad said to Javier, and answered himself: "Maybe later."

Tom found Lana in the kitchen, among the strewn cooking utensils and detritus of the night's meal. She was pouring herself a new tall glass of wine, and when she was done, she corked the bottle. Tom took it from her and struggled to pull the cork out for himself.

"You know what you're doing, I guess," Tom said, without judgment. He figured it was his obligation to check up on her. If nothing else, his concern added to the sense of juvenile drama.

"You have a problem with what I'm doing?" she said. She smiled a drunk, lizardy smile as some everyday part of herself immolated in the far recesses of her brain.

"It's not my problem," he said, shrugging. "You're a big girl."

"I am a big girl," she said, and took a large sip of wine. Her mouth and chin distorted behind the bubble of glass. She wiped her lips with the back of her hand. "And you know what? Big girl wants to fuck."

The last droplets of Tom's piss splashed into the bowl and the toilet's vacuum powerfully sucked the water away. He zipped and took a moment in front of the mirror, observing with detachment the harshly lit surfaces of his face. His lips were purplish from the wine, his eyes tired. Otherwise, not much to report. He splashed some water on his cheeks and dabbed them off on the towel.

Out in the hallway he spotted Diego and Lana at the head of the stairs leading to the basement den, engaged in a whispered negotiation of some kind. He averted his eyes, but couldn't help notice Lana's hand on Diego's elbow, or the appetite etched on Diego's face. Wordlessly, pretending Tom was not there, the two stumbled down the carpeted stairway into the gloom.

Tom drifted into the kitchen and piled a few dishes in the sink. Then, giving up, he wandered into the living room, which was empty save for Miles Davis. The lamp sent a balloon of light into the high corner, revealing a single strand of cobweb attached to the raw crossbeam.

The dining room was also empty, just the wreckage of the meal fastened to the tabletop. Tom could hear noise outside though, and opened the sliding glass door to find Conrad and Javier seated at the glass patio table, lit feebly by the living room window. It was getting chilly. They had located a deck of cards somewhere and Conrad was in the process of dealing a hand. Both of them were smoking new cigars pulled from Tom's stash.

"You boys doing all right?" Tom said, dragging a metal chair to join them, the legs vibrating madly on the wood. "You need anything?"

"We are excellent," Conrad said. He was scrutinizing his hand, rearranging the cards into a better order. "This is something we can both understand. Finally. We don't need to talk for this shit. We play cards. We do math. This is plain luck against luck. We don't need language for this. Am I right, Javier? Am I right?"

Javier, unaware he was being addressed, or not caring, grimaced at the hand he'd been dealt. A fuzz of mustache coated his wide upper lip, and the whites of his eyes stood out in the darkness. He licked his lips and fiddled with the cards. Conrad brushed a lock of blond hair from his forehead and returned to his hand.

"See? I'm right."

Tom watched the hand play out. They were playing five-card draw, which was almost absurd with only two people, but they went at it with intensity, and on Javier's part a kind of relief that the pretense of conversation was finally over. The shadows cloaked their faces, emphasizing the severity of Javier's bone structure. Bare triangles on his cheeks, a rectangle on his forehead. He had grown up in a village in Michoacán and now here he was, sitting on Tom's deck playing poker. It made the neighborhood seem strangely exotic.

The hand went to Conrad, and without pause, Javier took the deck and shuffled the cards expertly. The stiff riffle repeated three times. Without consultation, Tom was dealt in on the next hand.

"Okay. What are we betting here, anyway?" he said.

"Ten bucks to open," Conrad said, watching the cards.

Tom watched the cards, too. "That's a lot," he said. For Javier, he knew, it was an hour's wage. As host, he felt it was his duty to watch out for the well-being of all his guests.

"A lot?" Conrad said, scoffing. "What's the point, then? Come on, man. You want to play or what? Javier's cool with it. He's the one who set the ante. Not me."

"Is that true?" Tom said. He shifted his gaze to Javier.

As if to answer, Javier pulled out his wallet, a ruined slab of leather stuffed with dollars and cards and odd paper clippings, and emptied the bills onto the table. He picked out two five-dollar notes and pushed them to the middle of the glass. In the dim light, Tom could see a sharp intelligence kindling in his features, a fervid opportunism that had previously been hidden. For the first time Tom detected real will behind Javier's eyes. He might be the canniest one among them, he thought. Who knew what well of experience was hidden inside his Spanish-speaking head?

Conrad clapped his hands and rubbed them together. "Now we're talking. We're all men here. Doing what men do. I like you, Javier. You've got some iron balls. Are you in or what, motherfucker?"

Tom pulled out his wallet and floated ten dollars onto the glass. Then he lifted his cards and spread them into a fan. He was in possession of two threes, the queen of clubs, and the four and eight of spades.

The hand moved through its cycles and Tom folded with three of a kind. The other two kept going—Javier raising Conrad two dollars and Conrad raising Javier another three, then Javier raising four, Conrad five. In the end, Conrad showed his hand. He had a full house, which soundly beat Javier's three queens, and he took the seventy-four-dollar pot with relish.

Javier showed no emotion over the loss. Tom tried to read some clue into his style of play, some hint as to the outlines of his personality. Perhaps he had been bluffing, hoping Conrad would bow out. Or perhaps he had honestly believed his three of a kind was a winning hand. It was hard to say. He might be rash, or he might be clever, or he might be something else entirely, just testing the boundaries of his powers, taking control of the mental drama of the game from the gate.

"Boys," Conrad said, organizing the new bills in front of him, "I'm going to call that first blood."

"Rambo," Javier said flatly. The word came and went quickly, but there it was, his first casually offered response of the whole day.

"Rambo?" Conrad said.

"*First Blood*, dipshit," Tom said.

"Rambo!" Conrad said, pleased to have finally made verbal contact. "That's right, Javier. Me, Rambo. You guys, Vietnam. This guy knows more than he's letting on, Tom. Believe me."

"I don't doubt it," Tom said.

The deck had landed in front of Tom and he shuffled, enjoying the purr of the edges against his fingertips. He dealt proficiently and the men raised their hands. They chose not to speak anymore, even when the sound of Lana's hoarse laughter floated from deep inside the house, followed by the thunk of a heavy spill. They were inside the game, facing each other as equals. All the deference and tension and misunderstanding of the day sloughed away.

Conrad took two cards and Javier took one. Tom took three cards and ended up with another crap hand, two eights and change. He glanced at the other men but neither revealed any pleasure or displeasure on their faces. He folded, and once again the other two fought on, hitting back and forth until the pot reached fifty-four dollars. This time, Conrad won with a flush of spades over Javier's three kings.

"Second blood," Conrad said, and Javier grunted, indifferent. Whatever strategy he was pursuing remained unclear.

Conrad was on a streak. He took the next three out of five hands. Why the cards ran hot and cold was one of the great mysteries of the universe, but there was no question the cosmic weather was on Conrad's side. Soon, Javier was roughly pushing himself away from the table, shaking his head in self-disgust. He stared drunkenly at Conrad, searching for some visible sign of his powers, and then he scooted back to the table and looked earnestly at Tom. There was no need for talking. Tom pulled out his wallet and peeled out a hundred dollars, rounding up, and threw in a couple more twenties as a tip. The way Javier's luck was running, he figured, he would need all of it.

Javier made change with Conrad—twenties for tens, fives, and ones—and the game resumed. The first hand went to Javier, stoking thoughts of a wholesale turnaround, but then, immediately, the old pattern returned. Conrad hogged all the luck. Tom picked up a pot here and there, and Javier landed a small one now and again, but Conrad's good fortune was too much to battle. It was a force of nature, overwhelming. Soon, Javier was again back at the bottom, having lost a big bet on a good hand and then making some bad gambles, trying to turn his luck from the inside. From the way he gritted his teeth and pressed his elbows against his ribs, it seemed he had lost his hold on the circumstances. Under the glass his free hand was clenched tightly, tapping his knee.

Conrad won yet again. He pulled the pot to his chest with an air of near-apology. Even he seemed astonished by the duration of his streak this night. Tom considered offering Javier some advice, urging him to back off, but figured it wasn't his place to say anything. Javier was the captain of his own destiny. Reality had proven malleable on some fronts this day. Who knew where and when the next bend would occur? He seemed prepared to go all the way, though, to hit whatever wall, whatever floor, he was hurtling toward.

"Shall we continue the massacre?" Conrad said, emptying a tequila bottle evenly into the three glasses and mopping the spilled droplets with his shirttails. "I don't want anyone to say I didn't give them a chance."

"Don't flatter yourself," Tom said. "We're digging our own graves here."

"Very well then. We continue."

Javier dealt. He had enough money to ante up, but not much for the betting. If he could make a stand, he seemed to think, it might be possible that the whole world would pivot on its axis. The gods might yet change their minds.

Tom checked his cards. At first he saw nothing, just a loose bunch of red odds and ends. But then, as he arranged the cards in his fingers, they began to fall into a more promising order. The cogs clicked and the cards dropped into place and suddenly, to his pleasure, he found himself looking at a straight flush—hearts, six through ten. A mild buzz went through him. When he turned his cards moments later, he couldn't help but let out a moan of pleasure. Javier, however, made a strangled noise in his throat and scraped his fist against his knee.

"Let that be a lesson," Conrad said, tossing his cards on the table. "The god of poker is a bitch-goddess."

"No doubt about it," Tom said, taking his winnings.

Javier stood and swayed near the pine railing. He steadied himself, and with as much dignity as he could muster, he walked to the glass door, struggling comically with the screen, and continued down the hall toward the bathroom. The light went on, slapping the opposite wall with a block of color, and then the light was extinguished by the closing door.

"Bad run," Conrad said, gnawing his cigar.

"Tough breaks," Tom agreed. "More than one."

"I guess we're done," Conrad said.

"I think so."

Conrad relit his cigar and set about counting his night's winnings, shaping the mess of bills into a weathered pile. Tom picked up his cigar as well and replaced his own remaining bills in his wallet. The money organized, Conrad peeled off a chunk and tucked it in his pocket. Then, without a word, he took the remaining pile and slipped it into Javier's coat, a windbreaker lined with pilly fleece still draped on the patio chair.

"What are you doing?" Tom said. He was in the midst of relighting his stubborn cigar yet again, and the sweet taste of the skin clung to his lips. The tobacco caught the flame and his mouth filled with languid smoke.

"Nothing," Conrad said, pulling on his own cigar. "He was stupid tonight. The cards were against him. He should have quit a long time ago."

"You can't give it back," Tom said.

"Eh," Conrad said, and swatted the air with the back of his hand, causing whorls in the smoke cloud. "Payment for the pig."

The two sat for a moment and Tom watched Conrad with growing contempt. On the surface the gift looked generous enough. But underneath was something vaguely insulting. They'd established the rules, hadn't they? Someone had to lose. Just because Conrad wanted to make himself feel better was no reason to rob Javier of his hard-earned dignity.

Tom leaned over and reached into the coat pocket and found the wad of bills. He pulled them out and tossed them back onto Conrad's lap. "He's a man," he said. "He took his chances. This is yours."

"Fuck it," Conrad said, cradling the bills. "Let him have it."

Tom shook his head. He stretched his leg under the table and pushed the metal chair with Javier's coat out of Conrad's reach. "It's insulting."

Conrad sat there with the money in his hand, more puzzled by Tom's actions than anything else. "Come on," he said. "It's not a big deal. It's just a little cash."

"Don't do it," Tom said, an edge entering his voice. "I'm telling you."

Conrad glanced at the glass door. There was no movement inside. He took a deep breath, rounding his shoulders, and exhaled through his nose. He folded the bills and let them rest on his thigh, capitulating to Tom by degrees.

"You're a real fucking prick," he said, but he didn't move.

"He doesn't want it," Tom said, blowing a cloud of smoke. "It's yours now. Keep it." The smoke formed a bushy shape between them, and then drained upward into the sky, and was gone.

Inside, the stereo was silent. The house had a tired, hollowed-out feeling. The floor seemed slightly canted as Tom stalked the living room, straightening pillows, and it occurred to him that he had perhaps been somewhat compromised by alcohol.

After the living room he moved on to the bathroom to check

on Javier. He stood at the door but no sounds came from the other side. "You okay?" he said. Still nothing. Probably Javier was passed out on the floor, he figured, or curled around the toilet, safely ex-pelling the night's poison from his body. He saw no reason to bother him just yet. Around the corner Conrad could be heard picking over the remains of the food. The clatter of a fork hitting the floor followed by a whispered curse. Then, after stumbling foot-steps, the front door slammed and Conrad was gone.

Next Tom went downstairs, passing through the plush den— once the domain of his sons, the scene of many roughhousing tournaments and late-night TV sessions—until he arrived at the door to Billy's room. Cautiously, he turned the knob and a blade of light widened, revealing the littered floor and the ceiling plastered in ancient skateboarding posters, and then Lana and Diego laying in the twin bed, wrapped in an NFL sheet dotted with team logos. The sound of their mixed breathing was off-kilter: Lana's placid, Diego's rough and ragged with apnea. The room was muggy and close with the funk of sex.

Lana groaned and rolled over, clutching the sheet to her chest. Her eyes slivered open and she looked glassily at Tom. Her expres-sion was calm, or perhaps simply so boggled by alcohol she couldn't see straight. Her hair fell over her face, and she seemed unsure where she was.

Tom said nothing. He was already resigning himself to the idea of overnight guests. Whatever awkwardness they faced, they could face in the morning. He closed the door and went back upstairs, plotting to leave out pillows and blankets on the couch for Javier, although he would likely endure the whole night in the bathroom.

In the dining room, Tom poured himself a final Scotch and

soda and then sat down near the window. Outside, a single pin-prick of starlight was visible above the spire of the temple. Two clouds drenched in moonlight lurked near the horizon.

He left the lights off and surveyed the night's damage. The last strands of papaya were drying out. The scattered wine glasses caught bits of moonlight. The clues were tell-tale. A forensic detective would have to conclude that a pretty good party had occurred.

At the center of the table lay the remains of the suckling pig, by far the most gruesome reminder of the evening's progress. The bones had been completely stripped of meat, the entire spinal column visible. Little gobbets of fat were collected on the platter, mixed with the wilted pieces of parsley.

The only part of the creature that remained untouched was the face. The red cheeks, the empty eyes, the folded ears—all were just as they had started, lying on the cold metal, attached to a few bones glistening with fat.

Tom stared at the pig. He wondered about the rest of the litter, whether the brothers and sisters had survived, and if so, what had become of them. He wondered about the mother, too. What a life, he thought. Only a few weeks long, at best. Born to be devoured and nothing more.

He sipped his drink. A cloud moved and the pig's face brightened. The image was ghastly, but it didn't bother him so much. It made him think about the outlines of his own time on earth. On either end of his consciousness the edges resolved. The past tapered to nothing, the future tapered to nothing, and his hours became like a bright, tented wedge in the blackness. His boys, Elaine, Lana, all of them were there. And soon a new one would be coming, too, starting its own path from darkness to darkness. He and the new one would overlap only briefly, though. He was so far ahead he'd barely catch sight.

The moon dimmed and the shadows deepened in the pig's eyes. Tom sat perfectly still. He could tell he was entering a new country now, a solitary country, and up ahead the devouring maw was almost in sight.

The pig's remains gleamed in the darkness. Tom bowed his head and raised his glass. An ice cube popped.

It was late. The birds would be waking soon. He drank.

WORDS AND THINGS

AFTER TWO INTERVIEWS, neither of which were recorded and both of which took place at frowsy, dimly lit old-man bars, Jen still couldn't tell whether David, the critic, was gay or what. It didn't seem like it, although by all indications he probably was: good listener, well-groomed, verbal. But somehow, the way he looked at her and nodded and encouraged her to keep talking, drawing out all her best stories, it felt like something more than just professional interest on his part, maybe even more than just being friendly and well-bred and gay.

In the two interviews, the ostensible research for a profile David was writing in a regional art magazine, they had covered plenty of topics besides Jen's artistic career. They had talked about their mutual friends, of which there were many; and their families, which were profoundly unsimilar; and movies, which they more or less agreed on, barring his affection for post–*Animal House* boob-and-poop vehicles, which she explained she had personal reasons for objecting to, namely that her father looked remarkably like Chevy Chase and had poisoned a certain genre of smarmy, slapstick comedy for her simply by loving it so much. They had talked at length about their city, now seemingly evolving from its almost premodern slumber; they had talked about drugs. It all seemed like a prelude to something, the precise nature of which remained deliciously unclear. Tonight, if there was any logic whatsoever to their unfolding relationship as artist and critic, and if he wasn't gay, they would have their first kiss.

They were having dinner at Jen's house, though whose idea that had been was hard to recall. Jen tried to reconstruct the sequence of invitations while putting some mesclun in the lettuce spinner, but it was impossible to figure out. Had he invited himself over? Had she suggested it? In any case, he was coming, and she was glad. She had on her favorite safari shirt, with the embroidered daisies on the pockets, and her highwater denim pants, which she was happy to find she fit into this week. Her black hair was pulled back into two coiled pigtails, which she knew flattered her high cheekbones. She spun the lettuce spinner and listened to the plastic mechanism whir satisfyingly. What time was it? How prompt might he be?

Just as the last clicks of the lettuce spinner finished off, Jen heard the screen door rattle back and forth and David's deep voice delicately query the empty front room.

"Hello? Anyone home?"

"In here!" she said, and swung her head and shoulders into his line of sight. His shadowy outline hovered in the brightness of the doorway.

"I can come in?"

"Come in! Yes!"

David entered shyly, though not unconfidently, carrying a container of gourmet ice cream and the movie he had described to her a few nights before. That was the excuse, she remembered, to watch the movie, an obscurity from Canada. He was tall and lean, a fairly typical specimen of the gangly, brown-haired boys who flocked to her town like finches each year, and who generally got bored soon enough and left. The only difference being he was a native, and had no interest in going elsewhere. His eyes were slow-moving but alert, and beneath his jawline spread a rough, welted splotch of razor burn. His black pants and faded black T-shirt were a little wrinkled, his blue Adidas well-worn. He looked slightly flushed from his bike ride.

"Amazing!" he said, casting a curious gaze over the kitchen, almost clairvoyantly polite. "Your house is, like, incredible."

Jen smiled. Still holding the spinner, she took the opportunity to look around the room through her guest's eyes. Her kitchen, with all its cozy nooks, pleased her. The tile floor and weather-beaten table and antique bread box were hard-won totems of domestic order. She watched, oddly thrilled, as David crossed the room and put the ice cream in the freezer as if he already felt at ease inhabiting her space.

"It's a great place," he said. "I bet it was a lot of work, huh?"

"It was pretty run-down," Jen admitted.

"I wouldn't know where to start."

Jen was glad to recount the highlights of her past years' struggles: replacing the roof, taking out the mirrors that had been glued onto every wall, remodeling the bathroom, and turning the caving-in garage into a studio. She explained how her mortgage was less than most people paid in rent and how the property value had already at least doubled since she'd moved in. It was a kind of pitch for herself, she realized, revealing a pride she hadn't been aware existed, and David made appropriately enthralled sounds of attention throughout—his appreciation even for the mundane details of home refurbishment apparently genuine. As she went on, the plastic lettuce spinner in her hands dripped water onto the floor until a small puddle had formed, and finally it occurred to her that she was basically rambling. At last, she rummaged around quickly for something to tie off the thought.

"I guess I'm just building the architecture of the life I want," she said. "Hoping it shows up here someday."

"Aha," David said. He was staring out the window at a swaying fig tree in the side yard. Casually, he reached over and picked up a shallow ceramic bowl from the windowsill. Jen sensed she had said too much. David had detected the intensity of her need and already was preparing to flee. The bowl was filled with colored pieces of glass, and he tilted it under the light.

"My mom has a thing like this," he said. "A little bowl." He talked with a slight drawl, almost Southern in its languor. "Last time I was over there she had it filled with water and a bunch of unstruck matches. She said she wanted to throw the matches away. She didn't want them to spontaneously ignite in the garbage though." He turned and glanced at Jen sideways. "Is that pretty, or just paranoid? I don't know."

Jen shook her head and smiled, wondering if he had heard anything she said in the last few minutes at all.

Dinner was lovely. Jen served zucchini-basil soup with julienned ribbons of zucchini piled in the bowls as a final touch, oil-poached halibut with tomatoes and fennel, salad, and crisp rosemary flatbread with pleasingly jagged edges on the side. David was in good form, conversationally, delivering frank opinions about local curators, and, after that, they talked easily about their respective trips to the Prado and their shared love of Goya, especially the Black Paintings.

After dinner David insisted on doing the dishes. Jen dried, and when they were done, they moved to the living room, a cramped, in-between space, but which after dark could sometimes become kind of cozy. Her couch was soft and cat-scratched, and she set pillows on the coffee table for them to rest their feet on. They each had a bowl of vanilla ice cream with blueberries.

The movie was a campy comedy, mostly about incestuous passions in a repressed, Victorian town set in the peaks of a grandly artificial alpine mountain. David had seen it numerous times and gleefully ruined most of the good scenes by directing her attention too strongly, which she found somewhat endearing. It seemed like a funny movie, but Jen had trouble concentrating on its arc or intentions. She was more concerned with the distance between herself and David on the couch. They were sitting ambiguously close. Not so close as to be touching, but close enough to feel each other's heat and hear each other's breath. But it was a polite distance that could be interpreted in various ways.

Toward the end of the movie Jen gambled and placed her head on David's shoulder. It was a sudden move, she realized, but she felt bold, and her heart sank when David failed to respond in any way whatsoever. He just sat there immobile—so immobile, in fact, that she wondered if it was a sign of interest. Maybe he was that nervous, afraid to shift and give her a reason to pull away. Jen was stuck. She contemplated what the next move should be. Was it her job, as the interviewee, to initiate everything?

Painfully, the movie crawled on for another ten minutes, with Jen craning her neck on David's immobile shoulder and neither of them speaking or moving, but just listening to each other breathe along with the tinny, faraway sound of the television set. Finally, the movie ended, the avalanche was survived and the credits rolled, and Jen lifted up her head. David turned toward her and they looked at each other nervously.

"Would it be really unprofessional if I asked to kiss you right now?" he said.

"Maybe," she said, trying to flirt. He continued to hesitate. Finally, she just leaned in until their lips touched. Not gay.

Late in the summer, Jen took David to the mountain to visit a waterfall she knew. By then they had been dating for a few weeks, and they had even begun calling each other boyfriend and girlfriend on occasion. They drove in her car, an old Toyota van, and piled the back with sleeping bags and a cooler full of beer just in case they found a nice spot to stay. On the way out of town, the mountain gleaming on the horizon, they listened to Motown tapes, passing a bottle of water back and forth and sharing a bag of Fritos like old compadres.

"I read your book," Jen said. David was picking through the tapes in the glove box, lining up their next hour's listening. A few days earlier, he had given her a copy of a book he had written, a collection of essays about a single photograph by some obscure photographer. The essays were archly academic and cantankerously opposed to each other, and they argued passionately for a series of mutually exclusive interpretations as to the photo's ultimate meaning and importance. The trick was that all the essays were written by David himself, under various pseudonyms, and the photograph was just a snapshot he had found at a thrift store. The book was almost a hundred pages long, and he had published it himself at Kinko's.

"I liked it a lot," she said, even though she had ended up skimming the last chapter or two.

David murmured noncommittally, waiting for more.

"It was really interesting," she hazarded. "I thought it was interesting how the essays kind of wore away at the picture. You know what I mean? By the end I could barely see it anymore." This was a kind way of saying that the image, a pleasant, yellowing picture of a man at a podium in a Shriner's hall, had become cloudy and opaque the longer she read. It had become so burdened with interpretations its surface had seemed gouged and scratched with words.

David brightened. "Yes, exactly!" he said. "You get it. That's great."

Jen found this intriguing. His strange, indirect ambition for his art. She reached over and touched his leg.

"I really liked it," she said again, which was becoming more and more true, and they drove silently toward the looming mountain. On either side, the hops fields stretched toward breaks of parched poplars and maples and birch trees. Rounding a turn, the sunlight slanted at an oblique angle, diffusing in the white film of the windshield like a spiderweb. Two brown leaves swirled on the road. All at once the world had rolled into autumn. It was a subtle movement, just a degree of change, but Jen believed some profound axis had been crossed.

"Did you feel that?" David said. "It just became fall."

That fall, Jen had planned to visit New York, and it turned out David wanted to visit, too, so he bought a ticket that overlapped with her stay. He arrived a few days after her, and she met him on a cold, darkened street near her friend's apartment in Chelsea. It was almost ridiculous how cinematic the meeting was, with steam blowing across the wet street and neon lights blinking, her in a trench coat and him with his luggage. They smirked at each other, aware of their roles, the danger of their noirish love, and kissed and returned to her friend's empty apartment, where they stayed together the rest of the week.

David had many friends to see—most of his clique from college had moved east—and Jen went along to visit them in their dinky apartments and cruddy lofts. Afterward, David would fill her in on the more salacious details of their lives—who was sleeping with whom, who was addicted to what—which he thought would humanize them but which really just made them seem more distant. Every day they went out and looked at art, and every afternoon they took a nap.

One night they went to meet David's friend Bart, a blond musician who worked at an Internet magazine, for a drink on the rooftop of his apartment in the East Village. It was the first warm evening of their visit and Jen was glad to be outside. The masses of the city spread out in every direction, complex hues of gray and brown spiked with antennae and electrical lines. Traffic sounds washed up from the streets below—squealing brakes and car doors and alarms. The gold roof of the Standard Insurance building brightened gradually against the darkening sky.

The boys kept Jen in the conversation for as long as they could, but soon enough they were joking around about forgotten professors, and then the talk moved on to even more boyish things. Jen was happy enough to bow out. It was even relaxing in some way. She watched David against the skyline, unshaven, more disheveled than usual after their days of travel. He held a coffee mug of vodka tonic loosely at his hip, one finger looped through the handle, laughing agreeably. His encouragement was almost a reflex, she realized; he had a special talent for enthusiasm. For a moment, there on the rooftop, she glimpsed a whole life with David. A house together.

Separate studies. How utterly sane and well-proportioned it could be.

David left a day before she did. At the end of his visit, saying good-bye on the sidewalk, hard sunlight falling onto buckets of irises and carnations, Jen hugged David tightly. "It was nice being in love with you this week," she said, and meant it.

The article David wrote finally appeared in the magazine after the two had been dating for four months. It came in the mail a few days before Halloween, and Jen read it while waiting for yet another interview, this one on the community radio station, in prelude to her new opening. She flipped through the pages quickly, skimming over the sentences and comparing the photographs of her works with the other photographs in the other articles. Hers looked pretty good in comparison. The shadows beneath her own sculptures were crisply defined, the surfaces perfectly smooth and unblemished. She had been working on animals lately, and they had come out just as she had wanted: mute, seamless, and immaculately crafted. She had an eyeless horse made of cola-colored glass. A smooth felt sparrow sitting on a barren felt tree. A pink ceramic deer broken into four pieces and splayed on the ground. She felt proud of the work she had done, if only briefly, her pieces dignified by the sharp pages of the magazine.

Jen enjoyed reading the article that David wrote—it was a celebration, really—though she found it hard to understand why anyone else would be interested. Often it seemed less like a profile or a review than an essay responding to an essay that she had never read before, nor, for that matter, that she really wanted to read. In a way, it reminded her precisely of why she'd become a sculptor in the first place. Namely, her desire to make things that unquestionably existed in the world, real things that you could touch and care for and find comfort in. Not pictures of things or interpretations of things, or even clever commentaries on the vagaries of representation, as David relished, but things themselves. For things, Jen believed, at their most thoughtful and compressed, were inherently so complex that explanation seemed almost irrelevant. At their best, they made words disappear.

Writing, Jen thought, seemed like a very sad pursuit. Like painting, but worse. At least paintings had color. Writing, though, was just black marks on paper, standing in for people and objects and events that could never be seen or felt. It seemed pathetic in a way. Nouns were the saddest words of all, trying so hard to summon real objects to life.

In the middle of Jen's meditation the host of the radio show appeared in the doorway, an elegant, elderly woman with a beautiful cloud of white hair, a toothy smile, and a regal brooch on her apricot scarf. She was fixture in the local art scene, and Jen had admired her style as long as she could remember. "Are you ready?" she said.

"Ready," Jen said.

In the studio, waiting quietly for the previous DJ to introduce them, the host congratulated Jen on her new show and mentioned David's article, which she had read and admired. "It sounds like he fell in love with you a little bit," she said, winking.

"Is it that obvious?" Jen said. "It was kind of our courtship review."

"Only to someone sensitive," the old woman said, smiling ironically. "Like me."

After the interview, Jen was sorry to find that none of her friends had even listened to the broadcast. They had all been either asleep or at work. Her mom had been out of town; her dad couldn't find the station. David, it turned out, was the only one who had tuned in, and she felt slightly guilty for having thought of him disparagingly when she said, in response to a question about form and materials, that you can't touch a word.

As the weather changed, and the rains began, Jen realized she needed someplace to put the art equipment that over the summer had migrated into the open space between her house and studio. The patio was littered with wooden frames and sawhorses, not to mention the garden tools and outdoor furniture. And so one weekend she asked David to help her build an awning off the roof of her studio building. It was a simple enough project—just affixing long sheets of corrugated plastic to sloping beams extending from the eaves, and thus creating a dry storage space underneath.

Late in the morning, David showed up in his regular clothes and stood around waiting for orders. Jen, busily measuring out a four-by-four with a stub of a pencil from her toolbelt, didn't notice him at first. He tried kissing her but she backed away, too deep in her project to entertain any distractions.

"So what should I do?" he asked.

"You want to start hammering in the stuff up there?" she said. She pointed at the roof.

"OK," he said. "How should I get up there?"

Jen found him a ladder and watched as he tried to open it near the studio wall, planting his feet and bending his shoulders awkwardly. Eventually he climbed up to the roof and gamely started amassing his materials, his nails and a hammer and the plastic sheeting. He worked steadily, if inefficiently, but at no point seemed to take real possession of the labor.

Jen watched David struggle to control the objects around him that day. He looked stranded and helpless in his body, like it was burdensome somehow. Or maybe he was like a fastidious little prince, confronted for the first time by life outside the palace walls. He hammered at strange angles, contorting his long arms and rarely connecting with the nail. He lifted boards so that they dragged and wobbled against his effort. He was frightened to stride across the lattice of beams and instead crossed it by sitting down and scooting on his butt. Moreover, he seemed proud of his incompetence and complained about his deficiencies in a way that was more like bragging. He seemed to think his insufficiencies were charming.

When Jen learned that his parents still paid his car insurance for him, a certain mystery slipped away.

A few days later, Jen was standing in her garden, staring at the blond wood frame of her new awning, tracing the angle with her eyes and feeling for small discrepancies in the seam of the beam's bond against the wall. The satisfaction of the beam pressed flush against the wall was simple and profound. The brackets were screwed deeply into the wood's grain without a single head out of place. The corrugated plastic lay lightly atop the wood. She moved to a new spot and surveyed the structure again and still the pleasure remained, a good sign. She thought of David. He had been gone a few days, in Seattle on a press junket to the new museum wing, and she felt an extra pulse of affection toward him, too.

Jen was still admiring the new awning when her thoughts were interrupted by the sound of a dog whimpering. She tried to ignore it at first but the sound kept coming. It was a muted, strenuous kind of whimpering, like a sad question being posed over and over again, and when the sound didn't stop, she went to investigate.

Jen knew exactly where to look first. She lived on a corner lot, and she had a clear view of her neighbor's driveway and front porch. It seemed there was always something unsavory going on over there. She looked over the fence and spotted a tail poking out from underneath the Chevy Nova that had been parked in the front yard for the last year. A rope lead from the rear tire to the iron hand railing by the door.

Jen called her neighbor but no one answered the phone, so she walked around the block and crept into his yard for a better look. Under the car she found a young, charcoal-colored dog lying on a carpet of shattered glass. The dog was shivering, stranded without food or water, and its tongue lolled around its mouth, coated in white dryness. It rubbed its head against Jen's hand, panting. The dog's body was muscular and clean. It was probably a pit bull, she guessed. God knew what was in store for it. Jen went home and brought the dog a bowl of water and watched it drink, then took the bowl home.

The next day she visited the dog again, with another bowl of water and some cat food. It devoured both and then pressed its nose into Jen's hand for more. Its eyebrows assumed a sad, open expression, and its mouth smiled.

Jen looked around. The street was empty in both directions. Then she untied the rope and led the dog to her car.

She called David on her cell phone and told him what she'd done.

"Good for you," he said. He had just gotten back from his trip and he was amused by the news of the dognapping. They agreed to meet at a park toward the center of town.

Jen got there before David and unleashed the dog, watching her run in long, elegant arcs from one end of the lawn to the other, stopping sometimes to smell the ivy or paw at the dirt. She never barked and never traveled beyond Jen's line of vision, as if she already belonged to her, and the two shared some invisible filament of understanding. When the dog sprinted, the grass and bushes blurred in the background, her body suspended in a graceful economy of motion.

David arrived on his bike and stood to admire the dog.

"Are you going to keep it?" he asked.

"I don't know," Jen said. "Maybe. If I can."

"Wow," he said. The dog turned and smiled at them.

"What should we name her?" Jen asked, leaning into David's chest.

"How about . . ." David paused and half laughed. "How about 'Penis-balls'?"

Jen drew away. David's joke was repellent to her. She refused to mock the beautiful dog with a name like that. "That's awful. Something pretty."

"Okay, how about naming it after my grandma," David suggested. "Grandma Sadie."

"Sadie?" Jen said. She tried out the name on the dog with some optimism. Sadie was something she could work with. Sadie was antique but gracious, perfumed and yet tough. She liked the monocled, lacy, ruffled implications of the name. She imagined a sinuous, lacquered rocking chair.

"No, not 'Sadie,'" David said. "'Grandma Sadie.' Come here, Grandma Sadie! Com'ere!" David laughed as the dog halted in midstride and looked toward them. Jen could see, ruefully, the naming had been done.

Within minutes the dog's name had devolved to Grandma Penisballs, the words sliding around on some scrim between David and reality, some invisible Scrabble board in the air. Jen watched the dog's muscles bunch and stretch as she ran in long ovals around the grass. Her dog didn't need names anyway.

Soon enough Jen stopped listening to David and sat down on a bench. He had ruined the momentum of the day's events with his irony. She would take the dog to the Humane Society that afternoon and let them decide what to call her.

At the end of the month a spell of turgid, chilly drizzle arrived in town and continued for weeks without pause. It was like a cold lid placed over the sky, and the damp crept into everything. Jen couldn't keep her hands and feet warm. One day she opened the newspaper to discover that the region was entering a new, twenty-year cycle of rain.

She put her head in her palms. She wanted to buy a ticket to Mexico but she had almost no money. Her show had not sold very well, though it had been well-received, and the prop-styling work she did on the side wasn't coming through lately. The whole city was waiting for jobs, and all her friends were calling each other daily, trying to remain hopeful.

She stared at her kitchen table and took a slow index of its scattered contents: a pile of old bills, an ashtray full of thumbtacks, a ballpoint pen without its cap. The newspaper made a crazy quilt of pictures and type, and the cloudy light from the window caught in its grain. She could see tiny furrows and crosshatching in the paper, and the liquid blackness of the print embedded in its soft tissue. The walls of her breakfast nook were so pale that they almost seemed to have no color at all.

Jen had been in Portland for a long time. Ever since she was a little girl. And her energy for it was waning, as it always did around this time of year. She needed to move somewhere, she told herself. She needed to go where she could get something going, as an artist or anything else. Maybe it was New York City, maybe Los Angeles. It didn't matter that much. She had friends in both cities; she could land on her feet. She just needed to open her eyes and see some new buildings and trees.

As Jen sat at her table, plotting her escape, listening to the rain on the shingles, she slowly came to realize that her plans did not include David. She hoped he had guarded himself somehow, though she sensed he hadn't.

A few days later Jen took David to an art opening at a new gallery downtown. The white walls were high and immaculate and hosted a single row of small, brightly colored canvases at eye level. The crowd milling around was full of familiar faces, and it took a long time to actually get around to seeing the work.

David was drawn to one piece in particular, a blank canvas with the word "YO" written in italics. He claimed it induced some dyslexic effect in him, and kept flipping between "YO" and "OY." To him it became a dense semiotic commentary on racial identity, hip-hop's "yo" mirroring the Yiddish "oy." Jen, as usual, couldn't tell if he was joking or not.

"I think you're reaching," she said. "It's not that great."

"Not on purpose, anyway," he said. His excitement stalled and he went off to get a drink.

When the show was over, and after much back-and-forth between friends, a large group migrated to a bar a few blocks from the gallery. The bar was below street level, and candles flickered in wrought-iron holders. The low ceiling was decorated in a mosaic of broken glass and tile. The waiter, who knew most of them by name, pulled a few tables together and everyone made room.

Jen sat across the table from David and they got caught up in separate conversations. A few times she saw him trying to catch her eye but she pretended not to notice, and when he reached for her knee beneath the table, she lightly pushed him away. At one point David laughed loudly, and Jen looked over to see him engaged in an animated talk with their friend Dan. His eyes were narrowed and gleaming, his head shook in disbelief. She enjoyed seeing David laugh with people; he had such a gift for sympathy.

Later, Jen told the whole table the story about David's mother soaking her matches in water. The music was too loud and everyone leaned in closer to hear her. David rolled his eyes boyishly and told some other stories about his mother, all involving her artful obsessive-compulsion. It was like a parting gift to him, she thought, a gentle touch in the presence of others.

Jen and David said good-bye to their friends around midnight, drowsy and muddled from all the talking and beer. Their clothes were filled with the smell of cigarettes and their eyes stung from the smoke. They put on their coats and exited quietly, with David trailing a step behind.

Out on the sidewalk, beside the window of a closed restaurant, David reached out for Jen and drew her close. He bent to kiss her on the mouth but she limply turned her face toward his chest.

"What's the matter?" David asked. He seemed to think he could cheer her up with his own good mood. His face hovered in an expression of jokey distraction.

Jen hesitated briefly and looked down at the ground. She had been practicing what she should say to him for a week.

"Are you okay?" he asked, dutifully concerned.

She raised her face to look at David directly. "I'm not in love," she said. She stared straight into his eyes, leaving off the object of her sentence in a last-moment pang of guilt. As if her love existed apart from any real person or thing, like a math equation, or the echo of an echo. I'm not in love. "With you" was implied. She watched his face cloud over and darken.

David stood there silently and released her from his long arms. He stepped away and stopped expressing anything, but just closed down and appeared to think.

"Oh," he said, and stared intently into the darkness. Jen knew he wouldn't fight or lash out. He wouldn't make a scene. He would take this moment and wrap it up and carry it home to ponder from a distance. He would call her the next day with opinions and a variety of interpretations. He would make lists. He would experience this, as he did everything, only in dreadful retrospect. Jen could see David's past and future closing in tightly around him, disrupting his carefully maintained sense of not really being there at all.

She felt fine though. She watched him consolingly, caring enough to be gentle. She promised him they could talk in the morning, and then cried briefly when he cried. She walked him to his car and waited as he placed the key in the ignition, frowning, and pulled out briskly into the desolate street. The light turned green and soon he was gone. He was a sensitive person, she thought. He just had such strange ideas about what was missing from where.

Jen drove home alone. She felt calm and clear. The streets were quiet, and the sound of the engine vibrated around her. The porch light was on, as she had left it, and the screen door, which slammed too hard, slammed too hard behind her.

Once inside, she took off her coat and filled the teakettle with water. She crumpled a piece of paper and threw it across the floor for her cat to play with. She stood and listened to the stillness of her empty house.

While Jen waited for the water to boil, she picked up her phone to check the messages. There was one, from a few hours earlier in the evening.

"You have . . . one . . . new . . . message. Left . . . yesterday . . . at . . . nine . . . thirty-three . . . P.M." The robotic words sounded strange and staggered, dropped into their syntax like cans on an assembly line.

When the message clicked on, the first sound Jen heard was conversation and laughter. Then David's voice, slightly husky and affectionate and teasing.

"Hi, baby. I'm looking at you right now," he said. "You're across the room from me, talking to Mike."

Jen remembered talking to Mike at the gallery, and holding a glass in her hand, and laughing at something he told her about the caterer.

"Now you just laughed," David's voice said. She could imagine the scene from his vantage point, the sight of herself from across the room, in her flowered dress, which she was still wearing.

Then David's voice dropped to a whisper, and Jen imagined him cupping the cell phone with his hand in the room she had been in just hours before, and which was now dark and empty and elsewhere.

"You look so hot right now, Jen. Oy vey! I'll talk to you later. Bye." It was just like him, embarrassed and hurried and childishly unsentimental. Making some gesture but not knowing how to finish it.

She saved the message though, and listened to it one more time as the teakettle began to whimper on the hot coils. It was strange how David's words had waited for her like that, how they had been preserved in the telephone like actual objects with weight and texture. Like colored stones, she thought, stored in a metal box, hidden in an office building on the edge of some highway.

Jen poured the hot water into her cup and sat down at the table, watching the steam curl and disappear. The room was motionless, lit weakly by the yellow glow of a corner streetlight, and when the hum of the refrigerator stopped, everything became silent. The silence crackled on her eardrums.

Jen breathed shallowly as the silence shaped itself to the drying rack and the chairs, the narrow gap between the wall and the oven. When the whole room was filled with silence, and the tea had become strong enough, Jen lifted her cup and pressed its warm, hard skin to her cheek. Outside, a car was passing, and its lights swept through her garden and then were gone.

YOUNG BODIES

"I'M NOT SAYING you did it," Roy said. "I'm just telling you what Nathan thinks."

"I didn't do it," Kendra said. "He thinks I'm stupid. That's really what he's saying."

"I'm just giving you a heads-up is all."

Kendra Orlov stared at the paneled ceiling above her head. In the far corner of her bedroom a water stain the shape of Texas glared down at her. She was not happy. Moments earlier, her coworker Roy had called to inform her that the till at Express had come up short, and their manager, Nathan, assumed she was responsible. She was doing her very best to register her shock and disgust with some restraint.

"Is he around right now?" she wanted to know.

"In and out. You know how it is."

"God, what does he fucking do all day? No one knows."

"Okay. Well. You want me to say anything or what?"

"No," Kendra said. She tilted her head to keep the signal from breaking up. Across the street a crow landed on the back of a blue pickup truck with an awkward flapping of wings. "I'll come by later. I'll deal with it."

Kendra snapped the phone shut. She lay still and gazed at a brittle poster on the wall of Red Square at dusk, a gift from her father eight years before, and the last vestige of her childhood décor. Her teenage décor was barren walls. They were pale yellow, with an agitating fracture near the window. The sound of her mother vacuuming in the other room was another aggravation.

"Fucking asshole," Kendra said. The fact Nathan assumed she was the thief was infuriating. There were five other employees on duty throughout the day, and all of them could just as easily be considered suspects. What about Amy? Or Jennifer? They had it in them. Not to mention the ample non-criminal explanations as to why the day's count might be off: computer errors, human errors, magical incantations. The possibilities that didn't include her were practically endless. To single her out was an insult and revealed openly, at last, Nathan's long-held disrespect of her. He had been nursing it from the moment she came on. She had known it.

Kendra rolled over and climbed off the bed. She glanced passingly at herself in the mirror, sighting her wild, mouse-brown hair, her sultry but widely spaced eyes. She found her purse under a pile of towels on the chair and came back to the mirror and put on some eye shadow, a single tiny swipe of blue on each lid. Then she went to her drawer and withdrew a plastic box and popped open the clasp. Inside lay two worn twenties and a ten.

Yes, she had stolen the money. But did that give Nathan any right to suspect her of anything? As far as he knew, she was a model employee. She showed up on time every day. She was unfailingly polite. She was even responsible, she felt, for a goodly amount of return business, thanks to her charm and strong fashion sense. He had no reason to think anything but the best of her, and the fact he didn't was a kind of betrayal of trust, not exactly on par with her own betrayal, but a betrayal nevertheless.

She jerked on her socks and stabbed her belt through the loops of her jeans. She was angry at herself most of all. She had been sloppy this time. She had taken the money and neglected to ring in a fake return as she normally did. But how could she have? She'd been interrupted at every turn. First there had been the errand to the office supply store. Then she'd been stuck in the storeroom unloading new blouses for two hours. She'd never had a chance to cover her tracks, and she'd been waiting for the call from the store ever since.

Fuck Express, Kendra thought, applying lip gloss to her sulking mouth. Express practically forced her to steal from the till by paying such shit wages. And her own salary was only the beginning of its crimes. The corporation stole much more cruelly from the Chinese women who made the clothes. It stole from the sheep herders who made the wool for its sweaters. And for that matter, the sheep herders themselves stole from the poor animals they raised to harvest the wool off their backs. It was all robbery, up and down the line. Every step of the way someone was stealing from somebody, someone was profiting off somebody else's weakness. So she took a few dollars in the last moments of the cycle. She was only playing by the rules of the game as they had been established long before her birth.

Kendra dabbed cover-up onto the acne on her chin and evened the color. She did not feel guilty about what she had done, not in the least, but she did have to rectify the situation quickly. If Nathan made the effort to compare the weekly returns of the past three months to the inventory on the shelves, he would find upward of two thousand dollars missing. And that, she could see, would be a real problem.

Kendra pulled on her woolen pea coat and wound a scarf around her neck. With some luck, she thought, the whole situation could still be made to look like an overnight accounting error. Perhaps some cash had fallen under the register, or onto a table, or a few bills had drifted into a corner by accident. In any case, she had to move fast. The longer the money went missing, the more suspicious Nathan would become, and the more likely her punishment would be unavoidable.

The annoying vacuum drew near her door, banging against the baseboards.

"I'm going out!" Kendra yelled through the door.

"What?" her mother cried in Russian. After twenty years she still couldn't find their house on a map.

"I'm going out!" Kendra said again through the wall.

"Where?!"

"Work!"

The bus picked her up at the corner of 135th and Stark, in front of the Romanian Orthodox church, and slowly wended its way down the numbers, crossing through wintry Vietnamese neighborhoods, Laotian neighborhoods, Chinese neighborhoods, passing churches with Korean lettering and strip malls that could have been in Beijing. It was sunset by the time the oasis of downtown appeared, the pink and black and silver lacquered boxes nestled against the velvet folds of the West Hills, and Kendra's daily journey from Russia to Asia to America was complete.

In the Lloyd Center, the kiosks selling cell phone plans and zoom copters were already packing up for the night, and the high, windowed atrium was almost empty. Kendra hurried passed the ice rink, which was nearly empty too, hosting only a few elderly women dressed in peach and seafoam leotards. The smell of Cinnabon was still strong, but fading.

Express was located on the mall's ground floor, wedged between Portland Smash and Wild Pair. Within the mall's hierarchy it fell somewhere in the middle, more sophisticated than the teenybopperish Rave or Forever 21, less timeless than the blue-chip Banana Republic or the Gap. The interior was not bad—it was vaguely minimalist in design, its walls made of raw wood and white plastic, its floor a bleak white-linoleum tundra. Low pedestals displaying the season's belted shirt dresses, leopard-print pencil skirts, and merino sweater vests radiated outward from a mobile of broken mirror, all the elements combining to suggest, distantly, some New York City nightclub in its dead daytime hours.

From across the mall's main hallway, hidden behind a rack of basketball jerseys in Champion's, Kendra watched her boss, Nathan, fluffing the sweaters on the front platforms. How she loathed him. His meaty face shone with sweat, his coarse, wavy red hair needed cutting, and his overfed body looked absurd in the nearly chic ribbed V-neck and cuffed slacks ensemble he had assembled from the Express inventory.

A part of Kendra almost pitied him, too. He was not a smart or handsome man, nor talented in any way. Keeping up with the simple managerial directives from the central office was practically beyond him. But underneath the pity was mainly contempt. Kendra watched as he refolded a perfectly well-folded chimney-sleeve sweater, then shook it out and refolded it yet again. Here was a guy who had been given everything in life—a nice house, good education, cars, video games—and yet somehow he'd utterly failed to capitalize.

Around closing time, Nathan could be counted on to wander off the premises, leaving whoever was on duty to do all the work while he visited the blonde cashiers and stock girls at Nordstrom and Macy's, in hopes of some unlikely conquest. And sure enough, tonight was the same as any. At half past six, Nathan ambled out into the mall's thinning traffic, took his bearings, and disappeared, leaving the coast clear for what Kendra estimated would be at least twenty minutes.

She was just stepping from her hiding place, though, when someone called out her name.

"Yo! Kendra!"

She half-turned to spot her friend Bryan walking from the rear of the sporting goods store. Happy Bryan, with his cute little snub nose and square jaw, long brown hair tucked behind his ears, and perfectly proportioned arms swinging loosely at his side. Even his referee-shirt uniform looked almost good on him. Usually Kendra was inherently distrustful of people like Bryan, people so active and warmly welcomed by all. But over time she had come around to his normal charms. He was nice, and better, funny, and in the end the shared boredom of their adjacent retail jobs had proven more powerful than whatever social barriers might naturally have divided them. The fact was, too, she found herself flattered by his much-sought-after attention.

She would have been glad to loiter awhile, but today she had to keep moving. She waved and stepped briskly into the mall, hoping to outpace Bryan before he caught up and began his distractions.

"Hey!" Bryan said.

"Gotta go!" she called over her shoulder.

She couldn't escape so easily though. Bryan overtook her midway across the mall's aisle, clearly bored out of his mind. "I thought you were off today," he said, falling into step. His open face bobbed at the corner of her vision but she refused to meet his eye.

"Nope," she said, pressing onward.

"You heard about Doug?"

"Uh-uh."

"He wrecked his car last night," Bryan said.

"Huh," Kendra said, as the drilling drums and buzzing guitars of Express—its soundtrack of endless, listless pleasure—rose in her ears. The whiteness of the walls and floor glared from every direction.

"He was at Powers Park," Bryan said. "Pulled out and bam! Hit by a Volvo. His parents gave him the car last week for good grades. Total burn."

Usually Kendra would have cackled over the irony of the disaster, the material loss that was not her own. But today she had other things on her mind. She didn't respond, and thankfully Bryan didn't elaborate, having already lost interest in the story himself. "Cool sweater," he said, and peeled off to peruse the new inventory.

With Bryan out of her hair, Kendra focused on the task at hand. She sighted Roy sitting at the main counter, flanked by two huge posters of stunned-looking models in tenement hallways. Was he going to be an obstacle or an accomplice, she wondered? Behind his round glasses his face was as emotionless as milk. As if in answer to her question, he looked up from his magazine and wordlessly walked into the back room. Thank God. There was no need to go through the motions of pretend innocence with Roy. He knew the score. He was giving her the space to do what she had to do.

"Don't you have something to do?" Kendra said to Bryan, who had begun rifling through the shirt racks, loudly attacking the plastic hangers on the metal crossbars.

"Not really," he said.

"You don't have to close?"

"Eh. Kevin'll close."

"Because I've, like, got things to do," she said.

"Do whatever you want. I'm fine. Just ignore me."

Kendra didn't have time to argue. She left Bryan to his devices and strode behind the main counter, scanning the store for good places to plant the money. The till was one idea. She could simply slip the cash back in. The receipts from yesterday could conceivably have been miscounted. But she was confronted by the problem of her employee sign-in number. If she signed in, Nathan would know she had used the register on her day off, which would arouse suspicion. Better to sign in using Roy's code. But perhaps that was asking too much, shifting the burden of suspicion too soundly onto him. It was a bind.

Bryan, meanwhile, had begun talking about the day's gossip, not really caring whether Kendra listened or not. There wasn't much to report, he said. The scandal of the girl at Barnes & Noble whose strung-out boyfriend threatened her was ongoing. The question of whether the surveillance cameras actually recorded anything was unsolved. From there he shifted into his plans for the weekend, which were manifold, and included a mock-government meeting and numerous house parties.

Kendra cast around for another solution. The floor near the trash can? The drawer where the headphones were stored? Every option seemed a little flimsy. Her plan, she realized, depended far too much on the mercy of Nathan—and everyone else on staff—to succeed, their willingness to be deceived. She began to sweat as the drumming techno beats were joined by robotic backup singers.

"I'm bored," Bryan said, rummaging through the plastic bracelets and earrings near the front counter.

"No one forced you to come over here," Kendra said.

"Come on. Entertain me."

"I'll entertain you later, all right?"

Bryan didn't answer, instead making a show of reading the return policy laminated on the back wall.

Kendra opened the office supply drawer and checked the recess under the cabinets where the baseboard met the floor. Nowhere really worked though. Perhaps the best option would be handing the money directly to Roy and telling him she had found it in the back room. Maybe he could be convinced to say he had found the money on his own.

Kendra's scheming was cut short, however, by the sudden reappearance of Nathan on the scene. There he was, directly in front of the store, striking up a conversation with the girl from Jamba Juice and, judging from the girl's undisguised disinterest in whatever he was saying, their conversation could not last long. At any moment now, he might turn around and spot her.

She had to think quickly. If Nathan saw her, he would know immediately what was going on. She never visited the store on her days off, so her mere presence would be read as a confession of guilt. She would of course deny she had taken the money, but the damage would be done. And then what? At best, he would fail to prove anything and would carry his suspicion with him until the day she eventually quit. At worst, he would fire her on the spot, and she would have to find some way to explain yet another lost job to her parents, who were still unhappy about her termination from Barry's Chop House, a position they had viewed as a clear line to better things.

The best option, she decided, was to avoid contact with Nathan altogether. Thankfully, he was really dawdling, pushing himself on that poor, stupid girl, and Kendra seized the opportunity to act.

She stepped from behind the counter, grabbed Bryan by the elbow, and hurried into the back room to hide. On the way she passed Roy coming out of the bathroom, and he sighed, comprehending the whole situation at a glance.

"What are we doing?" Bryan whispered.

"Shh. Just be quiet," she said, tucking into a cove in the back room.

"But—"

"Shhh!"

Bryan obeyed. He stood quietly as Kendra pressed her ear to the wall and listened through the droning music. She only caught bits and pieces of conversation, but from what she could tell, Nathan was offering to close shop tonight. Roy, good friend that he was, was making an effort to retain the responsibility, but to no avail. They went back and forth a few times, and uncharacteristically, Nathan seemed to be insisting. Why, tonight of all nights, did he demand to carry his load?

Moments later Roy appeared in the back to retrieve his coat, gave Kendra a significant look, and then he was gone.

"What's happening?" Bryan whispered.

"Shhh," Kendra said.

A minute later the store's music shut off. Kendra and Bryan breathed shallowly into the raw silence, catching the occasional noises that trickled from the front. They heard the stapler pound and the chug of the day's receipts. They heard Nathan singing under his breath. Bryan's cell phone vibrated. He quelled it, then texted Kevin. The reply made him titter. And the whole time Kendra remained acutely aware of the clean, soapy smell drifting from Bryan's shirt and hair. If only she'd known she would be stuck in such tight quarters with anyone, she would have showered before coming in. She kept her elbows pressed to her body to make sure nothing escaped from her armpits.

The lights clicked off and Nathan's footsteps padded across the showroom floor. The iron gate clattered across the mouth of the store. The gate locked. Kendra and Bryan stood facing each other. The process of closing usually took her at least half an hour. Apparently Nathan had some shortcuts.

Kendra edged out into the back room. The mall's ambient noise of footsteps and calling voices and competing stereos had vanished, leaving behind a weird, enormous stillness to grasp. She crept across the floor, bumping into the edge of a table, and made her way to the back door. Not only was the door alarmed, but it was also padlocked and a heavy chain was wrapped around the crossbar—a clear fire hazard.

"What's going on?" Bryan called, beginning, slowly, to comprehend their predicament.

"We're stuck," she said.

"Hold on," Bryan said. "You're kidding me. Right?"

"Nope," Kendra said, peering out into the dim showroom. "There's only one key. I told you to go a long time ago."

"But . . . what's going on here?"

"I took some money yesterday," Kendra explained. "Nathan figured it out. I came back to return it. He never gets back from his walk that fast. I thought I had time."

She expected some kind of reprimand, but Bryan's response surprised her. He wasn't judgmental at all. In fact, he was mostly amused. "You dumbass," he said brightly. He was not the guilty one, after all; this was her problem. If anything, he was even somewhat thrilled by the situation.

They wandered out into the showroom. The shadowy clothes

hung limply from the racks, and the mannequins—their featureless, glossy white skin gleaming, their heads half razored off—presided like amputated sentinels. Kendra was glad she wasn't alone.

She walked to the gate and leaned against the cold bars. The cavernous nave of the mall was dark, barring safety lights and the distant glow of the neon signs in the food court. Across the way, beyond the sturdy living room settings at the center of the hallway and the urns of real but fake-looking succulents, a fleshy model for Lane Bryant beckoned, wearing a matching lavender bra and panties, her arm cocked behind her neck in the classic pose of bedroom seduction.

They postponed making any decisions while Bryan explored the store, looking for ways out. The back door was indeed impassable, he decided. He also checked the cupboards where the wrapping paper was stored and went through the closets and found some old photographs of a Christmas party. He spent twenty minutes in the storage room looking for air ducts.

Kendra, meanwhile, called her parents and told her mother she would be home in the morning. She said she was staying at Stacy's house. Then she called Stacy and cleared the story with her.

Bryan returned and fiddled with the gate again, confirming for certain there would be no picking the lock or slipping through the bars. They decided calling security was a bad idea. Yelling for a janitor wouldn't help either, as the janitors didn't have keys. Bryan searched the showroom for fire exits but found nothing. He even pushed a panel of the drop ceiling out of place in the accounting office to see if there was a vertical escape route, but the crawl space had no doorways. Whatever *Die Hard* fantasy he was entertaining fizzled.

He ended up at the gate again, staring out into the mall. Kendra stood nearby, watching him. Even Bryan's half-distraction was kind of attractive in its way, a promise of his complete attention when the time was right.

"I can't believe this," he said happily.

"You probably had some plans tonight," she said, granting him an opportunity to scold her.

"Nothing much," he said. "I'm getting hungry, though. I haven't, like, eaten any dinner. What are we going to do about that? Huh?" They had checked the refrigerator but there was only an ancient turkey sandwich and a box of baking soda.

"I have some Altoids," she offered.

Bryan scanned the mall again, as if some new idea might come to him from the hanging banners.

"Maybe someone would bring us food," he suggested. "Maybe Kevin would do it."

"The mall is closed," Kendra pointed out. "He can't get in anymore."

"The movie theater is open," he said. "He could come in that door and run something over. I'll call him."

"I doubt he'll do it."

But already he was calling. Kevin picked up, and after some convoluted explanations, it seemed a decision was reached.

"I'm in the mall," Bryan said for the fourth time. "I'm stuck with Kendra. Kendra Orlov. No, I can't really explain any better. It's too complicated. Just get it over here, dude. Yeah, right. Yeah, sure. You wish."

Bryan closed his phone. He grasped the bars and stared up at the gray skylight.

"Okay," he said. "He'll bring us some food."

"I guess we're set then," Kendra said.

"Stick with me," Bryan said. "Everything will be all right."

"As if I have a choice."

Bryan was wandering among the racks of merchandise, whistling, and sometimes sloppily throwing an item over his shoulder. Kendra, for her part, sat on the counter, organizing her purse. If someone was resourceful enough, she thought, they could almost live at the mall and never pay rent.

"It's all kind of eighties, isn't it?" Bryan said. He was holding up a white cotton blazer with narrow lapels that extended all the way to the bottom hem, scrutinizing it in the dark.

"Everyone loves the eighties," Kendra said.

"The eighties will never die. We're stuck there the rest of our lives, I guess."

Bryan lifted a particularly garish shirt from one of the sale racks and held it up to the emergency lights. The collar was green and the sleeves were purple, the buttons white along a piping of blue.

"Wow," he said.

"That's one of my favorites," she said.

"Maybe I'll try it on," he said.

"Go for it," she said. "Fitting rooms are right over there."

Bryan entered the dressing room and located an overhead light and emerged moments later newly garbed. The sleeves were much too long and draped over his knuckles, the silky fabric shaping to the swells of his shoulders. The jeans he had selected were also much too big, and the cuffs collected thickly around his ankles like elephant skin. When he walked, the fabric swished between his legs, but he still managed to box and karate chop with himself in the mirror.

"Nice," Kendra said.

"It's my new look," he said. "You like it?"

"I think you could do better."

"Huh. Maybe." Bryan shuffled around the store in search of another outfit. Kendra, not to be outdone, jumped from the counter and browsed the clothes, too.

She selected a few items from the sale rack and entered the stall next to the one Bryan was using. She latched the door and turned on the light and slipped off her shoes, then her pants, and eyed the pile of clothes she had deposited on the bench. One stall over, she heard Bryan return and latch his own door.

Kendra sifted through her clothes but had trouble making a decision about what to wear. Standing there, almost naked, feeling the public air brushing her body, she found herself thinking mainly about Bryan, and his naked body just a few feet away. Only a thin wall separated them, and she had to wonder if he was thinking about her own body, too. Listening to his clothes fall on the floor, the zip and rustle and shifting of weight, seeing her own bare flesh in the mirror, her slim shoulder and clavicle, the bumps of her nipples in her beige bra, the possibility of something happening seemed not impossible. The belated recognition of their total privacy hit her hard, a near nausea of anticipation.

"I've been needing a new look," Bryan said over the wall. "This one might be it."

"You already have a good look," she said.

"I don't have a look."

"Yeah you do."

"What's my look?"

"I don't know. You have a kind of hunter look. You look like an outdoor guy. The flannel shirts. The hiking boots."

"That's funny. I'm not one. I've never hunted."

"Here, put this on," she said, and tossed over a pale blue cardigan.

Moments later, the two emerged from their respective stalls, Bryan in five sweaters, leather gloves, long underwear, and plaid madras shorts from the sale rack; Kendra in a two-piece bathing suit under a down jacket with argyle socks.

"Well?" Bryan said, preening.

"Pretty good," she said. "What about me?"

"I don't care about your look," he said. He proceeded to hog the mirror until Kendra pushed him away and took over the work of self-admiration.

She turned in front of the mirror, tugging on the jacket, buttoning and unbuttoning the snaps, feeling his eyes on her. The air between them had become heavy with physical possibility.

"My boobs are all right, aren't they?" she asked. Her own brazenness was almost amazing to her, and she willfully ignored the creeping premonition of humiliation coming over her skin.

"Sure." He shrugged.

"One of them is a little bigger than the other," she said, opening the jacket and cupping her breasts, "but they both have good shape."

"Huh."

"This is my best feature, though," she said, lifting the jacket to show her butt. "You can touch it if you want."

"That's cool," he said, and swallowed, looking away.

Smiling effortfully, Kendra retreated to her stall. She had no idea what she was doing, or where her flirtation might be going, but the exchange had left a definite charge between them, an awkwardness that Kendra both loathed and relished, and that she exacerbated through the next few changes of clothes. She continued to suit herself in skimpy leotards and scoop-neck T-shirts. Bryan, meanwhile, became obsessed with pleats.

The queasy tension dissipated a little when they finally heard Kevin shuffling down the hall, and a moment later he appeared at the gate, trailing the scent of their Burger King order.

"What the fuck?" Kevin said, leaning his enormous skateboard against the wall. He was a toadlike kid, with curly hair squeezing from under a soiled baseball cap. "Nice pants, dude."

"It's my new look," Bryan said.

"That's cool," Kevin said. "Hey Kendra. How's it going?" Out of his backpack he pulled two warm, grease-spotted bags and passed them through the bars. Kendra slipped him a twenty.

"Keep the change," she said.

"Thanks," he said. "So what? Am I supposed to guess what happened or something?"

"It's kind of hard to explain," Bryan said.

"We got stuck," Kendra said.

"I could come back with a blowtorch, dude," Kevin offered. "Or a team of horses. We could tie the bars to a team of horses. Rip out the bars."

"That always works," Bryan said. "That's true."

"I'm just saying," Kevin said. "Give me the word and I'll break you dudes out."

"Cool," Bryan said, scanning the mall. "But hey. The security guard comes around pretty often, though. You should probably bounce."

"Oh, one more thing," Kevin said. He looked both ways and reached into his coat pocket. "This'll keep you warm. I'm a fucking saint." He handed them a narrow glass bottle. "Mr. Jim Beam."

"Wow," Bryan said, cradling the sealed bottle. "You're awesome." The addition of whiskey to the adventure made everything a degree of magnitude better.

Kevin gave them a salute. "Well, you kids have fun. I expect a full report in the morning. Don't do anything I wouldn't do."

"Yo," Bryan whispered hoarsely as Kevin shuffled back down the hall toward the movie theaters. "Don't tell everyone where we are. All right?"

"I won't have to," Kevin said over his shoulder. "I'll just tell one person. Everyone'll know after that."

They took the Burger King bags to the back room and had a picnic in the dark, wearing their new clothes. With Kevin gone, the tension between them began to gather again, but now it was tamped down to a simmer. They had lots of time, more than they knew what to do with. It was only nine forty-five.

For a while they talked about work and the degradation of their current jobs. From there the conversation wandered to previous jobs, and then to their childhood dream jobs—backup dancer for Mariah Carey, professional boxer, respectively—until, finally, organically, they came around to the subject of what their parents did for a living.

Kendra knew Bryan's father was a professional of some kind. She had once seen him from a distance, a hairier, lankier version of Bryan, wearing a tweed coat with elbow patches over a brown turtleneck sweater, a getup that had almost made her laugh out loud. She asked Bryan what he did in those clothes, and Bryan told her he worked for the EPA.

"EPA?" Kendra said. She was not ashamed to admit her ignorance to Bryan. In fact, she was almost glad to. She was happy to give him the opportunity to impress her with his worldly knowledge.

"He's a consultant," he said. "He works on water rights, mostly."

"That's cool," she said, although the words didn't clarify much. Neither consulting nor water rights were ideas connected to anything concrete in her mind.

"It kind of sucks, actually," Bryan said. "He says he's going to quit almost every day. But he sticks with it. He never thought he'd work for the government, but he thinks it's the only way to make a real difference. He's trying to change the system. You'd be amazed by the waste though. Everything you've heard about state workers is true."

The pride in Bryan's voice came as a surprise to Kendra. He seemed to respect his father in a way she could not really comprehend. There was no tension, no struggle there. The goodness of the family had apparently traveled between generations like clean water downhill. The strife of her own household would probably boggle his mind. Just the week before, her own father had come home so drunk he'd pissed his pants and fallen asleep on the living room floor. The week before that he had accidentally shocked himself and stabbed his hand while fixing the oven. Her mother was like a medieval troll, full of bizarre superstition and paranoia. For Kendra, her own resemblance to her parents was a source of constant shame and disgust. The fear that she genuinely belonged to them, that she would never escape the narrow parameters they had set, was among her worst.

"What does your dad do?" Bryan asked, much to her dismay. She had no one to blame but herself though. She had led them down this road.

"He drives a cab," she said. Among his various money-making schemes this one was the easiest to explain.

"Not many cabs around here," he said.

"They don't cruise the street so much. A lot of Russians drive cabs though." Bryan already knew the basic outline of her family history. Her parents' emigration to the United States. Their arduous road to citizenship. The gradual arrival of new relatives after Gorbachev. Her own utter disinterest in the language and culture of her heritage.

"Huh. He likes it all right?"

"I wouldn't say he likes it, no. But it's regular."

"He must see a lot," Bryan said, searching for some way to make the job of cab driving a dignified, socially redeeming activity. The education of cab driving! The human interest! He was sweet to try.

"He sees a lot of faggots and Mexicans," she said. "According to him, the whole world is faggots and Mexicans."

"Huh."

"Could be worse," Kendra said. "I mean, my cousin sucks dicks for money—that's a shitty job." As long as she was on the topic of family, she figured she might as well go all the way. The dysfunction was usually amusing to people, and she gained social points recounting the details. Plus, almost unconsciously, she enjoyed bringing the conversation back to sex.

"Wow," he said. If he was shocked by the news, he did a good job of hiding it.

"She says it's no big deal," Kendra said. "A hundred bucks for five minutes' time. Some water in her mouth."

"That's what she said?"

"That's what her sister told me."

"That's a bummer," Bryan said, shaking his head.

"What's the bummer?" she asked. She sipped the whiskey and the burning warmth spread inside her chest.

"I don't know. It's her body, you know?"

"It's money."

"Yeah. But would you do it?"

"If I had to." Then, gauging his reaction, she altered course. "No. I'm kidding. I wouldn't."

"So I guess you didn't get the money back into the register or anything?" he said, politely changing the topic. "That sucks."

"Yeah."

"So what are you going to do?"

"I don't know."

"You think you'll get fired?"

"No idea."

"You'd find something else."

"Probably."

"Hot Dog on a Stick. They're hiring."

"Fuck you!"

"Popeyes Chicken."

"No way."

"Arby's."

"Fuck you. I'll be eighteen next month anyway. I'll be fine."

"How does being eighteen solve anything?"

"I'm starting a porn site."

"A what?"

"A porn Web site," she said. "As soon as I turn eighteen, it's legal. I can be my own boss. Sell my own pictures."

"Oh Jesus."

"What? You think it's a bad idea?"

"I don't know. I mean, whatever. I don't care."

Kendra smiled, taking another hit from the bottle. "I'm totally shitting you," she said. "I know a girl who's doing it though. She's got a countdown going until her birthday. She gets massive hits. It's sick."

"Who?"

"I'm not telling you!"

"Someone at school?"

"Maybe."

"Your mom?"

"Duh. Yeah, my mom. My mom is seventeen."

Bryan reached for the bottle, the thought of Kendra's naked photos on the Web obviously turning at the forefront of his mind. Then Kendra took the whiskey back and sipped daintily, shifting her legs, giving him an easy avenue to lean toward her if he so chose. All the talk of exploitation was potentially a preamble to something. She was open to the idea, herself.

To her dismay the moment was broken by Bryan's cell phone. The old-fashioned rotary tone rang annoyingly. He fumbled in his pocket and inspected the number on the screen.

"Mmmm," he said. "I have to take this. Hold on a second." He stood. "Hi."

Cradling the phone and staring at the floor, he walked into the other room, leaving Kendra with the remaining fries and whiskey. The call was probably from Jenny Shepard, she guessed, the slightly bloated, orange-hued rich girl from Wilson who Bryan sometimes dated. Kendra didn't know her well, but she had her opinions. She imagined Jenny and Bryan's time together as a fantasy of all-American youth culture. Nights of bowling, drag racing, banana splits. Kendra, for her part, failed to see the allure.

From the other room Bryan's voice floated in and out of audibility. "No way . . . Really? . . . Yeah, I know where that is . . ." He began in a soothing tone, conciliatory, and gradually, to Kendra's pleasure, his voice became gruffer. The conversation rapidly devolved to a series of barks, sighs, and exasperated questions. The whole thing took almost twenty minutes, and he came back into the room looking slightly drawn.

"Sorry about that," he said, pocketing the phone. "That was Jenny. She says hi."

"Hi back," Kendra said, although she knew no greeting had occurred. She and Jenny were not friends, nor would they ever be.

Kendra dragged some cold fries through the remaining ketchup. The fire alarm glowed weakly in the upper corner of the room. Bryan sat down and sipped from the bottle. For whatever reason, the magnetism between them had dimmed.

They tossed the Burger King wrappers and wandered back into the showroom, searching for some new activity. Bryan made a few phone calls. Kendra left a few messages herself. They met up again at the register and recounted what they had learned about the outside world. Kendra had no news to report; Bryan had much. The party at Chris's was a bust, he said. The cops had already come twice. The party in the park, however, was well underway, with four kegs tapped. It didn't matter though. They would miss all of it.

"I wouldn't have gone anyway," Kendra said.

Bryan stared at the iron gate. His mood had dipped since the call from Jenny and the word from the world outside. The novelty of their situation was at last coming to an end, and he seemed to be counting the seconds of precious, privileged time he was wasting.

"Sorry this is such a bummer for you," Kendra said.

Bryan didn't answer. He just slumped on the counter, laying his head on his elbows.

"What's the matter?" Kendra prodded.

"Nothing," Bryan said.

"Come on. What?"

"Really, nothing." He paused for a while and the immense silence of the mall pressed in from the main hallway. "This place is just so fucking lame," he finally said.

"You're just noticing?" Kendra said.

"You know what I mean," he said.

Kendra shrugged, making eye contact with a mannequin. "I'm not sure I do."

"It's just a fucking façade," he said. He gestured generally into the darkened mall. "This whole society, man, it's based on crap. Fucking Limited. Fucking Old Navy. We're supposed to pretend it's all so fucking great. It sucks."

Bryan was more drunk than Kendra had realized it seemed. Judging from his muddled speech and boneless posture, he might even be very drunk. Kendra wondered if she herself was that drunk, too. She tested her lips and found they were slightly numb, which meant that most likely yes, she was that drunk.

She sat on a stool with her arms folded and listened as Bryan proceeded to hold forth on all the vices of American culture as he saw them. American consumerism, American piggishness, the moral injustice of the throwaway society. He hated the mall and all it stood for. He hated television and he hated the internal combustion engine. Most of all he hated George Bush. He hated him more than anyone alive. The hole Bush had dug for the world would take generations to get out of. The environment alone . . .

Midway through the diatribe Kendra stopped paying attention.

She didn't care so much for Bryan's political opinions. Listening to him, she heard mainly his gentle, wishful parents talking. The innocence was unbearable. What did they want, she wondered? What was the point in complaining? They would never change anything. They were all too invested, too wholly dependent on everything as it currently stood. Bryan and his family would die without George Bush, and on some level they knew it.

"At least you can say these things here," she broke in, finally. "In Russia, you can't even talk like that. Bush is nothing. You know that, right?"

"He would be if he could," Bryan said, losing none of his momentum. He was on a roll. He didn't even realize she was arguing with him yet.

"You have no idea," she said. "My dad talks about growing up in Russia. He couldn't even laugh on the street. His mom wouldn't let him. If the wrong person saw you laughing at something, you could disappear. Just gone. You can't even compare." If Bryan was going to mouth his parents' history lessons, Kendra figured she could do the same. Her father might be a loser, but his vantage point from the bottom of the world's heap gave him a certain, undeniable insight. At least he knew enough to blame himself for his own failures.

"Are you kidding?" Bryan said. The thought of minimizing the evil of George Bush was almost inconceivable to him.

"No," Kendra said, enjoying her role as the hard-bitten realist between them.

"So I guess this is the ultimate," Bryan said. "We're really living the dream. The pinnacle of civilization."

"Actually, yeah," she said, and out of spite she might even have believed herself. "This is it."

Bryan scoffed. "So this is it," he mused scornfully. "Wow. That's pretty cool."

Kendra didn't bother responding. The mannequins stood frozen in place, looking in all directions.

One thing they agreed on was that they were tired. They might as well go to bed soon. They returned the clothes to the racks and then piled some down jackets on the floor to serve as their bedding. The area was about as big as a queen-size mattress, and they used cashmere sweaters for pillows. Before lying down, Bryan set the alarm on his phone for a half hour before Nathan's expected arrival so they could hide and then scurry out when he went into the back room.

They lay down. The space between them was narrow, but no body parts were touching. The sound of a heating duct kicked on, implying an elaborate system of pipes and passages in the walls. Bryan's body heat was almost palpable. If something was going to happen between them, it was going to happen soon. They might have just had a fight, but Kendra was still willing.

She waited a long time for Bryan to make some kind of move. Some re-angling of his body. Some mere brushing of her skin. But he remained still. His harsh eyebrows were relaxed, his breath tranquil. She tried to remember the movement of their argument and whether she had perhaps thrown him off track with her antagonism, but the specifics were already getting hazy. Maybe he was waiting for some kind of signal on her part, some sign of forgiveness. Maybe it was her responsibility to get things started after all.

Why not, she thought. They were still drunk. It was dark. She could allow herself to be foolish. Anyway, time was getting short.

"Bryan?" she whispered.

"Uh-huh?"

"You asleep?"

"Not yet."

She didn't say anything.

"What?" he said.

"Nothing," she said.

"Come on. What?"

"Do you . . . How should I say this? Do you want a blow job?"

Her stomach clenched with nerves. She had expected a moment of flustered embarrassment on his part. A shocked, titillated grappling with the invitation. A stammering giving-in. But instead he seemed well prepared with his answer.

"That's okay," he said.

The distant vent cut off and silence collected.

"You're sure?"

"Yeah. I'm okay."

Rain pattered on the faraway skylights of the mall.

"Sorry if that was weird," Kendra said. "I just . . ."

"It's okay. Don't worry about it."

"I can sleep here next to you?"

"Sure. Of course."

They remained side by side. Bryan's body was as still as a statue. Kendra was too humiliated to close her eyes. What kind of person refused a blow job? What kind of superior asshole did he think he was? She had asked nothing from him. She only wanted to know he was human. She wanted to know he had a dick, and baser drives, like everyone else. The last thing she wanted was his pity, but that seemed to be what she had gotten. She never should have told him her father drove a cab.

She stared at the ceiling. She could still feel Bryan's heat emanating. He lay with his hands at his sides, and she watched the rise
of his chest and stomach, the inflation of the wet organs inside him.
He refused to open his eyes. Gingerly, she reached over and lifted
his shirt and touched his taut belly. His muscles constricted, then
relaxed.

"What are you doing?" he whispered.

"Shhh."

She unbuttoned his fly and reached under his waistband and
found him already hard. His cock knew what was going on. She
kissed his stomach. Late at night all the proscriptions of the day fell
away and anything became possible. Fuck his goodness, she thought.
Fuck his pity. They were two young bodies in a cage together, and
they would do what they pleased.

"Don't," he whispered.

"No one'll know," she whispered. She breathed onto the head
of his cock to torture him.

"I don't . . . I don't know."

He gave in the moment she took him in her mouth. She was
proud of her technique. She lubricated his cock with her spit and
rubbed the shaft for a few strokes. When his head hit the back of her
throat, she knew she was down in it, touching the venal root of the
world, discovering yet again what she had known all along. No one
was pure. No one was good. Anyone would fold given the opportunity and the cover of night. It was an important thing to understand. It was the secret of history itself. And knowing, she knew the
ground beneath her feet would never move.

She touched his balls and he came immediately. Afterward they
didn't say anything. They didn't kiss. She took the privilege of

cuddling beside him though. He could not deny her that. She had earned it.

Bryan snored loudly through the night. Kendra slept lightly, and she was awake when the occulus of the mall's skylight brightened with morning.

The floor was too hard, and she couldn't get comfortable. As the light increased, she got up and crept to the gate to watch the mall's interior gradually return to sight. Every store was protected by the same black ironwork—a zoo of commodities. The walls speckled and gained color.

Through the skylight, she could see the coursing gray clouds of an overcast day and flecks of water streaking the expansive glass.

She rested her elbows on the cold metal, ruminating on the day to come. Nathan might discover them hiding in the store. Or he might not, and still confront her about the stolen money when she came in for her shift in the afternoon. Most likely, he'd roll over and persuade himself to forget about it, in which case she would have the honor of going on with her pointless retail job as it stood. Maybe she'd be arrested. There was no way of knowing.

As for Bryan, he would pretend nothing had happened or he'd stop talking to her altogether, most likely the latter. She didn't see an attractive way through any of it. The one thing she could count on was her mother shrieking at her when she stepped in the front door.

Somewhere in the distance a rolling door rumbled. The mall, spacious and still, seemed to wait. Kendra expected a security guard or janitor to appear any moment, but she remained at the gate anyway.

She didn't care if anyone saw her anymore. In fact, she almost welcomed the discovery, the trouble it would bring, so long as the trouble delivered her someplace new.

No guard or janitor appeared though. Rather, the early-morning visitors turned out to be two old Chinese men wearing sweat suits and fishing hats. Chatting quietly, they drifted in from the mouth of the main entrance onto the shiny, beige floor of the atrium.

Kendra didn't bother waking Bryan, not even when two more old men appeared, and then three more. Soon twelve old men were there, sitting on benches, talking among themselves, changing their shoes and stretching their legs. At first Kendra was puzzled by the group, until she remembered the posters for early-morning senior tai chi sessions. Apparently they actually happened this time of year.

She watched silently as the old men spread out and spaced themselves into three equal rows and then, together, began carving their mysterious shapes in the air.

They lowered their hips and raised their hands, softened their wrists and pushed their palms outward. They craned their necks and raised their palms toward the sky. The poses flowed smoothly, one into the next, and watching them, Kendra began unconsciously to breathe in time, matching her own rhythms to the gentle arcs of the men's arms and legs. She inhaled as they opened their arms. She exhaled as they swept their arms across their chests. She inhaled. She exhaled.

If only the morning session could go on forever, she thought. The longer it lasted, the less she cared about anything else. She didn't care about the money anymore. She didn't care about Bryan.

Soon she didn't give a shit about anything at all. The only thing she found interesting was the old men, and the secret, graceful knowledge they seemed to have unlocked in their bodies. She watched them lunge, hands floating to their waists. She watched them pivot, crouching low in their centers of gravity. Someday, she vowed, she would greet the day with that kind of peace.

NEW SHOES

THE FACT THAT Guy was talking about the traffic in New York told Dan there was no real news to report. If there had been news, Guy, Dan's producer, would have said something already. He would have said congratulations, or sorry, not this time, or get ready, are you sitting down, this is going to take some explaining. But the longer Guy went on narrating his walk down Sixth Avenue, describing every odd detail of the passing pedestrians, the more certain Dan was that the fate of the movie, which was to say, the fate of his career, of his life itself, remained yet, as ever, undecided.

"This cab driver is actually getting out of his car," Guy said. Dan, sitting at his desk in the suburban hush, could hear honking and shouting on the other end of the line, a filtered hubbub of urban street noise, in stark contrast to the glazed fir trees outside his window.

"He's walking over to the dude in the SUV," Guy said. "They're yelling at each other. I swear to God, Dan, someone should make a movie about this. It's a true human drama happening over here."

"A movie about a pissed-off taxi driver in New York City?" Dan said.

"Yeah."

"I think someone beat us to it."

Dan waited through the distant noise of a jackhammer destroying concrete.

"Not with a Pakistani leading man, no one hasn't," Guy came back.

"So I guess we're still waiting?" Dan said.

"Still waiting," Guy said. "But hold tight, man. We should be hearing any time now. They love the script. Randy told me again today."

"They love it. That's nice. I'm glad they love it so much."

"Don't be sarcastic, man. Please. It's not helpful."

"I'm not being sarcastic," Dan said.

"Well don't be," Guy said. "This isn't the time for it. We need to keep our thoughts pure today. We're about to be rewarded for our long, grueling efforts. You know what they say about getting what you wished for."

"I guess so."

"That's right. Sometimes you do."

Dan hung up and put his computer to sleep. He paced to the window and stared through his fleshy, unshaven reflection at the pile of compost at the edge of the yard, watching the food scraps invisibly returning to the wet earth. Ever so slowly the organic material was being devoured by worms and bacteria, entering the downside of the endless cycle of creation and destruction. Life and death, life and death—they followed each other like day and night. At some point, the compost would rise in a new form—a tomato, a cherry blossom—and devour the world's nutrients in return.

Dan thought about checking his e-mail, but he had checked

only moments before. He thought about his credit card bill. He was having trouble keeping his thoughts pure.

So they loved it, he thought. Big deal. What does that mean? Ten months ago, when his screenplay had first begun making the rounds among financiers and casting agents in New York and L.A., word that a group of money people loved it would have been cause for excitement, but he'd since crossed too many false thresholds, approached too many false green lights, to get his hopes up. Along the way, dozens of people had proclaimed their love for the project before ultimately, grudgingly, with great regret, etc., passing. In the movie industry's spectrum of affection, Dan had come to find, loving something didn't actually mean that much. It was all hyperbole. If something was "good," it was generally terrible. If something was "great," it was not embarrassing. Merely to love something was a form of neutrality at best. It implied fear that someone else might see potential there, and thus it might be worthwhile to buy the author a few lunches, but it foretold no commitment of any kind. In a world of delicate egos, Dan could see how the hyperbole was useful. Loving ensured no one's feelings got hurt. But he was not deceived by the word anymore either.

The only word that meant anything was "special." "Special" was the highest praise. He never got "special."

Dan continued staring out the window. He was stuck. Without money, no actors would sign on, and without actors, no financiers would come aboard. It was a frustrating double bind, made more so by the fact he had worked so hard to write something with real commercial viability for once. This was not *Andrei Rublev* they were talking about here; this was *Animal House* meets *Mr. Smith Goes to Washington*, as the pitch went. The tale of a young, idealistic politician arriving in Washington, D.C., to board with a group of rambunctious elder statesmen at prankish war with the president. It was a broad comedy, and topical, but with the election only a year and a half away, the window of relevance was closing. Either the script would find its funding imminently or it would retire to the purgatory of Dan's hard drive forever, yet another unmade screenplay joining the rest in the digital lake of fire.

They loved it, whatever that meant. The decision was out of his hands. What could he do? His only idea was to go downtown and buy new shoes for his daughter, Celia.

Celia was in the living room, sitting on the couch in her sundress and a witch hat left over from Halloween, reading a book about North American fowl. Dan watched her from the doorway, marveling at the intensity of her concentration. She was a lithe, brown-haired girl, seven years old, with a fine, sharp nose, black eyes, and lips almost always pursed in contemplation. On the table beside her was a glass of water, and on the pillow at her hip a fat, purring calico cat.

Dan's mother had warned him that his child's youth would go quickly, and indeed it had. Celia was barely a child anymore. He'd missed certain crucial passages of development during his travels the last few years, coming home from New York or Australia to find an utterly changed creature in the house. But over the past months, being home all the time, he'd been able to witness her blossoming into full, functioning personhood, complete with her own advanced reasoning faculties and her own immutable impressions of the world's order. Every day she was onto something new. Recently, she had gone through dinosaurs, medieval castles, tropical flowers, and still the knowledge continued pouring in. Milton Berle, Tesla's coils, the Capricorn project. Where did it come from?

The information seemed to drift into her head from the air itself. Dan sometimes believed he could actually see her mind growing as the world traveled past her.

"Ahem," Dan said, but Celia, engrossed in her book, chose to ignore him. The cat, however, purred a little louder. "Ahem," he said again.

"Yes?" Celia said. Her pronunciation, as always, was amusingly precise, but still she refused to look up.

"I thought you were putting your jacket on," Dan said.

Celia continued reading, her eyes gulping down sentences. She shoved over the page to hurry to the next batch of words.

"I don't want my jacket," Celia said.

Dan watched her, weighing how best to bring her around.

"You might recall," he said, "we were going downtown to buy you new shoes today."

With a sigh, Celia looked up and met his eyes. "But why do I need a jacket, Dad?" she said. "It's not cold outside."

"It is cold," Dan said. "And you'll get sick without a jacket. And then you'll be sorry."

Celia appeared skeptical. Dan's logic was not so bad. To wear a jacket was to keep warm was to avoid a cold. But from her point of view, the true rationale for the order had not yet been exposed.

"It's not that cold outside," she said again.

"It's pretty cold," Dan said. "Colder than it looks."

"The car is warm," she pointed out. "The store will be warm. We'll only be outside for a few seconds, at most."

"We might have to park far away," he said. "And the car can take a long time to heat up."

"I probably wouldn't get a cold though."

"No, probably not," Dan admitted. "But let me put it this way.

Your mother would not be happy if I let you go outside jacketless in November."

"Aha," Celia said, drumming her fingers on the book's cover. "It's about Mom. That makes more sense." Which was true enough. Melissa was the stickler for rules in the house. And with that, Celia placed her tome on the end table and climbed to her feet, pleased she had uncovered the root cause of the issue.

Celia fed the cat, selected a scarf, and decided on a book by Lloyd Alexander for the road as Dan watched her from the foyer. She had always been a serious kid, and she went about everything with a sense of sober deliberation. "This one's been here before," the doctor had said, meeting Celia's suspicious gaze upon delivery. Dan still thought that might be true.

In the car, on the way to the freeway, Celia was full of questions about money. A week earlier, she had seen her first euro note at her friend Emily's house. She'd been struck by its size and coloring and the unfamiliar artwork decorating its surface. Since then she had become interested in monetary currency in general. Buckled into her seat, pink down jacket in her lap, she patiently interrogated him. Where did money go when it got old, she wanted to know. Where was it manufactured? Who designed money? What if everyone decided it didn't mean anything? What would happen if everyone stopped using it?

Dan did his best to provide decent answers, substituting general errata for information he lacked. Money was pulped when it got too old, he said. It was burned, to his knowledge. Some of the symbols on the dollar were remnants of the founding fathers' Masonic affiliations. Truly, money was an utterly arbitrary system, especially since the nation had abandoned the gold standard. There had been times in history when currencies became so devalued it took an entire wheelbarrow of bills to buy a single loaf of bread. He enjoyed Celia's probing curiosity, especially when he had some good nuggets to share. And moreover, he enjoyed being distracted from his own spiraling anxiety about the film.

· They reached 1-5 to find the lanes thick with traffic.

"Why is everyone driving at the same time?" Celia asked. Unlike Dan, she was more intrigued than aggravated by the congestion.

"The roads aren't really big enough anymore," Dan said. "Also, the bridge over the Columbia causes a bottleneck. They say this is one of the most congested stretches of 1-5. I don't know if that means anything to you. But 1-5 goes all the way down the West Coast. It connects us to San Francisco and Los Angeles."

"There's not always this much traffic on this road though," she said.

"That's true," Dan said. "Right now a lot of people are driving home from work, too. Rush hour starts very early in our town."

"Interesting." Celia watched a Range Rover merge into their lane. Dan could sense the levers and pulleys of her mind at work.

"Why do they all have to go at the same time?" she wondered.

"That's a good question," Dan said. "That's just how the business day operates. Everyone goes in and comes out at about the same time. Everyone depends on each other for their jobs."

"Some people should maybe go earlier," Celia said.

"You should write a letter to the city council."

Satisfied, Celia turned to the window and watched the passing scenery. The arches of the Fremont Bridge were approaching, and the radio towers in the West Hills pulsed against the clouds.

Dan drifted into the right lane, which of course slowed the

moment he arrived. Without Celia's questions, his own thoughts inevitably returned to the fate of the screenplay, the conversations transpiring on the other side of the continent at that very moment. He tried valiantly to ignore his fears, to discount them, to worry only about what he could control, but he couldn't help himself. His nerves knew something was afoot. The probability of good news was eroding by the hour. Good news came quickly. Bad news dawdled.

Bad news. Did this even qualify as truly bad news, he wondered? There was no death here. No blood or broken bones to deal with. But it did qualify, he believed. Making movies was the only dream he had ever nurtured, and he had pinned his whole identity on the objective. For years he had hoped only to steward certain images into the world—to invest his invisible thoughts with sound and color—and now, he saw, that plan might never happen. His secret visions would remain unformed. His work would remain unfinished. The loss he faced was not on the level of someone's murder or kidnapping, but it was nevertheless real. Otherwise, what was the point? What was the point of anything?

Traffic in all lanes halted completely. On the river, a tugboat pushed a weathered cargo ship to sea, grinding through the green waters.

If only there were a villain in the scenario, Dan thought, someone to blame for his troubles. But no one quite fit the role. There had been some assholes along the way, but mostly there were just insecure bureaucrats. The financiers were not monsters, after all. They weren't even stupid. They were all sharp, committed, well-rounded people who just wanted to be involved in projects that inspired them. They wanted to find good work, like anyone else. They took no pleasure in dashing the dreams of commercial directors in the provinces such as himself, even if that seemed to be their most natural talent.

Dan wished he felt entitled enough to be resentful and angry. Then he might turn his anxiety outward. He might lash out. But he was not that type. He was grateful for the opportunities he had already been offered. He was asking for a lot of money, after all. Millions of dollars. He had no right to complain.

"Dad?" Celia said, intruding on Dan's sadly familiar pattern of thoughts. The red brake lights ahead lit and extinguished nearly at random.

"Yeah," Dan said.

"What's the difference between a crow and a raven?"

"I have no idea," he said, and found he had lost some of his enthusiasm for questions.

Eventually, they crossed the bridge and siphoned into downtown, where Dan was dismayed to find the holidays already in full swing. It was only early November and the lights on the bus mall were up and the wreaths and ribbons were appearing in windows. It was depressing. Not so much because he disliked the holidays—he liked them fine, actually—but because the seasonal change only underscored the irreversible passage of time. At this moment one year earlier he had just been finishing the script, and he had seen only great possibility ahead. In his fantasy, his sturdy, conventional comedy was going to be the gateway to riskier projects, and in five years' time, with, say, two more films under his belt, he was going to be standing in the company of real artists. But a year later, in fact, he was no closer at all.

There was no parking on the street, so Dan swung into a garage. The ticket spit out; the arm lifted. They circled to the fifth floor and squeezed into a spot between indistinguishable Toyotas. They were still in the process of getting out of the car, collecting their sundries, when Dan's phone vibrated against his thigh, causing his heart to kick like a frog. It was Guy.

"Hi Guy," he said.

"Just wanted to let you know they're talking again today."

"They're talking? I thought they already talked."

"They did. That meeting went great. Today they're having a new meeting with Jeff on the phone."

"Jeff wasn't on the phone before?"

"They had to iron out some details before they bothered him."

"So the meeting before wasn't the real meeting?" Dan said.

"It was real. But it wasn't final."

Dan sighed. He understood the bizarre theater of conference-call meetings: the escalating levels of seniority in attendance, the Kabuki dance of ass-covering and sycophancy. He had become adept at the form himself over the years. He also understood their unpredictability and caprice, which worried him.

"Super," he said. "God knows what happens now."

"Don't get discouraged," Guy said. "It's just a meeting. It means things are moving."

"I'd been under the impression they were already moving."

"Well, they're moving faster now."

"Okay. Well, thanks for the update. Tell me when the ax falls. It would be nice to know if my head is still attached to my body tonight."

"Come on, man. Attitude. Mental toughness. Have it."

Dan closed the phone. Celia, cradling her jacket, lurked at the bumper, observing a dented El Dorado creep its way around the corkscrew of spaces, searching for a place to rest. She seemed to be gauging the efficiency of the entire infrastructure and finding it lacking.

"What's the matter?" Celia said, turning.

"What do you mean, honey?" Dan said.

"You sounded upset."

"No, I'm not upset."

"What are you then?"

"Just a little apprehensive is all." He locked the doors with a chirp and took his daughter's hand and they began their way to the stairs. From the concrete stairwell the tips of the trees in the park blocks made a damp, orange haze.

"What does that mean?" she said.

"Apprehensive?" He was surprised the word hadn't somehow found its way to her yet. "It just means I'm thinking," he said. "I'm trying to keep track of some things in my head."

Celia pondered this notion. Or perhaps another thought entered her mind; Dan would never know. She paused long enough that he assumed they were moving onto something else, but instead she stuck to the topic.

"Thinking about what?" she said.

"I'm expecting an important phone call."

"From who?"

"From some people in New York. That was Guy. You met Guy before. He's my producer."

"What is a producer again?"

Dan was happy to shift into more clear-cut territory. He almost never spoke to her about work, and it offered a comfortable batch of material. "A producer is someone who makes movies. Or TV commercials or Broadway plays. But in this case, movies."

"Uh-huh?" She expected more information.

"You remember how we talked about all the work it took to make a movie?"

"I guess so."

"Well, making a movie is a big, group effort. It can take hundreds of people sometimes. Some of them make the food, some of them write the music. Some people speak the lines of dialogue. Some people record the lines."

"A lot of people."

"Yeah," he said. "The producer is the person who kind of organizes everything. They make sure everyone knows what's going on. Actually, some of them just give money. But the one I was just talking to is more creative."

"It seems complicated."

"It's very complicated."

"And you're the director," she said.

"I'm the writer-director," he said. "That means I write the script, work with the actors, talk to the camera department, the costume person. I'm kind of right in the middle, telling people what to do."

"I thought that was the producer."

"It's both of us. I make the decisions and he carries them out."

Celia frowned. She was only partly satisfied with the explanation, but she was willing to let things stand for the moment. They arrived at the sidewalk and began down the street, passing a smattering of pedestrians along the way.

"So why were you upset?" she said.

"I told you, I'm not upset."

"Okay. Why are you apprehensive?"

"I'm waiting to find out if we get the money to make a movie. I might get it and I might not. I should be finding out really soon. And not knowing is hard."

"I'll say," she said. "Not knowing sucks." Dan figured she must be talking about school.

The smell of wet leaves and moss and cold earth drifted down from the West Hills. Dan took his time walking them through the park. They watched a hacky sack circle. Some skateboarders barreled through, testing their moves on the lip of an amphitheater.

They arrived at Meier and Frank, a stately, white building near Pioneer Square. It was among the last traditional department stores in town, and Dan generally preferred it to the mall. They pushed through the glass doors into the perfumed air.

"What is Meier and Frank?" Celia asked, as the doors sealed behind them.

Dan was puzzled by the question. "A department store," he said. "You've been here before."

"No," she said. "Meier and Frank. What does it mean?"

"The words?" Dan said. "They're people's names. Meier and Frank are the guys who founded the store. Meier and Frank. They were a team."

"Who were they though?"

"I don't really know," he said. He had never thought about the names as connected to actual people before. It was just the name of the department store he favored. The names were almost entirely abstract in his mind.

"Some Jewish merchants, I guess," he said.

"How do you know that?"

"Their names," he said. "They're Jewish names. Meier anyway."

"How do you know?"

"I just know."

Celia shook her head, frustrated by all the knowledge still outside her grasp. "I don't know how you can know that," she said.

"I'm a lot older than you," he said.

Walking through the cosmetics section and riding the escalator, Dan explained to Celia, as best he understood it, the history of anti-Semitism in the West. The Jews, he told his daughter, had been persecuted in Europe for centuries. They had been prohibited from owning property, which was to say from farming, and forced to live in squalid ghettos. They had thus turned to financial and mercantile trades, like owning department stores, for their living. Now they were hated because they were bankers and scholars. The legacy of political oppression, he suggested, played out in all kinds of unexpected ways.

His history lesson was cut short, though, when the escalator deposited them at the edge of the children's shoe section. The smell of new leather was heavy in the air, and the display pedestals formed a simple maze crowded with goods.

"We have arrived," Dan said grandly.

"Here we are," Celia said.

"Shall we commence looking?" Dan said.

"Yes," Celia said, "we shall."

They waded into the shoe department. Celia had a strategy, which involved making a first pass to get her bearings, then going back with a finer eye, and then going back again to winnow down the options. Dan followed at a distance, letting her take the lead and offering his opinion when asked, but mostly keeping out of it. He checked his phone to be sure he hadn't missed any calls.

Celia took her time among the fur-lined boots, the slick pink galoshes, the stub-nosed clogs, the buckles of every shape and size, and as the search dragged on, Dan's thoughts began to darken again. Perhaps, he thought, he had been fooling himself all along. He had never been in a position to make a feature at all. After five years as a commercial director, he thought he had accrued the necessary skills. He had executed successful campaigns for running shoes, deodorants, and first-person shooter video games. He had established the requisite connections. A feature had seemed like the natural extension of his craft. But maybe he was simply not good enough to make that leap.

It was in college that he had first decided to become a filmmaker. That was when he had first discovered the joyful science of montage, the thrill of placing moving images side by side. It was like magic. From two images a third meaning arose, and within each frame, a world of decisions. Composition, sound, color, performance. He remembered vividly that day in production class, checking out an album of sound effects from the library, carrying the sound of howling wind to the editing bay, laying the sound over his image of bleak, frozen pasture and naked trees, and feeling the chill of storytelling along his spine. The gift of sound and image. That was the whole thing in a nutshell.

To make movies for a living though—that had seemed unimaginable. Who did that? His father was a schoolteacher, his mother a pharmacist. No one in their world had ever made films. No one had ever made art in any way. It was like aspiring to be an astronaut or the president of the United States—utterly unrealistic, possibly even immoral. When the ambition had occurred to him, he had guarded his secret jealously. The idea was too terrifying to speak out loud. But to himself, in his most private moments, he promised to try.

He'd begun without fanfare, showing found-footage collages in music clubs and house parties around town, gradually amassing a repertoire of images—airplanes and flowers, animals and fire—that he screened alongside whatever music his friends were making at the time. He wasn't sure this was real filmmaking, but people seemed to think it was. The crowds in those days were very forgiving. They were looking for new friends, not great art, and most of the time they went home satisfied. Even as he moved further into music videos and experimental film and eventually advertising, his abiding self-doubts remained.

Dan still ran into some of the people from the old days. They popped up here and there. Tim Deller, for instance, had made it quite big. His second feature, about a family of meth addicts, was going into production in the spring. Dan had given him notes on the script. Julie Moore had also been successful. She practically lived on the festival circuit, receiving fawning attention from certain quadrants of academia for her odd documentaries. The doors had opened easily for both of them, and for good reason. Their talent had been so obvious from the start.

For Dan, the doors had opened, but less grandly. Five years ago—was it that long?—on borrowed money, using heads and tails of used film rolls, he had managed to complete an experimental feature, but the project had failed to land a distribution deal. No big surprise, considering its content. The movie had no characters, five elliptical dream sequences in a row, and voice-overs drawn from the dialogue of daily newspaper cartoons, all of which made for tough viewing, to say the least. Following that debacle came numerous aborted projects: a unicorn movie, a double-screen gunfighter epic, an improvised, single-set romance, none of which had gained any traction. At a certain point, his parents, previously supportive, had begun subtly to encourage him to find other avenues for his creative energies.

Dan sometimes reassured himself that everyone was a failure in some way. The great painter was a failed dancer, the professional baseball player a failed basketball star. He could see that in some ways he had done all right, achieving his dreams in the most bare-bones fashion. But the fact was, the failure was bitter. He put zero stock in his success as a father, a husband, a friend, a commercial director, all of which came too easily to command any real pride. Only film-making was meaningful, and his failure in that realm threatened his very inner glue. He had arrived at the perimeter of his selfhood, and sadly it was not as far out as he had hoped.

Trailing Celia through the shoe section, Dan gnawed on his failure. If his current film project capsized, what would he do? He had other movie ideas, certainly, but probably not the requisite faith and energy to pursue them to their final ends. He would continue making ads, most likely, and maybe that would be all. It was ironic. As a younger man he had been disgusted by advertising. He had fretted and wrung his hands about the effects of commodification in mass culture. He had imagined his own work specifically as a revolt against advertising, his images unsalable, his notions of beauty beyond market forces. But here he was, an ad man. Some of his colleagues thought of the work as a form of art, but he refused to fool himself in that way. The incredible tracking shot of a table of Nestlé products might be technically ingenious, but it was not art. It never would be.

He wondered what Melissa, his wife, would think if the movie were to go away. Would she lose her respect for him? No, he decided. If anything, she would be happy the thing fell apart. In the early days his ambitions had been attractive to her. Part of their courtship had involved wild talk about the possible movie projects he might direct, absurd plotlines to write, ridiculous stunt castings to engineer. But that was far in the past. She was tired of waiting any longer, and they were well beyond the point where his artistic fulfillment meant anything to her. They had a kid. At this point, Melissa just wanted him to get back to work.

When Dan thought about it really coldly, he could see that no one in the entire world genuinely cared about the arc of his filmmaking career. No one, that was, besides himself, and possibly Guy.

Celia made some eccentric choices. She was drawn to a pair of gaudy cross-trainers with blinking lights in the soles, a pair of slick patent-leather flats, and a pair of traditional, garnet-colored penny loafers. Dan instructed her to narrow the choices down, and she eliminated the cross-trainers. They had seemed unlike her anyway. And then they went to find the salesman.

The salesman was a wiry, rodent-like man, and he directed Celia to a bench near the cash register. He measured her feet, took her selections, returned carrying two boxes, and pulled up his stool. He sat down, tugging on his pant leg to reveal his black socks.

The salesman extended his hand, and Celia gave him her foot, allowing him to slide off the old shoes. He opened the first box and unwrapped the patent-leather flats and slipped one and then the next onto her stockinged feet.

"How do they feel?" he said.

"All right," she said hesitantly.

Dan watched as Celia stood and walked solemnly to the mirror on the pillar at the edge of the department floor. She stared at her feet. She turned around and examined the profile. She seemed to enjoy the slide of the leather soles on the carpet. Watching her, Dan was reminded of some Freudian theory about the genesis of the foot fetish. The sublimation at the moment of the castration complex. Someday, Celia would discover Freud, and God knew what she would do with that.

"You like those?" he said.

"I think so," she said.

"More than the other ones, you think?"

"I need to see."

She returned to the stool and the salesman asked if the shoes pinched at all and she said no, they were fine. She offered her foot, and the salesman slid off the flats and unwrapped the penny loafers from the tissue paper and placed them on her feet.

Celia again stood and again presented her feet to the mirror. She stood in front of the glass, watching her feet turn, seeing the light catch on the different planes.

"Well?" Dan said.

"I like these, too."

"What do you like about them?"

"I like these knobs." She brushed her hand against the burls of leather running along the seam. "But I like the color of the other ones."

"It's a tough choice," he said.

"It is," she said. She watched the shoes with penetrating attention. Dan wondered what thoughts were going through her mind, but she was already too old, too complex, to decipher. He would never fully comprehend her thoughts again, if ever he had. Her most simple actions had retracted into well-guarded mystery.

New shoes. Dan did not believe, as many of his colleagues in advertising did, that the choice of shoe was tantamount to a choice of identity itself. He did not believe the shoe made the person. But watching Celia grapple with her decision, he did see the glimmer of consciousness at work. He saw her taste forming, her distinction refining, her judgment strengthening. He saw the lotus of his daughter's mind opening to awareness, the petals of perception unfolding, seeking light. From there, it was but a small step to the world of imagination, that drawing forth of color and sound from the darkness. Imagination, the imitation of Godhead. The opposite of war. The holy vocation he had tried so hard and failed to attain.

Celia angled herself in order to see the backs of the shoes. She lifted one heel, pivoted. She turned again.

Let her always live inside the miracle of imagination, Dan thought. Let her come to worship this thing God had endowed. This was his prayer for his daughter, his benediction. He blessed her.

"So which ones?" Dan said.

"The other ones," she said, watching her feet.

"Very good choice," the salesman said. "They're very popular."

"You want to wear them out of the store?" Dan said.

Celia, watching her shoes, said, "Yes."

With proper reverence, the salesman packed Celia's old shoes into the new box and rang up the sale. Celia, meanwhile, walked back and forth on the hardwood floor, listening to the thin clack of her heels on the boards, enjoying a state of unconflicted happiness with her purchase.

Dan remembered the feeling. He still had the feeling, actually. The sense of completion that temporarily came with a new pair of shoes. Who said you couldn't buy happiness? You could, at least briefly. The idea that you couldn't was just a lie poor people told themselves to feel better.

They exited the store the way they had come, down the escalator, across the cosmetics section, out to the street, where the autumn sun was still shining. In the park the hacky sack game was still underway, and the skaters continued their revolutions around the amphitheater, epoxy wheels thrumming on concrete.

It was getting late. On the East Coast it was already well after seven, which meant they had gone another day without news.

They entered the bus mall, a canyon of shadow, and dodged the bums and bike messengers who crossed their path. Dan could tell that something was changing. He had finally crossed a boundary and there was no point in pretending otherwise. His movie had unquestionably entered the past tense. There would be no more meetings to schedule. There would be no more phone calls. There would be no more notes from prospective actors or financiers to address. And that, he had to accept, was all right.

The number 37 bus passed by, and Dan was at peace. He had nothing to regret, he told himself. He had pursued his project with the best of intentions, coming to it humbly, hoping only to participate in the pageantry of public life, and perhaps exert a small political influence for the better on the world. He had hoped to invest his daughter's universe with a little more meaning, a little more magic, and if no one wanted to give him the money for that, so be it. In the morning he would call his agent and tell her he was actively looking for ad work again, and he would proceed to do whatever was demanded of him. He could even become another person if necessary. If nothing else, at last, he knew his true place.

Dan and Celia walked over the gold leaves scattered on the ground. Up ahead, the mirrored walls of the bank building were shining with the last of the day's sun and sky. He didn't even notice at first when Celia tugged on his coat sleeve, seeking his attention.

"What?" Dan said.

"Your phone," she said.

Sure enough, the phone was ringing. It was Guy. Dan felt bad for Guy now. He had put so much time and energy into the project over the last year. He'd read so many drafts, made so many calls. He'd staked his own reputation on the gamble, and no doubt it was going to be a shame to see all that effort go to waste.

"I should probably take this," Dan said.

"Take your time," Celia said, and ambled over to the bus kiosk to read the schedules on the TV monitors.

"Hey," Dan said.

"Hey," Guy said. He sounded tired. "How's it going?"

"All right," Dan said. "You?"

"I just got off the phone with Jeff," Guy said.

"Uh-huh?"

"The meeting went long. But I've got some news."

Dan took a deep breath, testing the walls of his stomach, his chest cavity, happy to discover his serenity remained unshaken. The claws of hope had at last truly released him. There would be no news that could bother him anymore. No indecision that could cause him to lose another night's sleep. His only concern now was to help Guy understand that everything was okay. And after that, to shepherd his daughter, currently climbing onto a bench for a better view of the bus mall, home for dinner.

"So," Dan said, with divine resignation. "What's the news?"

"Are you ready?"

"I'm ready."

On the bench, Celia folded her arms, surveying the milling bus passengers. The number 35 grumbled behind her, the windows filled with reflections and half-obscured faces.

TRAIN CHOIR

VERNA COULD HEAR Lucy bounding through the long grass in the darkness. The dinging of her tags amid the chafing stalks gave away every burst of speed and change of direction. Briefly she was running toward the train trestle up ahead, a low bridge connecting two squat bluffs outlined against the high-plain night sky, and then she was doubling back toward the outskirts of town, a slope of tidy houses obscured by elm and pine and dogwood trees and hemmed in by the freeway to the east. Then the sounds stopped for a while, only to pick up again, tracing a path back toward the road shoulder, right to the spot where Verna, all alone, was walking.

Lucy emerged from the grass and plowed into Verna's legs, carrying in her smiling mouth a squat stick. The moonlight glowed on her small, muscled body, turning her yellow coat the color of pale frost. Verna wrestled with the stick until Lucy relinquished her grip, and after a pat on the head, the dog plunged back into the meadow for another sprint.

"We're only out here a little while!" Verna said. "Don't get too far. Are you listening? Stay close to me."

Verna continued walking. The wind in the grass mixed with the whisper of traffic on Columbus Boulevard and up ahead the yearning whistle of a passing train rose from the night. Verna breathed in the scent of sage and clean, arid earth, every step carrying her farther than she had ever been into the eerie, unpopulated landscape of the West. The clouds changed in the inverted bowl of the sky. The gravel crunched underfoot. For a moment, under the spilling stars, almost exactly halfway from Muncie, Indiana, to easy money in the Alaskan fisheries, she allowed herself a brief intuition of better times to come.

They were making good time. In four days they had driven almost two thousand miles, passing through the rusted sprawl between Bloomington and Chicago, the scabbed humps of Nebraska's Badlands, the dirt hills of Idaho. They had survived a torrential late-night storm in Iowa, the whole sky fractured by lightning, and a perilous climb through the Rockies when it seemed the car might shudder and collapse. They had seen more Pizza Huts than she knew existed.

In four more days they would be in Alaska. Alaska. Just the word sounded strong and pure. From what Verna had heard, a line worker in the canneries earned at least eight hundred dollars a week, housing provided, and with nothing to spend money on, it was easy to save at least five thousand dollars by the close of the run. For her, that would be enough to put a good dent in the Visa bill she'd racked up since her apartment had flooded in the winter, and possibly even get the collection agency goons off her back. If things went well, who knew? Maybe she would stay awhile.

Verna refused to let the fantasy get any larger than that. The notion of actually getting ahead was not even worth contemplating. All she hoped for was firm ground under her feet. The dream of a house with a fenced-in yard and rosebushes would wait for another time.

She passed a spooky mound of dirt and a fallen barricade of rail-road ties. The desert wind blew dry and cool. Down the road, Lucy emerged from the meadow and stood with her tail taut, ears pointed, sensing some subtle stirring of sound or motion. She looked around, first at Verna, then at the train trestle in the distance. And then, crazily, she bounded off, galloping toward the next electrical pole, and the next pole after that, making her way toward the looming shipwreck of the trestle.

"Hey!" Verna said, but Lucy had already disappeared, moving well beyond Verna's own comfort zone: a scream's length from hu-manity. Verna was a wiry woman, alert to the dangers at the mar-gins of an unknown town. She didn't want to go any farther. But as always, Lucy would have her way.

Around the next bend Verna spotted firelight playing on the under-side of the bridge, and moments later she heard faint yelps and laughter, mixed with tinny music from a portable radio. She sighed. If she had known anyone else was out there, she never would have let Lucy off the leash in the first place.

The land dipped, and a bonfire came into view. Through the low brush Verna observed a group of teenage kids—a proudly dirty bunch, their fingernails blackened, their hair clotted with knots, some with studs in their cheeks and even facial tattoos—feeding old pallets and the remains of a mattress into the flames. She'd seen members of their tribe throughout her journey thus far. They were lurking in every town, stalking all the highways. She'd always con-sidered them slightly absurd, but now, in the dark of night, bathed in firelight, they took on a sinister cast.

"Beyoncé!" one hollered, and for some reason the others laughed.

Lucy, that minx, was huddled in the arms of a fat girl with ropy dreadlocks who was barely sober enough to keep herself upright but nevertheless was scratching and petting Lucy expertly, the dog's hind leg thumping the ground in gratitude.

"Great dog," the girl said, as Verna appeared at the perimeter of firelight. "What's her name?"

"Lucy," Verna said.

"She's a sweetheart," the girl said. "You're a sweetheart, Lucy!"

Verna watched Lucy closely for some spark of affection, but her dog was too engrossed in the young girl's attention to look up, too busy giving herself away. Lucy panted heavily, her eyes half closed. She had no problem making friends on the road. Across the clearing, a boy had begun scaling the trestle, a beer pinned in his armpit. The rest of the kids huddled in pairs and threesomes, laughing and scheming among themselves. The darkness outside the fire's throw of light was impenetrable, but Verna tried to see into it anyway, already plotting escape routes in case the hobo scene turned ugly.

"What is she?" the girl said.

"Part Rhodesian ridgeback, part Lab," Verna answered.

"What's the closest store around here?"

"No idea," Verna said.

"Just passing through?"

"Yeah."

"Where to?"

Verna saw the query for a ride coming a mile away. "Alaska," she said, and added, "for work," as if that might draw some line between them.

"Oh," the girl said. "I'm going south." She nodded toward a grimy, well-muscled boy trying to break a two-by-four on his knee.

"Ben worked the canneries last year. Hey, Ben! This lady's going to Alaska!"

"Whoo! King salmon!" the boy called, and kicked his empty beer can into the bushes. He opened a new can with a splash and came trotting over.

"Where you going?" he said.

"Ketchikan," Verna said. Her curiosity about what the kid had to say outweighed her repulsion. She didn't want to dawdle though either. Ketchikan was only the most southerly of her options, and therefore the most likely place she'd end up.

"Ketchikan's good for greenhorns," the boy said. "Tell them Ben said to set you up. Don't tell Mike Murphy you met me though! He's the manager up there. Copper River is good, too. Farther north, but lots of work on the *slime line*." He relished the words "slime line," drawing them out as far as he could.

From there Ben launched into a rambling tale about his time up north and how boring it was, and the many methods he and his buddies found to kill the time. Verna listened for a while, hoping for any useful information, but it became clear he had nothing to offer. He just liked to hear his own voice. When his story turned to joyriding bulldozers on Kodiak Island, Verna had had enough. She shook Lucy's leash and the dog trotted from the dreadlocked girl's arms. Verna attached the leash and without a word they exited into the brush, Ben's bragging voice fading behind them.

"We couldn't stop the thing," he said. "It just rolled all the way across the construction site and snapped the retaining wires. Boosh! This huge spray of sparks. It was fucking amazing, man. The Cat went over the cliff head over heels, ass over tit, all the way into the water. It was probably a hundred-thousand-dollar piece of equipment, gone in four fucking seconds. They couldn't pin it on me though, man. I was gone."

Verna's car was a gray 1996 Camry with a dent in the driver's-side door panel and three missing hubcaps. It was the only car parked in the Walgreens parking lot on Lombard Avenue, which was the best camping option Verna had been able to find after pulling off the freeway. The surrounding streets were quiet, but just the right kind of quiet—quiet enough to feel empty and unattended but not so much as to feel outright dangerous.

Lucy scrambled into the back seat, taking her place among the piles of blankets and sweaters, burrowing a nook beside the cooler and some wadded sweatpants.

Verna pulled the map from the glove box. Lucy was not so interested in their daily progress, but Verna liked sharing the map with her anyway. She guided her finger along the spiny, brown mountains south of Salt Lake City up I-84 through Idaho and into eastern Oregon, to La Grande, east of the green welt of the Cascade mountains. The remaining distance to Bellingham, their next day's goal, was only about five hundred miles, and from there to Ketchikan, another seven hundred, mostly by ferry. The run started in a week, which meant they would arrive well before hiring was done.

Satisfied, Verna switched off the overhead light. Only one more task remained before she could sleep. In the darkness, she unbuckled her money belt, a soiled, flesh-colored corset, and counted out her remaining bills. She had $632 left. With fill-ups running almost $40 apiece, twice a day, and the ferry almost $300, that left $200, more or less, for her remaining food and sundries. It wasn't much, but it didn't have to last long. In Ketchikan she would be able to start drawing from her first paycheck immediately, and from then on she would be all right.

"Big trees tomorrow," she said, reassured by her nightly accounting. She reattached the money belt and reclined the seat to find Lucy already fast asleep. She lay curled in a ball, her snout on her paws. Verna clucked, and patted her dog's head. Then she closed her eyes, the road map spread out over her chest like a blanket.

Someone was banging on the window.

It was barely dawn. The windows were fogged with breath, and Verna couldn't see anything beyond the hulking, silvery shadow behind the glass. A quick check told her the doors were still locked, and judging from the sound of occasional traffic on the street, there were other people close at hand, which was something. Any crime that might occur would have plenty of witnesses at least.

Lucy barked and Verna didn't shush her. Perhaps the intruder would just go away. She could at least hope.

"You can't sleep here, ma'am," a man's voice said. "Wake up. You can't sleep out here. Not allowed."

"Yeah, yeah," Verna said, and huddled deeper in the warmth of her blankets.

The knock came again. "Hey! Wake up." The voice was sterner this time.

"All right, all right," she said. The initial shock of the awakening was already giving way to something more like grouchiness and irritation.

The shadow retreated. Verna roused and checked herself in the mirror. The reflection was not the most lovely she had ever seen. Her features looked harder than usual. Her eyes were hazy; her lips were thin; her jaw mannish and square. And the limp, unwashed blonde hair wasn't helping matters. Her skin was chalky white, with a faint blush of red at the tip of her nose and in the thinness of her eyelids—her blood aura, someone had called it. She tried brushing out the worst of the knots in her hair with her fingers, but there wasn't much to be done.

Verna cracked the window. Through the slit she spied a security cop a few yards away. He was a doughy, red-faced man, pushing sixty, with burst capillaries in his bulblike nose and a bushel of white hair under his too-small hat. His uniform, a gray suit with yellow epaulets, was absurd, but he wore it with a semblance of dignity, or at least resignation, hiding his eyes behind mirrored, wire-rim aviator glasses. Verna sensed immediately he had no real problem with her, just a job to do. She could understand that.

Behind him, the street that had been obscure was now visible in the morning light. The strip consisted of two check-cashing offices, a pawnshop, a barbecue joint, and a restaurant called King Burrito. Diagonally across the intersection was a darkened garage called Bill's, and next door to that was an Arby's. It was a good thing she had a map, she thought. This corner could be anywhere west of the Rockies.

"You can't sleep here," the guard said, crossing his arms.

"Yeah," Verna said, the sour taste of sleep in her mouth. Lucy had begun wiggling around in the back seat and her nails clicked on the glass. "Knock it off, Lu," Verna said, annoyed, and to the guard, "All right, we're going."

When Verna turned the key in the ignition, though, the engine gave a mangled, choking noise and refused to catch. She twisted the key again, and again the ugly sound came, followed by a dampened click deep under the hood.

"Fuck," she said. "What did you do, Lucy?"

The security guard stood waiting, hands in his pockets, and Verna checked the gearshift to make sure the car was in park. She pumped the gas a couple of times and tried the key again. This time nothing happened at all. She rolled down her window part way, feeling the bite of the morning air vacuum in.

"The car won't start," she said.

The guard frowned and leaned over. "You got gas?" he said.

"There's enough gas," she said. "Plenty of gas."

"Well, you can't park here," he said. "That's the rules."

"Yeah, I get that," Verna said. "It's probably the serpentine belt." Two days earlier, in Provo, she had gambled on a mechanic's warning, hoping to avoid the hundred and fifty dollar investment until after her first paycheck came in. It seemed the gamble had not paid off.

A car honked and the fluorescent lights inside the beige walls of Walgreens stuttered to life.

"You just have to get it off the property," the guard said, glancing at the store. "That's just the way it is."

"How far is the property?" Verna said.

"To the street. The street's public. You just have to get out of the lot."

"I'll need some help," Verna said.

The guard, grunting and puffing, lent Verna a hand getting the car to the side street, as Lucy raced from window to window, taking in every view like she had never been inside a moving car before.

"You know anything about that garage over there?" Verna said, guiding the wheel.

"Seems to get business," the guard said. "I guess that means something. Never talked to them though. He's close. He's got that going for him."

"How about a good store around here?" she said.

"Down the road there's a Keinow's," he said. "They've got everything."

With that, the guard wished Verna luck and ambled to his post beside the front door of the drugstore, under the neon mortar-and-pestle sign. Verna continued fiddling with the car, testing the key, pumping the gas, going so far as lifting the hood and staring at the occult machinery of the engine in case some incredibly obvious misplacement had occurred, but she had no luck. The car was dead. And to top it off, Lucy's bag of food in the trunk was down to a few crumbs rattling in the bottom-most wrinkles. Replacing it would run her forty dollars, at least, unless there was some kind of sale to be had.

"Getting tight," she said to Lucy, and the dog smiled.

Verna attached Lucy's leash and they crossed the intersection to Bill's Garage, a brown cinder block cube set on a balding, oil-stained lot, with two bays and a helmetlike roof of corrugated metal. The building was surrounded by cars in various states of disrepair, themselves surrounded by a new cyclone fence topped with razor wire. According to a sign in the window, Bill's not only specialized in lube jobs but also sold hot dogs and tacos. The sun-bleached sign listing the garage hours was almost unreadable, but from the sidewalk Verna managed to decipher what she needed to know. The doors didn't open until ten o'clock, still two hours away.

"Lazy," Verna said, tugging on the leash. "Come on, girl. Let's find that store. We gotta eat."

Lucy wagged her tail violently, happy for a morning outside.

The two headed down the sidewalk, passing the storefronts that had been shuttered on their way in—a lampshade shop, a video store, a nail salon. They stopped at a Texaco for the bathroom, and Verna tied up Lucy near the air pumps and told her to be good.

Verna let the hot water run for a long time, scalding the filmy sink basin as best she could. She washed her face with Softsoap and dried herself with a handful of rough brown paper towels. Stepping out, she noted that gas prices had once again spiked. Regular was up to $3.10 a gallon, having risen 5 cents in two weeks. Whatever distant events caused these upticks she had no idea; even the government couldn't seem to say for certain.

Verna kept her eye out for bottles and cans but the pickings were slim. A guy in a mobility scooter was already patrolling the road shoulders, and a couple of bums could be seen feeding the recycling machine at the one convenience store. Verna had never viewed these kinds of people as competitors before, which told her something about the spot she had come to.

Lucy dragged a dirty Pepsi can from the scrub and dropped it at Verna's feet, but she let it lie. One can wasn't going to change anything.

Keinow's was an old-fashioned, medium-sized place with bright, hand-painted signs in the windows and a coin-operated spaceship near the front door, and already it was doing brisk business. A steady tide of young mothers flowed in and out, carrying their bulging bags, with their children staggering in tow.

"You be good, all right?" Verna said, tying Lucy to a bike rack. "Don't bother anybody. I'll be right back with a treat." Lucy barked and Verna grabbed her snout and clamped her jaws together. "Hey," she said, sternly. "What did I say? No bothering. Don't be a nuisance. We don't want that."

Verna stood and waited as a rattling silver train of shopping carts rolled in the front door, pushed by a stout Mexican stock boy. When the last cart was inside, she followed in his wake.

The store's volume of inventory was immediately reassuring. Verna wandered among the bins of vegetables, the deep rows of fresh milk cartons and the multicolored boxes of breakfast cereal, feeling that all the fastidiously arranged food implied some well-organized system in place, the idea that someone, somewhere, was taking care that everything found its proper path.

She stopped at the bulk food bins and grazed on almonds and sesame sticks, loitering until a stock boy glowered at her and then moving on, but not before nabbing a last handful of mixed nuts. In the worst-case scenario, she figured, she could always steal food, but that was not the case with such things as gas or car repairs.

The dog food was in aisle six. Verna scanned for Lucy's preferred brand, Iams, and sure enough, there it was, bottom row, far left. The other brands were cheaper, but this was one place Verna hated to cut corners.

The forty-pound bag was not on sale, though, and at forty-two dollars it was significantly more than Verna could justify spending on such a day. She would have to buy a smaller quantity, she figured, just something to tide them over, possibly a few cans. She hated buying in small amounts—it was so much less economical in the long run—but under the circumstances it was the only real option. She and Lucy needed just enough to last a matter of days, that was all.

Verna stood around in the dog food section for a long time, comparing the different prices and weights and ingredients of the cans. There was chicken rice, mushroom and gravy, Purina and Kal Kan, growth, maintenance, and lite. Every fourteen-ounce can ran about a dollar-fifty, and all were approximately the same, ingredient-wise, mostly meat-meal and meat by-products, whatever that meant.

Three cans of premium dog food equaled almost two gallons of gas, Verna calculated, which in turn equaled almost fifty miles of road.

Verna glanced around. Down the aisle a stock boy was loading pints of ice cream into the freezer. In the front of the store two checkout girls were working the registers. Otherwise, the store was empty of employees. The other people were all customers like herself, none of whom had any real authority or any particular investment in anything she did.

Casually, Verna reached out and slipped three cans of Purina adult beef dog food into her bag and wandered away. She stopped at the chip aisle and made a show of examining the air-puffed packages, rejecting a series of possible purchases. The trick to shoplifting, she had found long ago, was in forgetting that one was doing it at all. A certain amnesia could hypnotize a whole room and turn one almost invisible to the public eye. From the chips she moved on to the magazines, where she loitered a few minutes, flipping through the perfumed pages, looking at snapshots of famous people. Only when Verna was fairly sure that no one was paying attention to her did she head for the front doors.

She could see Lucy grooming herself in the sunlight, tweezing with her front teeth at a small patch of hair near the base of her tail. What bliss, being a dog, Verna thought. They had no idea where they were or what was happening most of the time. As long as food showed up, they were happy. They had no comprehension of the whole system they'd been born into and from which they could never escape.

The point-of-purchase items drifted by, and Verna entered the alley of an empty cashier lane. She blanked her mind of all recent memory. She was just stepping onto the pad of the electronic doors when she felt a hand tighten around her upper arm and heard a man's voice speaking close to her ear.

"Do you have something to tell me?" he said.

Verna struggled but the man's hand refused to let go. Again his voice came, flat and deep, with a buried twang of sarcasm in the monotone. "You have something to say?" She tried to get away but the grip only tightened, pressing into the soft tissue of her biceps.

"Hey," Verna said. "Let go, all right? That hurts."

"You have something to tell me?" the man said once again, and expertly, without revealing himself, he maneuvered her into the produce section. Only when they had reached the oranges did he release his grasp and was she able to turn and get a good look at her apprehender.

He was just the stock boy from the bulk food section—a skinny kid in his early twenties, with small, mean eyes and a needle nose, his face flecked with acne and his thin, sand-colored hair brittle with mousse. The tag on his blue supermarket shirt said his name was Andy. The hatred she felt for him was immediate and intense.

"You have something to tell me?" Andy said.

"No," Verna said, and Andy grabbed her again and dug his fingers into her flesh. Across the produce section the other customers had begun to stare. One heavyset woman holding an avocado openly gawked like they were on television.

"Are you sure?" Andy said.

"Get away from me," Verna said.

"Fine," Andy said. "Then I guess you're coming with me."

"What are you talking about?" Verna said. "Where do you get off . . . Hey, come on. Let go."

With rough efficiency, Andy herded Verna down the Mexican food aisle before the eyes of the entire store. He pushed her through a pair of swinging doors in the back wall and into a musty sorting room full of stacked crates and pallets, and from there he marched her down a dingy stairway that smelled like rotten milk. Verna struggled but Andy was surprisingly powerful. He set his mouth and stared straight ahead, gripping her arm and refusing to let go.

They ended up in the manager's basement office, a small, windowless cell with wood paneling and rust-colored carpet. The furniture was sparse, just a blue metal desk and a few folding chairs, and on the wall hung a pristine calendar from 1983 stuck on the month of October.

"Sit here," Andy commanded, pointing at a chair in the corner. He went behind the desk and dialed the phone. "Mr. Hunt?" he said tersely. "This is Andy. We've got a problem down here . . . Uh-huh . . . Right. Good." The more Verna watched Andy, the more she despised him. What did he care if she took a few cans of dog food? Did the money come out of his pocket? No.

A moment later Mr. Hunt, the store manager, entered. He was a heavyset man with a dyed black mustache and a worried look in his shapeless eyes. His thick arms hung limply from rounded shoulders and he scanned the office with an expression of regret. He asked Andy what was the problem, and with tight lips Andy reached inside Verna's bag and placed the three cans of dog food on the desk.

"I wasn't done shopping yet," Verna explained. Mr. Hunt seemed like a person she could reason with, and moreover a person with little affection for Andy, her enemy. "My dog is outside. I was just visiting her."

"You were done," Andy said, his voice rising, and then to Mr. Hunt, "She was done. It was obvious what was going on."

"Okay, okay," Mr. Hunt said, chewing a hangnail. "We have two opinions here. I need a little more information—"

"Sir," Verna said, "this really isn't what your employee thinks—"

"You think you're special," Andy said, cutting her off. "You think the rules don't apply to you. Is that it?"

"No," Verna said calmly, addressing Mr. Hunt. "I made a mistake is all. I'm sorry about that. I understand it was a mistake."

"What was the mistake?" Andy scoffed. "Getting caught?"

"Andy," Mr. Hunt said. "Please."

"Mr. Hunt," Andy said. "This is exactly what we've talked about. You said we needed a more proactive—"

"I know, Andy," Mr. Hunt said. "Please. Just let me think." He continued chewing his nail, staring at the cans of dog food, unable to bring himself to look at Verna at all. Verna was silent. As much as she hated Andy and wished to make her case, she recognized the best course of action in a situation such as this was groveling, obsequious obedience to Mr. Hunt's authority. This was not a time for showing pride of any kind.

"I guess we should call Jamie," Mr. Hunt sighed, sitting heavily in the chair at his desk. He pulled a magazine from the top drawer and began flipping through the pages. He sighed again. "I guess we have to draw the line somewhere."

"But . . . this is a big mistake," Verna said. "I'm telling you, I was just going to check on my dog. I wasn't even done shopping yet."

Andy snorted. He'd already begun dialing the phone, and he told the person on the other end that they had a situation happening. "He'll be here right away," he said to Mr. Hunt.

While they waited, Andy took a Polaroid of Verna. Before the image had clouded into view he had added it to a wall of similar portraits, a grid of previously apprehended shoplifters, their faces blanched and almost unrecognizable in the hard light of the flashbulb. All the photos were dated on the bottom border. There were at least twenty-five of them, going back to the early nineties.

Soon the door opened and a policeman entered. He was extremely tall, with a small head and small white hands and a paunch around his hips that gave him a slightly womanish gait. He closed the door gently and took in the situation.

"Jamie," Mr. Hunt said. "Thanks for coming by."

"No problem, Mr. Hunt," Jamie said. "That's what she took?" He nodded at the three cans of dog food on the desk.

"Ask her," Andy said.

"Is that what you stole?" Jamie said. Verna was encouraged by his tone of disinterest and his thinly veiled dislike for Andy. She imagined a whole history of bad relations between them, an ongoing feud that might lead to a final splitting of judgments on this day. Her release and Andy's humiliation. It seemed very much possible.

"I'm very sorry for what happened, officer," Verna said. Her tone was scrupulously respectful. "I'm just passing through town. I walked out the door by accident without paying for those cans. My dog was hungry."

"If you can't buy your dog food, you shouldn't have a dog," Andy said. "Get it straight."

"Give it a rest, Andy," Mr. Hunt said.

"It was a big mistake," Verna said again, pushing her advantage.

"I'm very sorry." The apology flowed easily from her mouth. "I'm not from around here. I'll never come back again. I've learned my lesson."

"That would be real easy, wouldn't it?" Andy said. "That would set a real good example."

"I'm not even from around here," she repeated. "I can't be an example."

The police officer asked for ID, and Verna handed him her driver's license, which he scrutinized and handed back. Then the three men went to the far corner of the room and talked quietly among themselves. Judging from their mannerisms they were divided on what to do. Andy remained adamant about punishing Verna's crime, and Mr. Hunt and Jamie seemed unhappy to be bothered by the incident, resigned to whatever the other decided was the right course of action.

Verna fixed her face in a pose of abasement, emanating the full amount of remorse she could possibly muster. She hoped the suffering she was going through would be enough to make up for whatever monetary value her theft might represent. She even tried to influence the men through telepathy, planting the idea of her innocence, her goodness, her pitiable incompetence, in their heads. Jamie nodded a few times, and kept putting on his hat and taking it off again. It seemed like he was trying to reason with the other two, and he was gaining traction. Finally the three men parted and Jamie approached her.

"Come on," he said, handing over her bag. "Time to go."

"Time to go where?" Verna said. She stood and shouldered her bag, exuding further awful shame for her behavior.

"I'm taking you in," Jamie said. "The store's decided to press charges. Zero tolerance. We're going to the station now."

"What?" Verna was stunned. A few cans of dog food was barely worth the time they had already taken. What possible use could this punishment serve? "I didn't even do anything though," she stammered. "I never even made it out the door."

"No mistake," Jamie said. "Come on. We're going."

"My dog is out there."

"Let's go," he said.

Jamie prodded her up the stairs and refused to say anything more. He was not pleased by the turn of events either, but whether this was a mistake or not was no longer his concern. He guided her out the back of the grocery store and into the back seat of his patrol car. He locked the door and took his time filling out some paperwork and answering the radio.

"Please," she said, "you don't understand. My dog is out there." But Jamie just raised his hand for quiet.

"This won't take long," he said. "Don't worry about it. It's just a U-turn. Relax." He radioed headquarters and started up his healthy, revving engine.

Verna stared at the shotgun wedged in the front seat. The time had come to shut up and give in. She was in a car with a man in possession of an enormous gun and she should find a way to cooperate. The car crept around the building, past the graffitied walls, the abandoned milk crates. On the way into traffic Verna caught a glimpse of Lucy, still tied to the bike rack, dumbly watching the front door for her return.

When Verna finally made it back to the grocery store, it was almost dark. The whole day had been devoured by idiot bureaucracy. First she had been taken to the police station for fingerprinting. Then she had been forced to wait on a bench outside a bank of windows for three hours. When her name had finally been called, she had been transferred to another building and given the option of paying a fine of fifty dollars or coming back two weeks later for a trial with a judge. She had refused to pay until it was explained to her that by not appearing she would be committing a much graver crime than the shoplifting itself. With great reluctance she had given up the money, and even then she had been forced to wait another hour for more paperwork to clear. Eventually, with no explanation, she had been released. The police had put her on a bus—the wrong bus, it turned out—and she had ended up traveling the last half mile back to the grocery store on foot. When she finally arrived, the bike rack was empty. Lucy was gone.

Panic rising, Verna walked around the store calling Lucy's name, at first coaxingly, then angrily. She checked near the Dumpster and in the blackberry bushes, hoping her dog had burrowed into some hiding place and was waiting for her return. But Lucy was nowhere to be found.

Verna girded herself and strode into the store, figuring one of the employees had probably taken Lucy into the back room or placed her in the care of some neighbor. The first person she encountered was a bovine cashier girl.

"Has anyone here seen a dog outside?" Verna said. The girl shrugged, but the girl at the next register, an acned brunette, had a dim recollection. She thought someone had come and put Lucy in a van.

"Like a dog-pound van?" Verna said.

"Maybe," the girl said. "I don't know what a dog-pound van looks like."

Verna probed deeper, but the girl's memory only got worse. She had seen a dog, a German shepherd perhaps, hustled into an orange, but maybe white, truck. The truck had gone north, but possibly south. The time of day was definitely before lunch.

Verna abandoned the girls in disgust and made one more trip around the building, calling Lucy's name in her most seductive tone of voice. She was just getting sterner when the back door opened and Andy appeared, bearing a neatly stacked pile of flattened boxes.

"What are you doing here?" Andy said, putting the boxes beside the Dumpster.

"Looking for my dog," she said. "She's gone. I hope you're real happy."

Andy frowned and refused to respond. He stood beside the Dumpster and stared at the trees, pretending Verna was not there. She called Lucy's name, and a pair of headlights swept through the lot, followed by a wheezing Reliant driven by an older, addled-looking woman in a threadbare powder-blue bathrobe.

"Have a great night," Verna said as Andy climbed into the passenger seat. Andy and the woman in the car exchanged sulky words, and then the car rattled off into the dark.

"Your son is a real hero," Verna said, too late for the woman to hear. She kicked over the pile of boxes and knocked over a stack of milk cartons for good measure.

Reluctantly she gave up looking at the grocery store and began making her way back to Walgreens and her car. Her latest idea was that Lucy might have gone back to the parking lot. She was a smart girl, after all. It was a simple straight line from the grocery store to the Walgreens. If Lucy had managed to free herself somehow, it was perfectly likely she would have returned to home base.

The idea seemed increasingly plausible as Verna hurried down the road, passing the gas station, the video store, the lampshade shop, scanning for Lucy in every yard and alleyway. "Lucy!" she said. "Lu-cy?" The few people she passed—two Mexican girls, a kid with a blond, frosted flattop—dutifully ignored her, and by the time she turned the corner into the parking lot, she was brimming with expectation. The car was exactly as she had left it, sitting on the side of the street, and she closed the last distance at a trot. But no Lucy.

Verna stood beside the dead car, casting for a new strategy, a new plan, but she couldn't think of anything. Bill's Garage was closed. Apparently she and Lucy had missed its entire window of operations that day. The white-haired security guard was standing near the front door right where she'd left him, kindly pretending he hadn't noticed her arrival.

"Have you seen my dog?" Verna called, without hope.

The guard shook his head. "Not since I seen you. Nope."

"Is that fucking garage ever open?" she said.

He ignored the profanity. "Most days."

Verna sat down on the hood. A loose filament in the nearby barbecue restaurant's neon sign whined angrily. Against her will a sob worked its way from her chest into her nose and mouth, and passed from her body like a stone. What was Lucy going to do? What was she going to do without Lucy? She clamped her lips shut and swallowed hard and took a deep breath. She had to be in the pound, she told herself. This was exactly the kind of situation pounds were made for.

"You know where the pound is?" she called to the guard. "There's a pound here, right?"

"Not too far," he said, strolling closer, genuine concern creasing his brow. "You all right, honey?"

"Yeah," she said, wiping her eyes. "I just need to get to the pound is all."

"Sure," he said. "You just take Peninsular down thataway," he gestured at the cross street, "and when it dead-ends, you head right about three miles. You lost your dog? Is that it?"

"Looks like it," she said.

"Real shame," he said. "Somewhere around here?"

"That store," she said, flipping her wrist in the direction of the despised grocery store.

"Hmm," he said, having some trouble filling in the circumstances.

"I had to leave her for a little while," Verna explained. "She was right in front."

"Oh. Well, I'm sure someone's got her," the guard said. "I'm sure she'll be back soon. She can't be gone too long around here. Not that many places to go."

The guard's optimism was utterly unfounded, but Verna didn't mind the attention.

"I was gone a long time," she said, swallowing a violent breath.

"I'm sure it wasn't that long," he said. "I'm sure she'll turn up."

Verna struggled to control her spasming shoulders, and when it was over, she slid off the hood. She scanned the area somewhat blindly, prepared to begin walking in the direction of the pound.

"So I go that way?" she said. "And then right?"

The guard scowled, first at her and then at her broken car on the curb. He glanced at his watch. Distant laughter from a group exiting the barbecue restaurant drifted across the street.

"Pretty sure it's closed by now," he said. "I think you're going to have to wait until morning. The number four goes right there. You can catch it on the corner here. Starting at six."

"I think I'll just go now," she said, and began crossing the lot toward the street.

"It's definitely closed," he said.

"Jesus fucking Christ!" she said harshly, and slammed her feet on the ground, unsure what to do.

"If she's there, she'll be there in the morning," the guard said. "A night in the pound never hurt anybody."

Verna stood with her back to the guard, holding her elbows, not wanting to hear any more.

"If I see anything, I'll let you know," the guard added, retreating to his post near the front door.

Verna returned to her place on the hood of the car. For the next few minutes she and the guard entered into the fiction that the other didn't exist. Only once the guard broke the agreement to call out: "Hey. There's a hotel down the road. The Palms. They keep the rooms real clean."

"Thanks," Verna said. She would not be sleeping in any hotel that night, but she was glad anyone thought she might.

Verna remained on the hood as the last light faded from the sky, building scenarios in her head that might rationally lead to Lucy's safe return. Maybe some child had untied her and taken her home. Maybe the girl at the store had remembered something and was currently trying to track her down. She should have left more information at the store, she realized, but then again, she had no phone number or address to give.

The parking lot emptied and the foot traffic tapered off. Verna called her sister from a pay phone, but as soon as she got on the line, her sister started complaining about money and Verna understood there was no point in asking her for help. Verna didn't even bother telling her what was going on. At eight o'clock, the store closed and the guard went home. Verna forced herself to eat some corn chips. When the streetlights came on, she climbed into the car and sat behind the wheel, the smell of Lucy all around her.

She couldn't sleep. Her stomach hurt and her chest ached. Every few minutes she was certain she heard Lucy padding on the pavement or scratching at the door, but when she checked, the dog was never there. At one point Verna climbed all the way outside, positive that she heard the jingle of Lucy's tags, but the street was empty in both directions.

The night passed excruciatingly slowly. Plains of aggravating silence were interrupted by bursts of unexpected noise. Sirens wailing. Planes descending. The ripping sound of rubber on asphalt. The streetlamp filled the car with piss-colored light, casting oblong blocks over the seats and dashboard. She would never forgive herself. Everything about Lucy—her smile, her nose, her mere existence, elsewhere—sent shock waves of pain through Verna's body.

Around midnight, a group of teenage boys materialized outside her window, talking loudly about their friend Josh, who, Verna involuntarily learned, was fucking someone named Tina. "Oh, shit, dude," one of them said, bumping Verna's door, "there's a lady in there!" and the boys shrieked with laughter and hurried away. The ache of Lucy's absence was like a limb being severed over and over again.

Finally, after what seemed an eternity, the sky began gaining some color. The dome of blackness warmed to dull gray and the sound of birds returned. Verna got up, shivering, and walked to the Texaco station to use the bathroom. She brushed her teeth and took off her shirt and washed her armpits with a wet hand towel, which she kept in a plastic bag, and changed her pants, a pair of corduroys for a pair of jeans. Then she went outside and waited at

the bus stop in the growing dawn, sheltered by a plastic kiosk decorated with white slashes of graffiti.

The traffic thickened. Men and women sailed by on their way
to work, drinking their coffee, listening to their radios, and Verna
felt utterly out of sync with all of them. The tomblike garage remained locked, but Verna didn't care. The car had become a distant second priority.

Forty minutes later the number four bus heaved into view, just
two minutes behind schedule. The doors flopped open, exhaling
bleached, heated air. "Does this bus go to the pound?" she asked,
not wanting to waste any time on bad directions. The driver
grimly nodded, and so she climbed on board.

The bus rolled through the neighborhood she and Lucy had
walked together only two nights before and turned right alongside
the railroad tracks as promised. The meadows that had seemed so
mysterious in the dark were revealed as bland, vacant lots. The trestle was a trestle, not a shipwreck or the bones of a dead dinosaur.
The young hobos were all gone, scattered beyond the city's ragged
rim, out into the hostile high desert of dust and sage.

The pound was a low-slung brick structure wedged next to an
abandoned sugar factory, tarted up with a row of tulips and some
new bark dust. With a prayer, Verna pulled the plastic cord and descended from the bus.

The lobby was a drab room with a low drop ceiling and puke-
colored walls, the air permanently tainted with the smell of urine.
Verna took a number—two—and sat down on a plastic bench,
trying to feel some premonition of Lucy's presence nearby, any
telltale sounds or smells, but nothing was powerful enough to register as a clue.

Incredibly the pound's line was already at a standstill. The day's first customers, a haggard woman and her pubescent son, were standing at the intake desk, dominating the lone employee with a long, sad story about a squirrel they had discovered the night before. Apparently, Verna gathered, the squirrel had fallen from a tree in their backyard and broken its hind legs, and then a dog had bitten off its nose. During the night the woman had given it morphine to end its suffering but it had somehow survived. She and her son had brought in the squirrel, which was under a hand towel in a hamster cage, in hopes that someone at the pound could do something to help.

Verna stared at the woman and her son with a mixture of impatience and grudging respect. Who would bring a squirrel to the dog pound? It didn't make any sense. On the other hand, where else would one go? And how many people would make the effort at all? She almost admired them.

Mercifully, just as the boy pulled away the towel and unveiled the scabbing blank spot of the squirrel's mauled face, another employee arrived behind the counter. She was a short, wide woman with smudgy tattoos on her collarbone, and after a brief moment of shuffling papers she called for number two.

Verna rose. As efficiently as possible, she recited the story of Lucy's disappearance, withholding the shoplifting part, but delivering the other salient details of time and place and physical description.

"I don't see anything that matches," the woman said, fingering a recipe box of three-by-five cards. "But come on, let's take a look in the back. You never know. Follow me."

The woman led Verna down a short, bright hallway leading to a large, hangarlike room. The room was cold and fluorescently lit, divided into a maze of cages by cyclone fencing that ran from dirty floor to dirty ceiling. The smell of wet hair and dog shit was strong, and in most of the cages a single animal huddled far at the rear, awaiting discovery.

Verna and the pound employee walked the path in front of each dingy cell, checking the inmates. They saw a rottweiler, two retrievers, a beautiful, blue-eyed malamute with a chewed-up ear, a greyhound with a wound on its leg, and an Irish setter half covered in mud, but not Lucy.

"Front and center, kids," the woman said, clapping her hands, and a few of the dogs trotted to the wire, but most lay still, eyeing the turds on the floor. Verna did her best to ignore the suffering. She had room only for Lucy's suffering this morning.

"How long do you keep them?" Verna asked.

"Four or five days," the woman said. "Then they're evaluated for behavior and sent to the Humane Society." The other option she left unstated. "We suggest you check back every three days."

"Is this the only pound?" Verna asked.

"Only pound for fifty miles, yep," the woman said. "If any dog gets picked up in the vicinity, this is where it would be. Sometimes it takes a while to find them though. You want to be patient."

They reentered the lobby to find the squirrel was gone, replaced by a mutt that had just vomited on the floor. The woman handed Verna some paperwork, and Verna stood at the desk to fill it out, answering as many of the blanks as she could about Lucy's breed, her sex, her color, her age, whether she had a chip implanted, if she was neutered. As she worked through the form, the front door opened repeatedly, ushering in new emergencies. An elderly couple searching for a bulldog named Josephine. A woman crying with her crying baby. The waiting room got louder and more crowded as the morning progressed, but always remained somehow desolate.

Verna managed to fill in all the information except two important lines at the top of the form—the lines asking for an address and a phone number. Their blankness stared back at her. Without contact information, it was hard to see how the system could work.

"I think I need to find another way of doing this," she said.

"No address?" the woman said, inspecting Verna's form. She frowned. "No phone either?"

"Not right now," Verna said. "I'm just passing through."

The woman hummed, expressing something between irritation and sympathy. "How about a previous address?" she said. "We need something there."

Verna gave her an old street address in Indiana. "We had some floods this winter," she explained. "I had to leave."

"Huh," the woman said, date-stamping the papers and clipping them together. She shifted them to the stack of papers in an outgoing bin.

"They made the national news," Verna added, as if that might help her case.

"No kidding," the woman said, rounding up a blank Lost Dog poster and a worksheet for looking for a missing pet.

"The animals got it the worst," Verna said. For some reason she wanted to complete her story. "A dog in the neighborhood, when the rescuers found him, he was swimming in circles right above his house. He had an electric collar and he was afraid to leave the stun radius."

"That's terrible," the woman said, shaking her head, but Verna could see her interest was already waning. The woman had seen every kind of animal torment imaginable and nothing Verna could say would make an impression. Her eyes were deadening, the air between them was de-energizing. Embarrassed, Verna stopped talking.

"Keep checking in," the woman said, handing Verna the colored papers. "It'll be your responsibility to stay in touch now."

"You think you'll find her soon?" Verna said. She wanted to exit the pound on a good note. It seemed important somehow. The woman was already clutching the next number and one of the dogs in the waiting room began barking.

"They all get found sooner or later," the woman said. "That's the best I can tell you."

As Verna turned and picked her way through the crowded lobby, the woman called number twelve.

The bus deposited Verna back at the intersection a little past noon, and everything was more or less as she'd left it. Her car was still in place, with a new splash of birdshit on the windshield, and a group of men were clustered at a bench, sharing the contents of a brown paper bag. The security guard was still standing against the wall a few paces from the front door beside a sloppy tag reading "Seahawks."

The garage was open. She could see across the intersection that the gate was unlocked and the main door was rolled up, and floating on the lift was a red town car. Verna gathered her registration and license from the glove box, discarding some old food wrappers into the gutter, and headed over to deal with the problem of the car. There was no point in waiting.

Inside, a distracted kid was tinkering with the chassis of the upraised car, but Verna ignored him, following instead a voice that emanated from deeper in the building. She walked down a dim hallway, through a waiting room that smelled of acrid, stale coffee, and ended up at the business office, where a tired, fleshy-faced man in a jumpsuit was seated at a desk, making grunting sounds into the receiver of a phone. Verna paused in the doorway and he waved her in.

"Uh-huh? Uh-huh?" he said. "No. That's not what I'm saying. What I'm saying is each of the three phases has its own windings in the alternator. You know what I'm saying? Its own pair of diodes. Each one can fail and the alternator can still charge the battery, but without all its original capacity. What? Nah, I don't think so." The man's voice was almost absurdly deep, with the warm, phlegmy resonance of a late-night DJ.

Verna stood near the door, waiting. He narrowed his thumb and first finger to suggest the coming end of his conversation, but there was no spark of emotion on his face, no welcome.

"Set the voltmeter to the DC scale, all right?" he said. "You measure the voltage across the battery terminals. The voltage should read around fourteen volts, okay? If it reads less than twelve, you might have a problem. What? Just turn on the heater, the defogger, the radio, whatever draws power. Then you rev up the motor. If the voltmeter reads lower than fourteen, your alternator's probably no good."

The language was far beyond Verna's comprehension. In some ways the mechanic's expertise was heartening, but in other ways it was cause for concern. Verna was entering a realm ruled entirely by this man's authority and where her own intelligence was basically useless. The danger of being fooled or intimidated was significant.

The mechanic finally hung up and scribbled something on a yellow legal-sized sheet of paper, which he buried under a stack of manila envelopes. Without glancing at Verna, he opened a file cabinet and flipped through some hanging folders. Verna could see it was going to be her responsibility to initiate contact.

"Excuse me," she said.

"What's up?" the man said, examining a sheaf of papers. "Start talking. I'm listening."

"I think my serpentine belt is cracked," Verna said. She hoped to show some baseline competence regarding her own car, but somehow the effect was just the reverse, a broad declaration of ignorance. "Someone said it would run about a hundred fifty dollars for a new one?"

"You were driving with the air-conditioning on?" he surmised. "The engine jerked? Steam came out? That kind of thing?"

"No," she said. "It just won't start. It sounds bad."

The mechanic sucked on his lip, opening a new folder. "What kind of car are we talking about here?"

"Camry," she said, pleased to be able to provide a correct answer. "A 1996. It's across the street."

The mechanic stood and peered out the dirty window. Finally she seemed to have his attention.

"So what's the problem exactly?" he said. "Start from the beginning."

"I turned the ignition yesterday and there was a bad sound. Now it's just dead."

"You checked the battery?"

"The battery is okay," she said. "The electrical works."

"And you think it's a problem with the S-belt?"

"The last guy said it was cracked. He thought it might hold out a little longer though."

"Easy enough to replace the S-belt," he said. "I don't know why the engine would freeze up though. Who knows. Could be the S-belt."

"How much would a new S-belt be?" she said. Before committing to anything she wanted to hear an official estimate for the job.

"About a hundred bucks," he said. "A hundred twenty-five. Depends if we have to order a new one. I'll have to check stock. And fifty for labor. That's the best price you'll find. I promise that."

The price was no bargain, exactly, but it was close enough to what she'd been expecting that she was willing to accept it. Food was going to be a problem the rest of the drive, but she could find a way. "Okay," Verna said.

"We'll have to tow it over, too, I guess," he said. "That adds another fifty dollars."

"It's just a block away," Verna said.

"It's always fifty," he said. "Plus mileage. But there's no mileage here. So it's just fifty."

Verna pondered the added fee. She touched her money belt under her shirt. The extra fifty more or less wiped her out. But what choice did she have? The fee would likely be the same anywhere else, with more miles to rack up, and the idea of pushing the car across the street herself, which was to say organizing the men in the parking lot to help her, sounded impossible. Assuming gas prices held, and no more major problems developed, she would still be okay. They would have a couple lean days, but they would make it.

"Thirty bucks," the mechanic said, interpreting her silence as negotiation. "That work for you?" He picked up the phone, signaling the price wouldn't drop any lower.

Verna nodded.

"Good. We'll pick up the car this afternoon," he said. "We should have it ready for you first thing in the morning."

Verna returned to her car to collect some of the items she would need over the night. She took her jewelry box, her toothbrush, a quilt, and a pillow, all of which she stuffed in an army backpack she pulled from deep in the trunk. She found it a little embarrassing that the mechanics would be seeing all her crummy possessions, the garbage bags of clothing, the chewed dog toys, the depleted brick of Top Ramen, but there was no choice in the matter. She hoped they wouldn't look too closely, and locked the doors.

The trip to the garage had taken an hour, which meant it was a good time to check in with the pound again. Conveniently, the nearest pay phone was located directly beside the front door of Walgreens.

"How's the dog?" the guard said as she passed by. He was wearing the same uniform and leaning against the same spot on the wall as the day before. His hands were deep in his pockets and his glasses reflected the parking lot. Verna was not actively unhappy that he was there.

"No news yet," Verna said.

"How long's she been gone?" he said. His interest would have been more touching if he wasn't clearly just bored out of his mind, but Verna would take what sympathy she could get.

"Yesterday," she said. A man with a huge hole burned in his coat sleeve wandered out of the store.

"That's nothing," the guard said, lifting his glasses. "I had a dog left for a week before he came back. They'll find her. They always get their dog."

"I hope so," she said.

"My name's Jack, by the way."

"Verna."

"Good to meet you, Verna."

"Good to meet you, too."

Standing at the pay phone, her backpack leaned against the brick pillar, Verna searched her purse for loose change but only managed to turn up a few pennies and nickels. She tried the pockets of her backpack, from smallest to largest, but they only yielded a few hairpins and some lip balm. The idea of breaking a dollar bill seemed like a defeat, but it also seemed there was no other option. Before unbuckling her money belt though, she took another good look at Jack, scrutinizing him closely.

He looked like a harmless guy, a little older than she had realized. His skin was half pickled and his eyes were foggy, but his face revealed a kind of friendliness that she guessed had been beaten into him over the years. It was a form of weakness, she believed, a way of hedging his bets, of gaining favors, but it was friendliness all the same, maybe even purer for the lack of power behind it. She might as well try to get something out of him.

"You got fifty cents?" she said.

"Hmm?" He was surprised to be addressed. "Oh. No change," he said, "but . . ." Jack patted himself down and extracted a silver cell phone from his breast pocket. "Here. Lots of minutes. I'm out here all day. Feel free. No one uses a pay phone anymore."

Verna inspected the phone, wondering if she would have to pay for this gesture someday, but she doubted it. The gesture, coming from this man, scanned clean.

"Thanks," she said.

"Hate to think a dog's out there," he said. "That's not right."

The pound had no news for her. They were not unencouraging though. The woman told Verna to call again later and urged her to put up the Lost Dog posters in the area where Lucy had last been seen. Verna was skeptical at first, but the woman said the posters were an effective method of aiding the process. It was quite impressive how often they worked, she insisted. Verna thanked her and handed the phone back to Jack.

"So how late are you out here anyway?" Verna said. She had a new question for him and she needed to work her way into it.

"Eight," he said. "Every day. Eight to eight. Thereabouts."

"Hunh," Verna said.

"Better than the last job. I'll tell you that."

"Not many jobs around here, I guess," she said.

Jack laughed. "I don't know what these people do all day. Used to be a mill. But that's been gone a long time now."

"You can't get a job without an address anyway," Verna said. "Without a phone. That's why I'm gong to Alaska. I hear they need people up there."

"You can't get an address without an address," Jack said. "Can't get a job without a job. It's all fixed."

Together, they watched a pickup pull into a parking space near the trash cans. Verna was having trouble formulating the question she wanted to ask. She didn't know quite where to begin. But then, mercifully, Jack helped her along.

"You know," he said, "if you need a number for those posters, Verna, I'm just standing here all day. You can use this one if you want. I heard a little of what you were talking about. My phone's your phone if you need it right now."

Verna watched the light at the intersection change from yellow to red, and the light perpendicular change a beat later from red to green.

"I might do that," she said. "That might be good. Yeah. Thanks."

She ate a quick lunch off the dollar menu at Arby's and filled out the Lost Dog poster to the best of her ability, using Jack's phone number as her contact information. Her writing was not pretty, but the important data was all there: name, breed, and even a picture of Lucy sleeping on the grass that Verna kept in her pocket at all times.

From there, she went to Walgreens and made copies, ten cents apiece, and spent the rest of the afternoon canvassing the neighborhood. She hung posters in the supermarket and all the storefronts along Lombard, with a few forays into the more populated residential streets to either side. How people managed to pull together a down payment she would never understand. She would never understand any of it.

Every hour or so she returned to the parking lot to check in with Jack and make sure the pound hadn't called, but always without success. On one of the trips she saw her car getting hauled away and slotted into place among the others at Bill's Garage. Now Lucy would have no place to return to, she realized. Home base was gone. She called the pound once again, and this time they asked her please to stop calling; they would be in touch as soon as they had news.

At eight o'clock Jack departed, and Verna was cut adrift. She made a trip to the train trestle and found the charred remains of the mattress, but that was all. No kids, no dogs. They had all managed to keep moving.

She returned one more time to Walgreens and tied a shirt to the base of a tree near the spot where the car had been parked, something for Lucy to get a scent from, and then wandered to a park where she had seen children in the playground earlier in the day, scouting for a good place to spend the night. Overall, she thought, the park seemed like a decent place to camp. It was the best of bad options, at the very least.

She found a spot at the park's far edge, just over the lip of an embankment, a shallow slope overlooking the train yards, dotted with oak trees that would shelter her from the wind and most prying eyes. The sun went down, and the sky curdled with orange, and she dragged flattened boxes to the base of an oak tree. She ate two tacos from King Burrito and tried her best to be thankful that the weather was warm and dry.

Somewhere, she knew, she had gone wrong, but for the life of her she couldn't tell where. Images of her new couch—destroyed by the flood—plagued her, and she tried to banish them from her mind. She peed a few yards from her campsite and barred herself from thinking about the fact that even at the end of the road waited only more body-crushing work.

Verna was exhausted, but she had trouble sleeping. Her nerves were buzzing. The traffic in the train yard never entirely stopped. Numerous times she was on the brink of sleep, only to be awakened by the sound of rumbling boxcars. At one point, well after midnight, she was finally beginning to dream when the horn of a slow-moving engine filled the air. It was like a church choir, the sound of many voices blended into a single sustained song of praise.

Angels, she thought, half waking, and it took two more long, harmonic blows of the horn to place the source. No, it was not angels. It was no shimmering, golden curtain of praise. It was just a train heading out, following the rails into the dead emptiness. When she eventually did sleep, she dreamed of Lucy drowning in an Arctic bay.

It was sometime in the dark morning hours when she half-woke again, and immediately she knew that someone was there. She could hear breathing, rustling in the grass, and she knew without thinking it was a man. She could smell the reek of the sweat in his clothes, the stale alcohol on his breath.

Verna jolted awake, immobilized with fear. Her cells turned into helium and the sound of her own blood churned in her ears. Out of the corner of her eyes she could see the man's hunched form moving among her stuff. The noise of her backpack unzipping was deafening as each tooth decoupled from its partner, opening the pocket into a gaping hole.

She could see the man's hand dipping into each pocket, brushing the seams for whatever he could find. He pulled out her clean socks, her toothbrush, her sweatshirt, and scattered them onto the ground. All the while Verna remained utterly still, replicating the breath of a sleeping person. In her mind she was already projecting herself deep in the future. Whatever happened in this desolate place was already over and done with. She was already well into forgetting the event had ever occurred.

The search went on and the man became more careless; at one point he lost his balance, pitching from his squat onto his side.

"Fuck," he said. "Bull fucking shit."

The man stood up and brushed himself off. At last Verna got a clear look at him. He was a thin, unshaven man, hair combed into a hard shell, and small, reptilian eyes sunk deep in his head. In his stubby hands he was holding her jewel box, unaware that the contents were just rhinestones and glass.

The moon came out and the ground brightened.

"Fucking cunt," he said, staring at her. He swayed, barely keeping upright. "You don't have shit, huh?"

Verna couldn't speak. She choked on her own dry breath and felt the double pump of her heart in her ribs. The money belt cinched around her waist was burning into her skin.

"Don't look at me," the man said, and Verna obeyed, shifting her gaze onto a patch of dirt near her nose. She looked so hard at an ant walking by she thought she could see the moon reflected in its eye.

The wind blew and clouds glided across the sky. The shifting trains banged in the yard. Thoughts of Lucy filled Verna's entire body. All this time she had been worried about Lucy's safety, but what about her own? The man lowered himself into a squat a few steps from her quilt, ominously calm.

"This is a steep hill, ain't it?" he said. "Those kids on the cardboard are having some fun." There were no kids anywhere in sight though. No more cardboard either. "You know what I mean?" he said. "If the cardboard wasn't so worn out, they'd slide a lot better, right?"

Verna tried to nod but she was unable. Her voice was a dream whisper: "Yes."

"I don't like this place," the man said, rocking back onto his haunches. "It's the fucking people that bother me. God, they have attitude. I'm out here trying to be a good boy, and they just don't want to let me. It's like I don't have no rights. They don't know I've killed over seven hundred people with my bare hands."

The man reached into his back pocket. Verna thought it was over. But he only pulled a flask of cheap rye from his back pocket and took a sip.

"Everywhere I go, man, the cops are just rude," he said. "Move it along, move it along. I just spent three weeks in jail out in Nebraska. Wasn't that bad. Pretty good to have a place to sleep. I told them, 'Be nice. Be nice and I won't kill you.'

"I had to teach one boy a lesson," the man said. "You don't want to get fucked with, you make an example. That's the way it is. I didn't make the rules. This boy, he got in my space and I had to step up. They smell the weakness on you. I started out by ripping his ear off. Believe me, it ain't that hard. The body's ninety percent water. After that he didn't want to fight so much. If he did, then it's his eyes. If you can't see me, can't fight me. You know what I mean?"

A satellite slid slowly over the sky's clear blackness, following the curve of the atmosphere.

"We're never gonna win this war," the man said, watching the stars. "Fucking A, no. Those people, they don't want us over there, man. They're gonna keep fighting until we get out or every one of them is dead. Doesn't matter what we do. I know what I'm talking about. Down in El Salvador I cut off a baby's head and what did that get us? Bullshit. We lost, man. Fuck if I know."

The man stopped talking. The sound of Verna's shallow breath was the only thing marking time. Somewhere in the dark a branch shook with the weight of a settling bird.

Then, without a word, the man stood. He staggered a few steps into the grass, paused, and continued down the hill. His footsteps receded, and the wind ruffled the grass, and he was gone.

As soon as Verna was certain he was not coming back, she packed her things. She threw what she could find into the bag and tucked her pillow under her arm. Then she walked, then ran, through the park toward Walgreens. The houses of the neighborhood, splashed with wicked light from the streetlamps, shook at the edges of her vision. A cat racing from a laurel hedge almost scared her to death.

The intersection was empty when she arrived, and the streets were grimy and obscure. She walked in the middle of the road, keeping space on all sides, and visited her car, locked securely behind Bill's cyclone fence. The car's body was coated in fine droplets of mist, and the starburst of a streetlight's reflection whitened the roof, every spindle and crosshatching perfectly distinct in her vision.

A car passed, washing her with the headlights, and her shadow grew wildly on the wall. She felt she had to get out of sight.

The only place open at that hour was the Texaco, a hard oasis of white fluorescence surrounded by pitch desert blackness. Verna crept along the wall and slipped into the bathroom, bolting the door. Under the rancid, overhead light she splashed water on her cheeks and stared into the slab of metal that served as a mirror. Only a blotch of pallid whiteness was visible.

Alone, Verna succumbed to the panic she had been holding inside her. Black terror descended like bats, sucking her breath away, and dry lightning flashed across her skin. She gasped for air and sweat streamed over her forehead and back. The world her visitor had emerged from was not so far away. It was only a few steps in either direction. At any moment, around any bend, she could be claimed by it.

Verna braced herself against the sink. With effort, her breath returned to normal. The heat receded from her brow. She steadied herself by staring at the white shape on the metal.

"Hang on, girl," she whispered. "Don't give up. I'm coming. I'll be there soon."

When the sun rose, Verna was already at Walgreens, exhausted and disheveled, waiting for Jack to make his appearance. She had slept only a few minutes in the Texaco bathroom and evacuated as soon as the first customers began coming around. By eight o'clock she had already seen a whole parade go by. A man with a carved walking stick. A woman with a beehive hairdo. The near rear-ending of a Ford Contour followed by drifting plumes of fresh rubber smoke. She took all this in with equanimity, though, not as signs or portents. Having barely slept in two days she was getting looks herself.

The daylight had wiped away the worst of the last night's fear, and the pattern of commerce had resumed its unshakable pace. The only reality she faced now was the chore of the coming day.

Jack did not arrive at eight, as he'd said he would. Nor at eight thirty.

A few minutes past nine o'clock, a Lincoln Continental bounced into the parking lot. In the passenger seat was a pale woman with red hair and a white turtleneck, and in the driver seat, revealed as the glare vanished from the windshield, was Jack. With both hands on the wheel, he piloted the car to a space and then turned off the engine. He leaned over and pecked the woman on the cheek.

"Howdy, Verna," he said a moment later, jingling the change in his pocket. He was not wearing his uniform this morning, but a pair of creased blue jeans and an olive T-shirt. His white hair was unhidden, and it shone in the open light. "You all right? You look a little stricken."

"I was here at eight," Verna said, as if that answered anything. "Where were you?"

Jack paused, just long enough to acknowledge that Verna had taken a liberty but not so long as to shame her.

"I had to take Holly's kid to school," he said, pointing at the car. "It's always a big production over there, you know, just getting everything done. It's my day off today."

Verna glanced at the woman in the car, feeling vaguely betrayed by the life Jack had outside the parking lot, the life he had been hiding from her. She had come to imagine they shared something, that perhaps they might even have something to offer each other. But she could see now that was not the case. She could see he was not nearly as bad off as her. He was not nearly as bad off as she'd hoped.

"You got a call this morning," he continued. "Good news. I told them I'd track you down ASAP."

"The pound?" Verna said. She had been preparing herself for a long wait before any contact from the lady at the pound.

"Just a little while ago," he said, presenting the phone to her. "I told you they'd call."

Verna tentatively took the silver lozenge from his palm and stepped a few feet away for some privacy. Verna hastily recited her lost-pet number. The woman informed her that Lucy had been found.

"Oh God," Verna said. "Don't be joking."

The woman was a little sheepish. She was not joking, she said. Apparently Lucy had been processed the very day she had been lost, but she had been placed in a foster home, which was why they couldn't find her. It had been a mistake, and it had taken a little while to make the connection.

"She's in a good place," the woman said. "4567 Farragut Street. You just need to come in first and pay the lodging fee. Then you're free to go pick her up."

"Lodging fee?" Verna said warily.

"Five dollars a night."

Verna laughed. Ten dollars was nothing. After the valley she had traveled through during the night, she could care less about a few dollars. The whole world seemed to brighten around her. Maybe she had finally reached higher ground. Maybe, at last, the worst was behind her.

"Fine," she said. "I'll be there soon." She handed the phone back to Jack, who was beaming, unable to disguise his pleasure in her good news.

"Everything all right?" Jack said.

"Real good," she said. "They've got her. She's fine."

"Told you they'd find her," he said. "Let that go on the record."

"It's on the record," Verna said.

"Well," Jack said, stepping off the curb. "I guess this is it then. You'll be heading out."

"I guess this is it. Yeah."

"I hope it all works out for you, Verna. I know it will."

"Thanks," she said. "You too."

"Just take care of yourself," he said. He pressed something into her hands and closed her fingers. "Take this. Don't argue. And hey, if you're ever through here again, be sure to stop by."

"I will," Verna said, smiling. She wanted to say more but the time was all wrong. Jack had to go.

Verna watched Jack cross the parking lot to the car. The woman was applying lipstick in the rearview mirror and she began talking as soon as he closed the door. The engine coughed to life, and with a final wave, he pulled into traffic and was gone. She opened her hand to find six dollars.

The garage would be open at ten, so Verna waited in Arby's among the late commuters, granting herself an order of French toast sticks in celebration of the day's turn of events. According to the map, Farragut Street was only about two miles away, and she was tempted to take a bus there right away, but she held tight. Assuming all went well, she and Lucy could still get on the road by lunchtime. Once she had the car in her possession, they would be out of town in a matter of minutes.

Verna withdrew her money belt and counted out two hundred and five dollars for Bill's. That left only a few dollars to spare, but she was not that worried. She could always sell her plasma or pawn her one remaining brooch when she reached the ferry if she really had to. She only needed to hold out a few more days. Ketchikan had tent cities for everyone who got hired, and from what they said, everyone got hired.

It was almost ten thirty when the potbellied mechanic came shuffling along in his blue jumpsuit. Verna watched as he unlocked the front gate and looped the chain around the post, shifting a white paper sack from hand to hand. She gave him a few seconds' head start before following. Above the metal roof, the sun was turning a cell phone tower bright gold among the pine trees.

Verna located the mechanic at his desk, preparing to eat a breakfast sandwich. The white bag was flattened as a place mat, and his napkins and plastic utensils were arranged neatly on either side. He waved her in.

"Morning," he said. "You're up early."

"Morning," she said.

"You want some coffee?" he said. "I think the first pot's ready." Without waiting for an answer, he rose and found a cup on the windowsill and blew in its basin. He picked up the pot from a burned ring on the heating pad and poured. He handed the hot, weak coffee to Verna.

"Indiana plates," he said. "You're a ways from home, aren't you?"

"Long way to go, too."

"I've never been to Indiana. I hear it's nice."

"It's nice for some people," Verna said. She didn't need a personal connection at this point. She needed to head out. Her silence was a form of inquiry into the business at hand.

The mechanic took a bite of his sandwich and chewed slowly. Out the window a sparrow landed on an electrical line.

"The guy was right about the serpentine belt," the mechanic said, swallowing. "It's cracked all over the place. It was just a matter of time before it gave out on you."

"That's what he said," Verna confirmed.

"He wasn't wrong," the mechanic said. "But he wasn't all the way right either." He picked at a piece of congealed cheese on his wrapper. "The S-belt's worn out, but that's not why the car wouldn't start."

"No?" Verna said. Her stomach was tightening. The mechanic's blasé tone could only be a prelude to bad news. But how bad could it be? After the past two days she felt almost impervious to obstacles. The world could throw down what it wanted, she thought. She would take it. She and Lucy would walk away.

"You've got milky oil here," he said. He bent over and picked a small plastic container from the floor and handed it to her. A layer of brown fluid like chocolate milk coated the bottom.

"I didn't want you to check the oil," she heard herself say.

"I'm just telling you," he said. "I hate to be the bearer of bad news."

"Bad news," she said.

The mechanic nodded his head sadly. "I hate to say it, but you snapped a piston rod. Actually, you blew the head gasket first, and then water got into your cylinder. The rod can't compress, and there you go. You end up with hydrolock, they call it. You'd have to re-build the whole engine if you want the car to drive again. And honestly, I don't think it's what you want to do. It would end up costing more than the car is worth, probably."

"How much?" Verna said. She wanted a price. She wanted a precise number on this impediment.

"Two thousand," he said. "At least two thousand. Like I said, more than the car's worth. On the other hand, it's less than a new car."

Verna didn't say anything. Two thousand dollars might as well have been two million dollars. She returned the plastic container to the mechanic, who placed it on top of a pile of pink receipts.

Overhead, the lights seemed to flutter, and for a moment she worried the whole world might disappear. But in fact nothing hap-pened; the world remained as it was. There was no thunder. No lightning. Outside, a couple strolled by, the girl in a pink sweatshirt, the boy in a green windbreaker. Her problems had no discernable effect on anything beyond herself whatsoever.

The mechanic sipped his coffee. He crumpled his place mat and tossed it in the trash can.

"So what happens now?" Verna said.

"Fix the car. Buy a new one. Or I could junk it for the title."

Verna sat down on the bench. Then she stood up and drifted toward the door, pulling on her lip.

"I don't know," she said. "I need some time to think."

"Look, I know this is bad news," he said. "It's not what anyone ever wants to hear." He looked uncomfortable, for what that was worth. "The thing is, though, the car's taking up space out there. I need to know what to do. I can't just leave it. You can understand where I'm coming from."

Verna said nothing.

"I need to know what to do," he said, rising. "Look. Call it fifty even. For the tow and the junkyard. We'll take care of everything and that'll be it. But I can't let you leave here without paying the bill."

Verna emerged from the bus into the low slanting sunlight of Farragut Street. In her hands she carried two plastic bags of belongings. The rest of her things she had consigned to be junked. It was almost surprising, she'd discovered, how little was in fact impossible to leave behind.

With four hundred ninety-five dollars in her pocket, Verna realized her future had narrowed down to a measure of days at best. She now had barely enough for a bus ride to Alaska, and with a dog in tow not enough for anything even close. The next leg of their trip was going to demand some kind of miracle.

Verna paused on the corner to get her bearings and let the two plastic bags drop to the ground. A chewed-up golf ball rolled from the blue bag and wobbled ominously over the concrete, coming to rest in the dirt.

The neighborhood she'd come to was poor but tidy, a collection of small bungalows with groomed yards and a few new duplexes on the main street. Midway down the block two girls were washing a pickup truck, and two boys were circling them on dirt bikes. All of them averted their eyes as Verna walked by scanning the house numbers.

The address she was looking for appeared at the end of the block—a modest ranch house clad in aluminum siding, with duct tape on one window and purple morning glories climbing in the cyclone fence. Behind the house the land dropped to the rail yard—a scalding field of enormous, shifting, multicolored machines—beyond which lay the ancient yellow hills on the horizon.

Verna stood on the corner, unsure what to do next. In the yard beside the house, a handful of dogs were happily romping and grooming themselves. One gnawed on a plastic chicken leg. Two mutts napped under a cedar tree. Three more were fighting playfully over a deflated rubber ball, and it was among that group that Verna spotted Lucy, padding beside a pert black poodle, gamely trying to fit in. The dogs tumbled over the patchy yard, lost in the scents and colors and textures of the dirt and grass.

Verna almost cried out but she managed to hold herself back. Now was not the time for making a scene, she realized. It was a time for caution and level-headed planning. If she expected to walk away from this neighborhood with Lucy in tow, she had to play it smart.

She gauged the height of the fence, the length of the street, the proximity of the neighbors. The gate was locked, she noted, but Lucy could hop the fence easily given the proper encouragement. From there they could make a quick escape into the trees.

And then what, though? Where would they go? Back to town? The freeway? This was where the plan became hazy. They could hitchhike the rest of the way up north. Or they could stow away on a passing truck or train. What other options were there? Verna thought of those gypsy kids and how they managed to keep them-selves going. If they could move from place to place, it seemed reasonable she and Lucy could, too.

Verna was still pondering the next step when suddenly the dogs began barking. The whole yard went up at once, a mess of hoarse, adamant, unintelligible voices. At first Verna assumed the dogs were barking at her, the nearest intruder, but then the real culprit became clear. The sliding glass door had opened and the foster dog owner emerged, bearing a huge bag of dog food. It was feeding time.

The foster owner was about what Verna expected. An obese woman with stringy black hair and a yellow velour sweatsuit, barely able to move beyond a shuffle. It took her almost three minutes to empty the bag into the row of plastic bowls on the patio, and the whole time the dogs clambered all around her.

Lucy was right there in the thick of it. She got knocked off her stance a few times, but more or less managed to hold her own, swal-lowing down a solid portion of meaty kibbles. The feeding lasted a few minutes, at which point the dogs began peeling off from the group, trotting to separate parts of the yard to digest. Lucy ambled to the far end of the lot for a patch of sunlight near the base of the cedar. Within moments her eyes were twitching with dreams. For a dog, this was not the worst kind of life. It wasn't nearly as bad as Verna had imagined.

The foster owner busied herself hosing down the apron of ce-ment, forcing the hair and kibbles onto the ground, and then recoiled the hose and lumbered back inside. Moments later she exited the front door and drove away in a bottle-green station wagon.

The street was silent. The smell of sage suffused the warm air. The sun had moved a few degrees in the sky, and some of its heat had softened, but the land was still scoured of shadows. High above the hills a hawk rode a thermal in widening circles.

Verna crossed the road, coming to a stop outside the fence.

"Lu," she said. "Lu, wake up."

Lucy lifted her head and smiled, her tongue lolling from her mouth. She barked once. She didn't seem surprised by Verna's sudden appearance. Verna called her name again, and this time she stood drowsily, shook herself, and trotted over to rub herself against the braided wire of the fence. Verna scratched the dog's ears and worked her way down to the base of her tail as she spun around, trying to lick Verna's hands and continue the petting at the same time. Their opportunity to escape was limited, but first they had some greetings to go through.

"You miss me?" Verna said. "I missed you, girl."

Once the initial petting was over, Lucy turned and padded a few steps into the yard and lay down, telling Verna she expected some work on her part.

"Come on," Verna pleaded. "We have to go. We'll play later. All right? All right? Come on, girl."

But Lucy remained where she was. She wanted attention. They had been apart two days, after all, and she deserved something. Verna knew there was only one way to please her in this kind of situation.

Verna searched around until she found a decent branch, thick and unforked, and after two quick feints she tossed it into the yard.

Lucy scrambled and returned the stick, refusing, as always, to let go. But Verna was patient, holding on until Lucy relaxed her grasp.

"You like that?" Verna said. "You want more? Okay. Here. Here it is."

The next throw went long and Lucy had to fend off the attack of her friend the poodle. She trotted back, adjusting the stick in her teeth, and rose on her hind legs, placing her paws in the loops of the cyclone fence. "One more," Verna said. "That's all. Okay?"

The next toss never touched the ground. Lucy caught the stick midair, and the moment of her musculature flexing in the sunlight, her whole spine snapping to return her feet to the earth, was one of the most beautiful things Verna had ever seen. Spontaneously, she clapped her hands.

"Good girl!" she said. "Good girl! You're so good. Such a good catcher."

Verna crouched and let Lucy lick her face through the holes of the fence. The game was done, but for some reason Verna found herself rooted in place. Her fingers refused to let go of the metal wire. The pebbles on the ground dug into her knees.

A dog could love anyone, she thought. A dog could be happy almost anywhere. They just needed food and water and affection. They were not picky about who delivered it.

And by the same token, a dog could forget anyone, too. They were loyal, but only to whoever was around.

And people, they just had to stick dollar signs on everything.

"Pretty nice, isn't it?" Verna said. "Nice yard. This isn't so bad."

The tears began gently, but then, quickly, came with more power. Soon Verna's whole body was quaking. She felt like rusty nails were being pried from her chest. She crouched there and let the sun hit her. The sun was still free, she thought, though probably not for too much longer.

"I lost the car, Lu," Verna said, sobbing. "I'm sorry . . ." And already the decision was made.

Woodenly, she got to her feet. There was no need to wait any longer.

She walked alongside the fence until she came to the front door, and under the metal awning she attached a photo of Lucy to $30, folded it inside a Lost Dog poster, then slipped the whole package into the mail slot. It wasn't much, but hopefully enough to guarantee decent care for a while. Verna felt a martyr-like thrill as the mail slot slammed shut.

From there Verna circled around the house and skidded down the dirt incline to the edge of the train yard. The fence was open and she walked inside. The many tracks intersecting each other made a crazy scrawl of metal and gleamed whitely under the sun.

Across the yard an engine pulling a chain of boxcars and gondolas and flatbeds was chugging its way toward the gate. Verna walked over and stood there as the train picked up speed. Sunlight through the open doors of the empty boxcars slapped her in the face again and again. She needed to move, and this machine was moving in her direction.

A ladder swept by. A toothed metal foothold. An empty platform.

Down the line, a ladder approached. Verna emptied her mind and tossed her bags onto the trundling platform, then heaved herself on board behind them. The rocky ground blurred underneath her feet.

Verna arranged her bags and stationed herself at the corner of the doorway, her hand gripping the rattling jamb. Already the foster home was receding in the distance. A juniper bush whipped passed. She was traveling ever deeper into a sterile, bone-dry planet of rock and sky.

Verna lay down on her side and pulled her knees to her chest. Far ahead, the engine's whistle blew, full-throated and remorseful. And then it blew again. Verna watched the ball of sun wobble in the sky. She knew she was going to be chasing that sound for a long time now.

ACKNOWLEDGMENTS

The author wishes to thank: Ben Adams, Julia Bryan-Wilson, Jennifer Carlson, Colin Dickerman, Steve Doughton, Dan Frazier, Todd Haynes, Justine Kurland, Camela Raymond, Mattathias Schwartz, Storm Tharp, and everyone at Bloomsbury. And, especially, Kelly Reichardt, for seeing something here.

A NOTE ON THE AUTHOR

Jon Raymond is the author of *The Half-Life*, a novel, and co-writer of the films *Old Joy* and *Wendy and Lucy*, adapted from stories in this collection. He is an editor at *Plazm* magazine, and his writing has appeared in *Bookforum*, *Artforum*, *Tin House*, the *Village Voice*, and other publications. He lives in Portland, Oregon.